ARY

GW00471404

LIS
→ LIS 7/21

one and all · onen hag oll

CORNWALL
COUNCIL

24 HOUR RENEWAL HOTLINE 0845 607 6119
www.cornwall.gov.uk/Library

100 CHILDREN'S BOOKS

that inspire our world

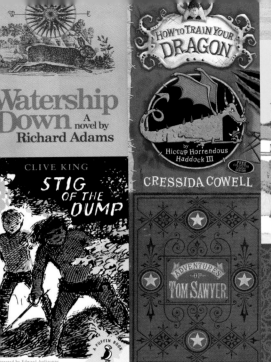

Watership Down
A novel by Richard Adams

HOW TO TRAIN YOUR DRAGON
by Hiccup Horrendous Haddock III
CRESSIDA COWELL

Lost and Found
Oliver Jeffers

Richard Scarry's
WHAT DO PEOPLE DO ALL DAY?

Dick King-Smith
The master of animal adventures

THE RED BALLOON
BY A. LAMORISSE
DOUBLEDAY

ALEX RIDER MISSION 1: STORMBREAKER
ANTHONY HOROWITZ

A Bear Called Paddington
Michael Bond

CLIVE KING
STIG OF THE DUMP
A PUFFIN BOOK
Illustrated by Edward Ardizzone

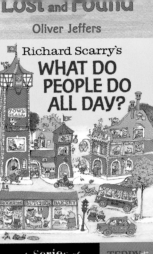

ADVENTURES OF TOM SAWYER.

A Series of Unfortunate Events
by Lemony Snicket
BOOK THE FIRST
The Bad Beginning

TERRY PRATCHETT
the fantastically funny
TRUCKERS
The first book of The Nomes

We're Going on a Bear Hunt
Michael Rosen   Helen Oxenbury

The Jungle Book
By Rudyard Kipling
With Illustrations by
J. L. Kipling, W. H. Drake, and
P. Frenzeny

MARY NORTON
THE BORROWERS
A PUFFIN BOOK

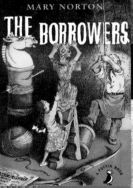

HOLES
LOUIS SACHAR

A BOOK OF NONSENSE
BY EDWD LEAR

Where's Spot?
Eric Hill

JUST SO STORIES
RUDYARD KIPLING

GOODNIGHT MOON
by Margaret Wise Brown
Pictures by Clement Hurd
Harper & Brothers, Established 1817

MIKE MULLIGAN AND HIS STEAM SHOVEL
STORY AND PICTURES BY
VIRGINIA LEE BURTON

Shirley Hughes
DOGGER
The classic story about losing your favourite toy

MARK HADDON
THE CURIOUS INCIDENT OF THE DOG IN THE NIGHT-TIME
WINNER WHITBREAD BOOK OF THE YEAR

Pienkowski
HAUNTED HOUSE

Carrie's War
NINA BAWDEN

JEAN DE BRUNHOFF
THE TRAVELS OF BABAR
RANDOM HOUSE

Kipper's little friends
25 years

R.L. STINE
Goosebumps

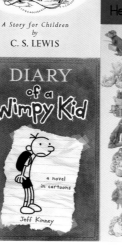
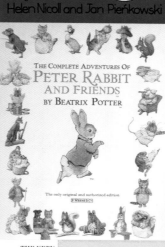
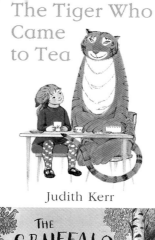

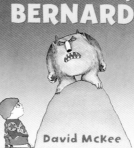

Published in the United Kingdom in 2020 by
Pavilion Books
43 Great Ormond Street
London, WC1N 3HZ

Produced by Salamander Books, an imprint of Pavilion
Books Group Limited.

© 2020 Pavilion Books

All rights reserved. No part of this publication may be
reproduced, stored in a retrieval system, or transmitted
in any form or by any means, electronic, mechanical,
photocopying, recording, or otherwise, without prior
consent of the publishers.

10 9 8 7 6 5 4 3 2 1

ISBN: 978-1-911641-08-7

Printed in China

100 CHILDREN'S BOOKS

that inspire our world

—

Colin Salter

Edited by

Hetty Hopkinson

PAVILION

Contents

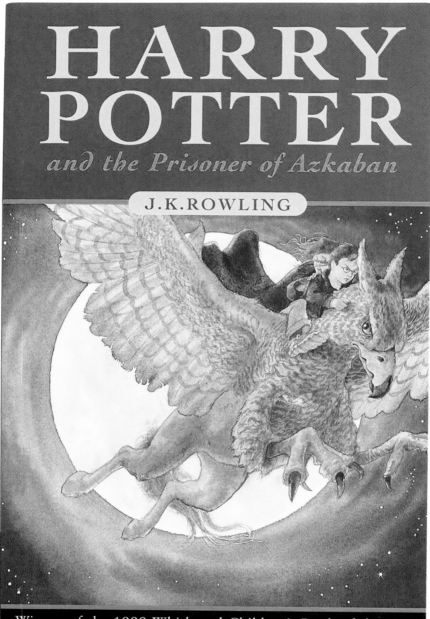

Winner of the 1999 Whitbread Children's Book of the Year

ABOVE: J. K. Rowling's Harry Potter *series is the bestselling book series of all time with sales of over 500 million. The original book,* Harry Potter and the Philosopher's Stone, *has sold in excess of 120 million worldwide, although* Le Petit Prince *by Antoine de Saint-Exupéry is reputed to have sold 140 million copies.*

Introduction

This book aims to present the finest children's literature and illustration for children of all ages. And that's a broad remit. There's a world of difference between a two-year-old and a teenager, between a young infant and a young adult. But children's literature caters for everyone in this wide age range, like a staircase of books to ascend, each step broadening their minds and their understanding of the world.

Books written for children began to appear during the mid-to-late eighteenth century, as the Enlightenment normalised education among children, and adults began to differentiate childhood

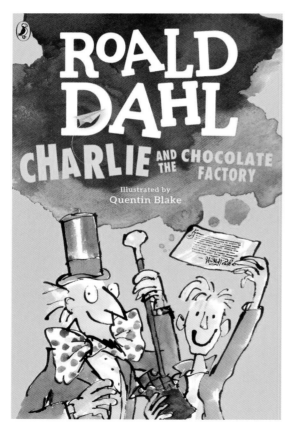

ABOVE: Illustrator Quentin Blake has long been associated with the works of Roald Dahl, but they only collaborated from halfway through Dahl's novel-writing career.

from adulthood as an important stage of development. The earliest entries to the canon were simple illustrated ABCs, number books, and instructions on correct behaviour and good manners. Oral traditions – nursery rhymes and fairy tales – had already started to appear in print, but at first there was nothing in the way of original material written specifically for the young. As consumer culture increased, however, a new genre of children's literature emerged, and the publishing industry saw the value of producing books, journals and magazines for children.

Things have changed in the intervening centuries. Modern children's books rely on humour and delight to encourage reading and writing. Picture books like *Spot* or *Kipper* have become shared activities between parent and child. Writers are now challenging the very format of a book with die-cut openings, flaps and inventive pop-up features, as in Jan Pieńkowski mock-scary *Haunted House*. Sound, touch and light are used to create multi-sensory experiences: some books have pages made of a variety of textures; stories with push-button audio clips are commonplace.

Light moral messages about the consequences of actions still underlie many stories for the young. Be nice to your friends; work together; share your toys as Bella does with her brother Dave in Shirley Hughes' *Dogger*. At the other end of the age range, however, the dilemmas are much more complex. The introduction of morally ambiguous characters and situations in young adult fiction works against the idea that there is always a clear-cut difference between right and wrong.

Today children are treated with respect for their capacity to experience and understand. Books, such as Michael Morpurgo's *War Horse*, have proved that young people are perfectly capable of handling fictional horrors. Some children's books have, however, been

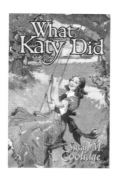 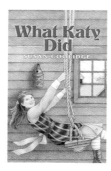   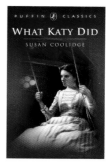

modernised for contemporary audiences in later reprints: Enid Blyton's *The Faraway Tree* now tells the story of Joe, Beth, Frannie and their cousin Rick, rather than Jo, Bess, Fannie and Dick; and all references to Dame Slap's use of corporal punishment have been removed in favour of Dame Snap, who instead punishes misbehaviour by yelling.

Traditional rollicking adventures have always been popular, from Robert Louis Stevenson's piratical *Treasure Island* to Anthony Horowitz's junior James Bond in *Stormbreaker*. One particularly noticeable trend in recent times has been the rise of children's fantasy series. Two centuries ago children's literature featured fantastical elements, such as faeries and other folkloric creatures, but it was not a genre in its own right. In the twentieth century it was the alternative worlds of Tolkien and C. S. Lewis – more fully conceived but still populated by witches, hobbits and Aslan the lion. But in the final decades of the last century a host of new fantasy realms opened up – among them Diana Wynn Jones' *Chrestomanci*, Suzanne Collins' *Hunger Games*, Eoin Colfer's *Artemis Fowl* and, of course, J. K. Rowling's *Harry Potter*.

We live in a filmic age these days. Through the use of CGI,

ABOVE: Classic children's books, such as What Katy Did *by Susan Coolidge, have received a wide variety of cover styles over the years, but the girl on the swing is by far the most popular theme.*

BELOW: Judith Kerr reading from her book The Tiger Who Came to Tea *at the Hay Festival in May 2018, when she was ninety-four. With so many nonagenarians in this book it would seem the way to a long life is to become a bestselling children's author or illustrator.*

cinema and television series can transform imaginary worlds into 3D near-reality. But the result of this remarkable technical ability is that it actually leaves less to the imagination. How many films have you been to after reading the book, which omitted your favourite parts of the novel.

There's no formula for writing a successful children's book, but there are some recurring plot devices and characters. For the very young, toys feature heavily, either anthropomorphised as, for example, in A. A. Milne's *Winnie-the-Pooh,* or come to life like Margery Williams' *Velveteen Rabbit.* Bears and rabbits are popular – Michael Bond's *Paddington,* of course, and Dick Bruna's rabbit *Miffy.* Dogs are common too, appearing more frequently than cats. Imaginary creatures also fire the imagination – Julia Donaldson's *Gruffalo* for example, Maurice Sendak's *Wild Things* and, for older children, David Almond's *Skellig.* And as Oliver Jeffers' *Lost and Found* proves, you can never go far wrong with a penguin.

When it comes to human protagonists, it always helps to have a young person as the central character. Authors have proved themselves ingenious in finding different ways of separating a child from its parents in books – through adoption, death, neglect, illness, overseas travel. Orphans abound in children's literature.

Why isolate your leading character in this way? The use of absent parental figures as a plot device forces fictional children to fend for themselves, overcoming danger by their own wit and ingenuity. Maia in Eva Ibbotson's *Journey to the River Sea* is one of many examples among our 100. Elsewhere, Emil of *Emil and the Detectives* is left on his own in Berlin after bungling an errand; Carrie in *Carrie's War* is one of many fictional children separated from their parents by evacuation during World War II and the Baudelaire children in the Lemony Snicket novels are orphaned by the death of their parents under suspicious circumstances.

Fictional children demonstrate for real children how to overcome the real challenges of life – their first school, a new home, the loss of a grandparent, darkness, the unknown. Some fictional characters, like Jeff Kinney's *Wimpy Kid* and Jacqueline Wilson's *Tracy Beaker*, show the author's extraordinary understanding of the absurd concerns that preoccupy growing young minds. Judy Blume's books and Louise Rennison's unforgettable heroine Georgia Nicolson delve remarkably, and often uncomfortably deeply, into the minds of teenage girls.

So how did we choose *100 Children's Books That Inspire Our World*? It wasn't an easy or swift process and thanks (or blame) must go to the staff at Pavilion Books who contributed lists of their early reading. A favourite question of mine to friends and family for many months would be: "What are your most-loved children's books?" The question was asked in the hope and expectation they would reinforce the strong core of titles we had already gathered, but occasionally there would be a surprise when someone mentioned an overlooked classic. My editor woke in a cold sweat one night muttering "Peter Pan!" and the list had to be jostled to accommodate J. M. Barrie's *Peter and Wendy* published in 1911 after the success of the stage play. The fact that Pavilion Books sits opposite the Great Ormond Street Children's Hospital to which the play's royalties were given, would only accentuate the shame of its omission.

You may completely approve of fifty of the titles in this collection, you may profoundly disapprove of the rest. Every one of these is *someone's* favourite, and all of them have had a significant impact on the books we give our children to read today. If there are stories here that you know and love, hooray. If there are titles or authors you've never heard of, then why not give them a go? You're never too old.

Colin Salter
Spring 2020

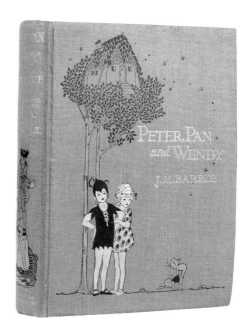

TOP: *After first appearing as just* Peter and Wendy, *publishers subsequently added the "Pan" to J. M. Barrie's book title.*
ABOVE: *Anne Fine's book made the long list – see page 215 for a further fifty titles that could arguably have been included.*

Tales of Mother Goose

(1697)

Charles Perrault (1628–1703)

Charles Perrault retold traditional folk tales with a modern twist in the seventeenth century. He paved the way for the better known stories of the Brothers Grimm in the eighteenth century and Hans Christian Andersen in the nineteenth.

During the reign of Louis XIV of France, Charles Perrault played an important part in the establishment of several of the country's académies, the institutions devoted to excellence in various fields of human achievement. He reorganised the Académie de Peinture in 1661, directing the visual arts to the glorification of the king, and in 1663 he was the first secretary of the Académie des Inscriptions et Belles-Lettres, dedicated to the humanities.

But his most famous contribution to the world of literature was the relatively low-brow collection of folk tales that he re-imagined, published in 1697 as *Histories or Tales from Past Times, with Morals*, or *Tales of Mother Goose*. The origins of the eight stories which Perrault presented are still the subject of debate but his modernisation of them made them very much his own work. They include: *The Sleeping Beauty, Little Red Riding Hood, Bluebeard, Puss in Boots* and *Cinderella*.

Using the courtly language of the day and contemporary settings, such as Versailles, Perrault introduced rhyming morals at the end of each story. They were immediately popular and went to four editions over the next three years. The first English edition was published in 1729; only one copy survives, now held in the Houghton Library at Harvard University.

Perrault combined his influence in the French court with an interest in old stories when he advised Louis XIV to build thirty-nine fountains in a maze in the gardens of the Palace of Versailles – one for each of the

characters in *Aesop's Fables*. The jets of water symbolised the conversations between the various figures, and in 1677 Perrault was the author of the maze's guidebook.

Despite his admiration for the Ancient Greek storyteller Aesop, Perrault was at the forefront of a heated cultural debate known as the Quarrel of the Ancients and Moderns. The argument concerned whether it was possible for contemporary authors to outshine the classical literature of antiquity. Perrault was a leading spokesman for the Moderns, arguing – perhaps with one eye on his pension – that the reign of Louis XIV was proving to be a golden age for the arts, whose académies he had been so influential in setting up.

Mother Goose's tales reflect highly Christian morals, as well as a traditional view of wickedness and gender. Women are depicted as passive and responsible for the Original Sin. *Sleeping Beauty*, for example, is punished for curiosity by being put to sleep, and her mother-in-law is a child-eating ogre. Girls, like Little Red Riding Hood, are vulnerable to predatory men. But boys, like Puss in Boots, are encouraged to be heroic fighters. Bluebeard kills all his wives except the last in the course of his Tale.

The *Tales of Mother Goose* have had a lasting influence on the modern fairy tale. Several of Perrault's stories were reworked by the Brothers Grimm, who in turn influenced Hans Christian Andersen. All three of these giants of the genre have created the foundation stones of storytelling for the young right up to the present day.

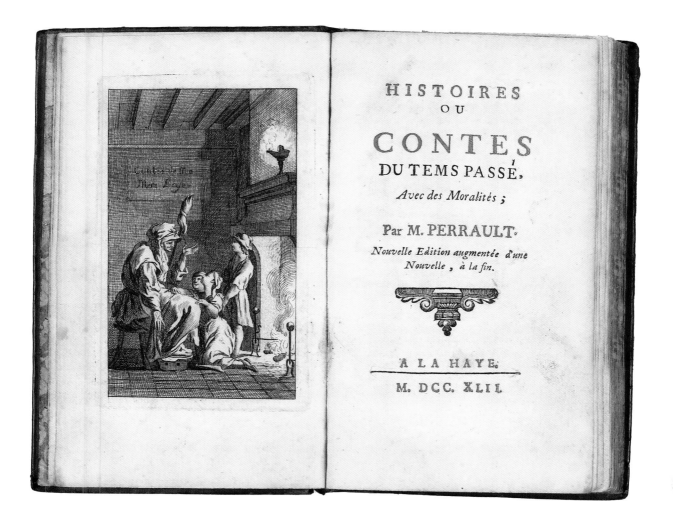

HISTOIRES
OU
CONTES
DU TEMS PASSÉ,
Avec des Moralités ;

Par M. PERRAULT.
Nouvelle Edition augmentée d'une
Nouvelle , à la fin.

A LA HAYE.
M. DCC. XLII.

ABOVE: A frontispiece from an early printing, without
the subtitle, Contes de ma mère l'Oye,
*(*Tales of Mother Goose*).*
LEFT: In 1671 Perrault was elected to the prestigious Académie
Francaise, the body concerned with the regulation of the French
language. Two books earned him this honour: La Peinture,
dedicated to the king's favourite painter Charles le Brun, and a
1670 work dedicated to the king's mistress.

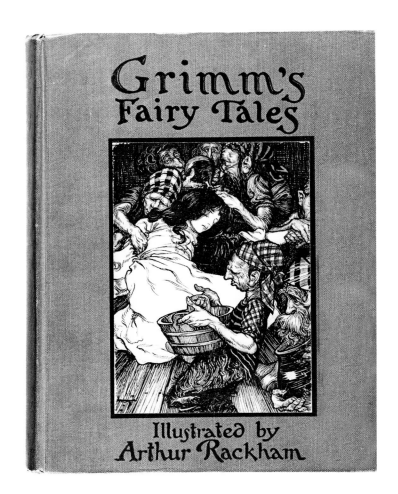

ABOVE: *Leading British book illustrator Arthur Rackham developed a reputation for pen-and-ink fantasy illustration with* Fairy Tales of the Brothers Grimm *and* Gulliver's Travels *(both 1900).*

LEFT: *Lucy Crane translated the Brothers Grimm's* Household Stories *collection from German to English in 1882 and they were illustrated by her younger brother Walter.*

Grimm's Fairy Tales
(1812–1857)

Jakob (1785–1863), Wilhelm (1786–1859)

With their universal themes – life and death, good and evil, love, greed and selflessness – folk tales have emerged to describe all aspects of the human condition. They strike chords in all of us, young and old.

The brothers Jakob and Wilhelm Grimm had a disrupted childhood. They studied law in Kassel, central Germany, following in the footsteps of their magistrate father. But following the successive early deaths of their father, grandfather and mother, they found themselves financially responsible for their younger siblings.

They worked hard in their studies to make the best possible provision for their family. In the course of their academic work, inspired by their law professor Friedrich von Savigny, they developed a love of German literature. In their homeland they are celebrated not only for their fairy tales but for a landmark comprehensive *German Dictionary (Deutsches Wörterbuch)*, which they only completed as far as the word *frucht* ("fruit") and which was finally finished by later scholars in 1961.

Jakob and Wilhelm set about collecting their famous folk tales at the request of a publisher. The first edition in 1812 contained eighty-six stories; the seventh edition, in 1857, 211. Not all of them are fairy tales, and some of them are quite literally grim: there are no charming Disney animations of *The Girl Without Hands, Death's Messengers*, or *Hansel and Gretel* involving cannibalism.

The Grimms were not collecting for children but out of academic interest. Fear that industrialisation would erase these folk tales from memory led the brothers to create their anthology of fairy tales as a preservation measure. Methods used to record the stories would become the basis for later folklore studies. They were also working on the theory that a nation's traditions reflected its character, at a time of a growing sense of German-ness – the German Confederation, which brought together thirty-nine German-speaking principalities in central Europe, was established in 1815, only three years after the first edition of the Grimms' collection.

Such nationalism can have unintended consequences. It chimed at first with the general spread of romantic nationalism in many European countries. British delight in all things German in the Victorian age, influenced by Queen Victoria's German husband Prince Albert, encouraged early translations into English. But Adolf Hitler's admiration for their supposed embodiment of Arian virtues resulted in them being banned in Allied-occupied Germany after World War II.

Children's literature only really took off in the nineteenth century. Before then very little had been written specifically for the young. After excising the most gruesome stories and sanitising others, parents saw the value of the Grimm tales as useful moral life lessons for their young readers. *Grimm's Fairy Tales* became a cornerstone of any children's library.

From the very first German editions they have been fully illustrated, and the tales have attracted the very best artists to decorate their pages. Arthur Rackham and Arts and Crafts graphic artist Walter Crane both produced memorable illustrations. Walt Disney's interest in the stories was really just an extension of that tradition of putting pictures to the words. His first animated feature film, *Snow White and the Seven Dwarfs* (1937), is a Grimm brothers tale, as well as *The Princess and the Frog* (2009), and *Tangled* (2010), based on the fairy tale of Rapunzel. Though the Grimms also collected stories such as Cinderella, Sleeping Beauty and Tom Thumb, they were derived from earlier written French folk stories.

Some of the best known of Grimm's Fairy Tales: *Rapunzel, The Elves and the Shoemaker, Little Snow White, Cinderella, Hansel and Gretel, Thumbling (Tom Thumb), The Goose Girl,* and *Little Briar-Rose (Sleeping Beauty).*

Fairy Tales

(1835–1872)

Hans Christian Andersen (1805–1875)

At first simply embellishing traditional stories, Danish author Hans Christian Andersen later began to create his own. Today his original tales are as familiar around the world as those handed down across the generations to him.

Andersen began, like the brothers Grimm, by retelling the folk tales of his youth. He had greater literary aspirations than his German counterparts, however, and his interests were not confined to fairy tales. He was also a novelist and poet who penned a briefly popular pan-Scandinavian national anthem. He travelled widely and wrote travelogues which combined local observation with philosophical passages about the role of fiction in travel writing, and about his own role in the genre as author. Some of his travelogues also included folk tales.

Andersen was born into a poor family. His mother could not read, but his father (who had fairy-tale notions of being related to the Danish nobility) used to read stories from *The Arabian Nights* to young Hans. When he was eleven years old his father died, and Hans had to start earning his keep and his school fees. He worked for a weaver and a tailor; perhaps this is where he found the inspiration for one of his stories, *The Emperor's New Clothes*.

With the backing of some supportive benefactors Andersen travelled through Europe in 1833, gathering folk tales and writing short stories as he went. In Rome he wrote a semi-autobiographical novel based on his own life and travels called *The Improvisatore* (1835). Its success, followed by two more novels in consecutive years, launched his writing career. *The Improvisatore* was published in the same year as his first collection of fairy tales, however they did not sell well, despite the inclusion of some of his best-loved stories such as *The Emperor's New Clothes, The Princess and the Pea, Thumbelina* and *The Little Mermaid*.

Still, Andersen persisted with his fairy tales. He was rewarded when in 1845 a translation of *The Little Mermaid* appeared in a popular English literary magazine called *Bentley's Miscellany*. This introduced his storytelling to the English-speaking world, and in 1847 he undertook a tour of England during which time he was introduced to his idol, Charles Dickens. "I was so happy to see and speak to the living English writer whom I love the most," he wrote.

There was a mutual respect between the two authors since both wrote about the poor and the ordinary in society. But when on a subsequent visit Andersen outstayed his welcome in the Dickens household, he was asked (after five weeks) to leave, and Dickens stopped answering the Dane's letters.

Andersen, socially awkward, never understood why Dickens dropped him. He never married, despite becoming serially infatuated with a number of women, including the Swedish opera singer Jenny Lind. He once proposed to her, and was inspired by her to write the story *The Nightingale*. It is claimed that her nickname, the Swedish Nightingale, followed its publication. When he died, his friends found a letter from a childhood sweetheart, Riborg Voigt, clutched to his chest. If his own life lacked a fairy-tale ending, his fairy tales never did.

Some of the best known of Hans Christian Andersen's fairy tales: *The Emperor's New Clothes, The Princess and the Pea, Thumbelina, The Little Mermaid, The Steadfast Tin Soldier, The Wild Swans, The Nightingale, The Ugly Duckling, The Snow Queen,* and *The Little Match Girl*.

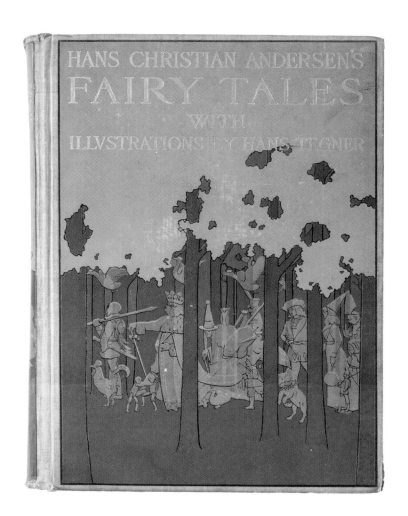

ABOVE: The international edition of Fairy Tales *(1900) illustrated by fellow Dane Hans Tegner.*

LEFT: In the late Victorian and early Edwardian periods, many deluxe illustrated editions of classic books were published; this one was illustrated in 1911 by Frenchman Edmund Dulac.

There was a Young Lady of Sweden, who went by the slow train to Weedon;
When they cried, " Weedon Station !" she made no observation,
But thought she should go back to Sweden.

TOP: A later edition of Edward Lear's A Book of Nonsense. *The original was
published under the pseudonym 'Derry down Derry'.*
*ABOVE: Lear was a great exponent of the limericks but didn't invent them. The first
known book of limericks is* The History of Sixteen Wonderful Old Women *(1820).*

The Complete Nonsense of Edward Lear

(1846)

Edward Lear (1812–1888)

Edward Lear had a poet's love for the sheer beauty of words, real and imagined. Their sound, their shape, their construction – they all mattered more to him than their mere meaning. As a result he wrote some of the most delightful nonsense verse in the English language.

The Complete Nonsense of Edward Lear is a compendium of two books published during the author's lifetime – *A Book of Nonsense* (1846) and *Nonsense Songs, Stories, Botany and Alphabets* (1871). The former was a collection of his famous limericks and the latter included his most well-known work, "The Owl and the Pussycat."

Nonsense verse is a delightfully childish form. The young, starting to make sense of the world, find its absurdity hugely entertaining – adults too for that matter. What better antidote to the mundane, rational everyday than

> There was an Old Man with a beard,
> Who said, "It is just as I feared!
> Two Owls and a Hen,
> Four Larks and a Wren,
> Have all built their nests in my beard!"

Lear did not invent the limerick, which was already current in the eighteenth century. But he certainly popularised it and, it must be said, sanitised it. The limerick was generally a vulgar thing with a rude punchline; Lear's, parents will be happy to know, are all family friendly.

For all the amusement that Edward Lear has given to others, his was a troubled life. He was the twentieth of twenty-one children, and raised by his elder sister Ann, who was twenty-one years older than him. His health plagued him throughout his life, suffering from epilepsy, asthma and frequent bouts of depression. Driven indoors by these afflictions Lear was a polymath: he was a fine landscape artist who published many illustrated journals of his European travels, one of the finest painters of birds of his generation, and a gifted musician on several instruments. He composed music for his own poetry (including "The Owl and the Pussycat") and that of others, notably Alfred, Lord Tennyson. But his personal life was incomplete and he never married.

Not content with writing nonsense with real words, Lear often made up his own. "The Owl and the Pussycat" contains probably his most famous invention – the runcible spoon. "Runcible" is such a satisfying word that one wonders why it hadn't been invented earlier. It now appears in several eminent dictionaries. Disappointingly, it's now defined more clearly than Lear ever intended: according to the Penguin English Dictionary it is "a sharp-edged fork with three broad curving prongs."

Where's the nonsense in that? But there exists an online tribute to Lear in the form of OEDILF, a community project to define every word in the Oxford English Dictionary In Limerick Form. Now that's nonsense.

Other books by Edward Lear: *Journal of a Landscape Painter in Greece and Albania* (1851), *Tortoises, Terrapins, and Turtles* (1872), *Nonsense Botany* (1888), *Tennyson's Poems, illustrated by Lear* (1889), and *The Quangle-Wangle's Hat* (1876).

Alice's Adventures in Wonderland

(1865)

Lewis Carroll (1832–1898)

Alice in Wonderland, as the book is commonly known, is one of the most influential children's books of all time. Its extraordinary turn of events liberated the fantasy genre from logic, while John Tenniel's original illustrations defined an unforgettable cast of characters.

Lewis Carroll's book, first told to young Alice Liddell and her sisters during boating trips on the River Isis in Oxford, is generally classified by academics as literary nonsense – a genre in its own right balancing the absurd with the sensible to subvert logical reasoning. It might be better described as a literary flight of fancy, to which normal rules of behaviour and possibility do not apply. By allowing his imagination to become illogical, Carroll could play with time and space for the amusement of his receptive young audience. A book which opens with Alice falling down a rabbit hole can go anywhere.

The succession of characters whom she meets down in Wonderland are memorable precisely because of their incongruity. Many have entered into the English language as idioms in their own right: the March Hare – "I'm late! I'm late!" – and his pocket watch; the Mad Hatter's tea party; the dormouse in the teapot; the Queen of Hearts with her playing card guards and her cries of, "Off with his head!"; and the grinning Cheshire cat who disappears *almost* altogether, leaving only an enigmatic smile.

Central to the story is Alice, whose journey through Wonderland and encounters with the above are on multiple occasions complicated by her abnormal growth and shrinkage as a result of the food she has recently ingested: a bottle labelled "DRINK ME", a cake with "EAT ME" spelled out in currants, and a mushroom of two halves, one to make her tiny and the other to make her neck stretch like a snake. In the final courtroom scene she expands without any help at all.

There is no evidence to suggest that these distorted changes in perspective, and the hookah-smoking caterpillar sitting on top of the mushroom, are evidence of Carroll's use of psychedelic drugs. The theory only emerged during the growth in use of hallucinogenics in the 1960s, (aided by Jefferson Airplane's song *White Rabbit*) long after Carroll's death. His interest in Alice Liddell has also been called into question. Given his own overactive imagination (and self-conscious stammer), it is perfectly possible that he simply got on better with the young, whose ability to fantasise had not yet been constrained by adult convention.

Alice's Adventure's in Wonderland was followed by *Through the Looking-Glass, and What Alice Found There* (1871), in which Alice enters – through a mantelpiece mirror – a checkerboard world populated by characters from traditional nursery rhymes, including Tweedledum and Tweedledee and Humpty Dumpty, and by the Red and White Queens. *Through the Looking Glass* famously includes Carroll's great nonsense poems *The Jabberwocky* and *The Walrus and the Carpenter*.

Lewis Carroll's surreal worlds have been a magnet for book illustrators through the ages. Carroll's own sketches are sprinkled through the original hand-written drafts of *Alice*. Since John Tenniel's definitive illustrations of the first edition, others trying their hand have included Arthur Rackham (1907), Mervyn *Gormenghast* Peake (1946), Ralph Steadman (1967), the great surrealist Salvador Dalí (1969), Max Ernst (1970), Peter "Sgt Pepper" Blake (1970), Tove "Moomintroll" Jansson (1977), and Helen Oxenbury (1999).

Other books by Lewis Carroll: *Through the Looking-Glass* (1871), *The Hunting of the Snark* (1876), and *Sylvie and Bruno* (1895).

The Hatter opened his eyes very wide on

"Well then," the Cat went on, "you see a dog growls when it's angry, and wags its tail when it's pleased. Now *I* growl when I'm pleased, and wag my tail when I'm angry. Therefore I'm mad."

"*I* call it purring, not growling," said Alice.

"Call it what you like," said the Cat. "Do you

ABOVE AND LEFT: Charles Lutwidge Dodgson (Lewis Carroll) didn't set out to write a children's book. At Alice Liddell's urging, he wrote down the story he had told the three Liddell girls on a rowing trip from Oxford, adding a few drawings to the text. Novelist Henry Kingsley, picked it up at the Liddell's home and suggested it should be published. A surprised Dodgson asked author George MacDonald for his advice while friend Robinson Duckworth suggested he commission Punch cartoonist John Tenniel to draw what would become the definitive Alice and Mad Hatter.

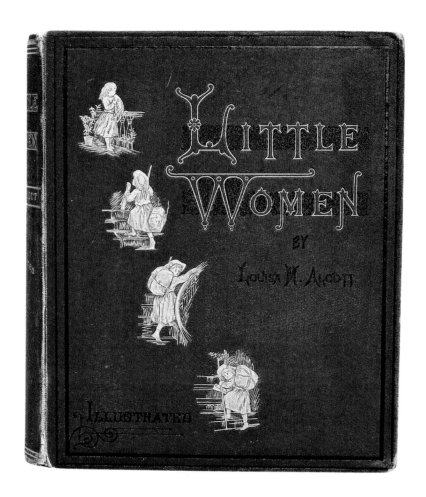

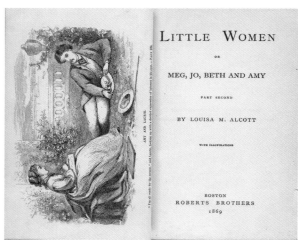

ABOVE: While some children's books, such as Alice in Wonderland, *took time to become popular,* Little Women *was an instant success, selling out the initial 2,000 print run in 1868.*

LEFT: The follow-up book to Little Women *was simply titled "Part Second" in the United States, whereas in Britain it was published as* Good Wives *to distinguish it from its predecessor.*

Little Women

(1868)

Louisa May Alcott (1832–1888)

Louisa May Alcott's classic coming-of-age story of four sisters was written at her publisher's request for little women – girls on the cusp of puberty and adulthood. But perhaps adolescent boys could learn a thing or two by reading it.

Little Women follows the fortunes of four sisters of the March family – Meg, Jo, Beth and Amy – as they come to terms with the adult world of work, love and death in Massachusetts. The book's strongly drawn female characters are landmarks of realism in children's literature.

They are based on Alcott herself and her three siblings Anna, Lizzie and May. Louisa, like Jo, was the second child, a tomboy; and Jo is the principal protagonist of the book. Beautiful Meg, like Louisa's eldest sister Anna, gets married first. Beth, like Lizzie, brings tragedy to her family through ill health. May and her fictional counterpart Amy share a desire to become an artist.

Both the real and the fictional family lived in Orchard House. The March family, like the Alcotts, lived in relative poverty, although the March girls' father had respectable work as an Army chaplain. The Alcotts often went hungry thanks to the shortcomings of their father. Mr Alcott was a harsh perfectionist who met with constant setbacks in his efforts to establish an experimental school and community, based on the thinking of his philosophical friends Ralph Waldo Emerson and Henry David Thoreau.

Emerson and Thoreau encouraged Louisa Alcott's writing. Her father's lack of employment, disapproval of tomboy Louisa, and general attitude to women created a strong female bond between the girls and their mother. By contrast the character of Professor Bhaer in *Little Women* is Alcott's idealised father figure. His capacity for affection and support for Jo's writing career showed a more nurturing, feminine side than Louisa's father ever did.

Alcott was at first reluctant to follow her publisher's advice. She did not feel competent to write a novel either

for or about girls, knowing few apart from her own sisters. In any case, when it came to children, she preferred boys to girls, and furthermore she preferred to write short stories. Her main source of income was from newspapers, to which she submitted articles about her life experiences.

She had written novels before – mostly serialised gothic potboilers to earn money, under the pen name A. M. Barnard, such as *Pauline's Passion and Punishment* (1863) and *Behind a Mask, or, A Woman's Power* (1866). But her latest, *A Modern Mephistopheles, or The Fatal Love Chase*, had been rejected, and her confidence in the novel form may have been dented. Even after its completion, neither she nor her publisher were convinced of *Little Women's* quality, but in trials with younger readers it won approval, and they went ahead with printing.

It was an immediate success, and lifted the Alcott family out of poverty at last. The realism of the March girls engaged readers completely, to the extent that they wanted to know more about them. Fans would write to her as "Jo" or "Miss March", and she would reply in character.

Little Women was promptly followed by a sequel, *Little Women Part Second* (1869). Two further books about the March sisters continued their stories: *Little Men* (1871) and *Jo's Boys* (1886). Unlike Jo, Louisa – a passionate feminist – never had boys or girls of her own, and never married.

However, her book about the importance of strong female friendships remains relevant in a modern context, and is why it has become a classic, and why there have been so many adaptations.

Other children's books by Louisa May Alcott: *Eight Cousins, or, The Aunt-Hill* (1875), *Rose in Bloom: A Sequel to Eight Cousins* (1876), *Under the Lilacs* (1878), and *Jack and Jill: A Village Story* (1880).

What Katy Did

(1872) and sequels

Susan Coolidge (1835–1905)

What Katy Did was to break the mould of the conventional narrative for young girls, which in the Victorian period placed them firmly at their parents' side as mother's little helper or father's junior housekeeper. Katy broke the rules, and through the "School of Pain" learned to become a better person.

Tomboy Katy Carr dreams of fame, success and beauty, and "to be good if I can". The latter is difficult because of her nature and her strict Aunt Izzie, who raises Katy and her siblings with a firm hand in the absence of their late mother and hard-working father. If Katy had obeyed Izzie, she would not have fallen from the unsafe swing in the barn and lost the use of her legs.

Bedridden, Katy bitterly rejects the company of her family until her cousin Helen, herself an invalid, explains that she is learning the lessons of the School of Pain – among them how to remain cheerful and make the best of things. Katy rediscovers patience and hope and, following the death of Aunt Izzie, steps fully into the role of head of the Carr household.

Katy returns in *What Katy Did at School* (1873) and *What Katy Did Next* (1886), and the rest of the Carr family feature in two further novels, *Clover* (1888) and *In the High Valley* (1890).

Coolidge based the Carr children on herself and her siblings. She chose herself as the model for fiercely independent, headstrong Katy. Katy's cousin Helen was named after Coolidge's lifelong friend and travelling companion, the author and activist Helen Hunt Jackson, whom she met while they both served as nurses during the American Civil War.

Susan Coolidge's father died in 1870, just after her first short story was printed in *Heart and Home* magazine and two years before she wrote *What Katy Did*. Many of the central characters in her novels are also coping with the loss of a parent. Katy is without her mother; in *Eyebright* (1879), Isabella Bright – I. Bright, or Eyebright –

must deal not only with the death of her mother, but the unemployment and depression of her father and their enforced move to a run-down farm. Coolidge reversed the plot of *Eyebright* for *A Little Country Girl* (1885), in which an orphan from the country is sent to stay with wealthy relatives on the East Coast. She teaches them her wholesome rural values while she learns from them some urban sophistication. In Coolidge's last novel, *Rule of Three* (1904), three sisters struggling to keep house for their widowed father must now come to terms with his remarriage and the arrival of their stepmother.

After the death of her father, Coolidge and the rest of her family travelled around Europe for two years. The places they visited provided the setting for *What Katy Did Next* and another Coolidge novel, *Guernsey Lily* (1880), in which Lily, like Eyebright, is of necessity uprooted from the comforts of home to an unfamiliar place and life – in this case from England to the Channel Islands for the good of her mother's health.

Susan Coolidge shared a publisher with Louisa May Alcott, the author of the *Little Women* series, and Alcott edited Coolidge's first book, *The New Year's Bargain* (1971), a collection of short stories. Like Alcott,

Coolidge satisfied a new demand among the reading young for more realistic stories whose protagonists experience the real challenges of life. *What Katy Did* remains popular because it provides a snapshot of the times in which it was written, and because of the realism of its headstrong central character with all her qualities and flaws.

ABOVE: Katy Carr has been progressively updated on book covers since publication. This edition, illustrated by Paul Hardy in 1903, owes a lot to the style of Edward Penfield, designer of classic Harper's *magazine covers in the 1890s.*

OPPOSITE: A sporting Katy from the 1920s.

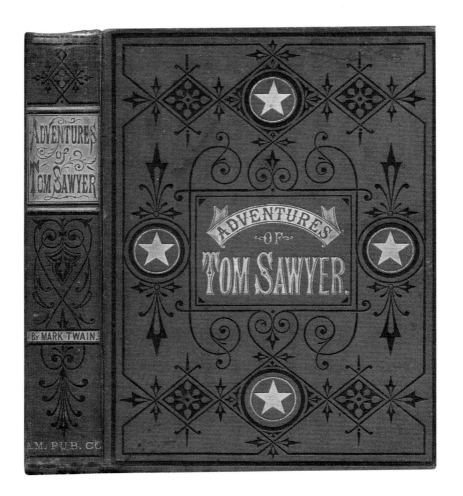

ABOVE: *The first edition of* Adventures of Tom Sawyer *published by the American Publishing Company.*

LEFT: *The frontispiece of* Tom Sawyer, *by True W. Williams, showed the eponymous hero fishing. His partner in crime, Huckleberry Finn, was based on Tom Blankenship, son of the Hannibal town drunk, who couldn't afford to go to school. In his autobiography Twain said: "He was the only really independent person — boy or man — in the community and by consequence he was tranquilly and continuously happy and envied by the rest of us."*

Adventures of Tom Sawyer
(1876)

Mark Twain (1835–1910)

Mark Twain's bestseller during his lifetime was the tale of young boy Tom Sawyer's adventures around, on and in the mighty Mississippi river. Inspired by Twain's own youth, the book was – like Twain's career as a novelist – not an immediate success.

Twain first came to national prominence in 1865 when his short story *Jim Smiley and his Jumping Frog* was accepted by a New York literary newspaper, *The Saturday Press*. Newspapers and magazines across the country reprinted it, quickly introducing Twain to a very wide audience. For many years thereafter he built his reputation not on fiction but on travel journalism. His observations of his journeys through America and Europe were wry and entertaining.

On one such trip he met Charlie Langdon, who introduced him to his sister Olivia. Twain and Olivia were wed in 1870 and after a brief spell as a newspaper editor in Buffalo, New York, settled in Hartford, Connecticut where Twain entered the most productive and successful period of his career. He continued to write his popular travelogues, but now they were interspersed with novels such as *The Prince and the Pauper* (1881) and *Pudd'nhead Wilson* (1894).

His first effort failed to impress the critics. It was the result of a bet with a neighbour Charles Dudley Warner that they could write better fiction than the romantic novels which their wives were reading. The result was a joint effort, *The Gilded Age: A Tale of Today* (1873), whose co-authorship – reviewers felt – made for confusing, disjointed prose. His next novel was a solo work, *The Adventures of Tom Sawyer*.

As with his travel writing, Twain drew on his own experiences. The book's fictional setting of St Petersburg is based on Twain's boyhood home Hannibal, Missouri; and many of Sawyer's adventures are based on Twain's childhood memories. In *Tom Sawyer* Twain sees the adult world through a child's eyes, and this makes the story live for young readers. The opening episode in which Sawyer has to whitewash his aunt's picket fence as a punishment for skipping school, and persuades other boys to do it for him, is one of the best loved passages of American children's literature.

Tom Sawyer introduces us to iconic characters like Tom's girlfriend Becky Thatcher, his partner in crime Huckleberry Finn, and the villainous Injun Joe. Becky was based on Twain's childhood friend Laura Hawkins and Joe was based on Joe Douglass, who in real life lived to 102. Tom and Huck's adventures include buried treasure and labyrinthine caves, childhood sweethearts and murderous adults.

Tom Sawyer is notable for being one of the first novels written on a typewriter. Twain was fascinated by printing machinery, thanks to his early days working as a typesetter for his brother on the *Hannibal Journal*. He invested heavily and often unwisely in new technology such as the Paige Typesetting Machine, which swallowed $300,000 of his writing income before becoming obsolete with the invention of linotype.

While *Tom Sawyer* portrayed the innocent school days of rural America, the realities of slavery took *Huckleberry Finn* and Twain's fiction into the adult realm. Its depiction of runaway slave Jim and Huck's moral dilemma over turning him in raised controversy over the book in the nineteenth century. Its use of language has taken it off children's reading lists in the twentieth and twenty-first, but it moved Ernest Hemingway to describe Twain as "the Lincoln of American literature".

Twain returned to the character in *Tom Sawyer Abroad* (1894) and *Tom Sawyer: Detective* (1896) but nothing equalled the impact of those two books written in razor sharp Missourian vernacular.

Other children's works: *The Prince and the Pauper* (1881), *The Adventures of Huckleberry Finn* (1884) (1885 in the U.S.) and *A Connecticut Yankee in King Arthur's Court* (1889).

Black Beauty

(1877)

Anna Sewell (1820–1878)

Black Beauty is one of the bestselling children's books ever published. But Anna Sewell never intended her only novel to be for children. She was writing with a campaigning zeal to expose man's cruelty to both men and beasts.

Anna's life was shaped by her Quaker faith, her family's precarious finances and an injury she sustained at the age of fourteen. She sprained her ankles in a fall; but the treatment she received was inadequate and she never recovered to full health or mobility. From then on it became easier for her to travel by horse and cart than on foot, and to observe at close quarters their treatment.

Her family made several moves, either in pursuit of employment for her father or in the hope that a change of air or treatment might suit her better. As her health declined further, she travelled around the spa resorts of Europe in search of cures. By the time she settled in Norfolk in 1866 at the age of 44, she had lived in some eight or nine different villages and towns the length of Britain, from Brighton on the south coast of England, to Wick at the northern tip of Scotland. And she had travelled by horse-drawn vehicle between them all.

So much time behind the reins gave her a shocking insight into the standards of animal husbandry. Cruelty was commonplace and, for low-paid workers, animal welfare was not a priority. From her sickbed in the village of Old Catton near Norwich, she began to write *Black Beauty* in 1871. "A special aim," she said, "was to induce kindness, sympathy, and an understanding treatment of horses." Sometimes she was too ill to lift a pen, and had to dictate chapters to her mother, whom as a child she had helped to write evangelical children's stories for their Quaker congregation.

Black Beauty is the autobiography of a horse, known to its successive owners as Black Beauty, Darkie, Black Auster, Jack, Blackie and Old Crony. It is written in the first person, and describes Black Beauty's changes of ownership and activity from youth to retirement. He is owned by a gentleman, an earl, a cab driver and a corn merchant among others.

Sewell's accurate descriptions of Beauty's working conditions as seen through the horse's eyes are gripping. The good practices are so well described as to serve as a manual for the care of animals; the bad practices are brought home so vividly that in the years following publication some of them were discontinued. The use of bearing reins, which force the horse painfully to hold its head up, straining its neck, was phased out.

In the U.S., animal welfare campaigners took to distributing *Black Beauty* among those who worked with horses to get their message across. In London, besides its contribution to the husbandry of horses, *Black Beauty* had an unexpectedly beneficial effect on the working conditions of the city's cabbies. Her reporting of them as overheard by Beauty led to a lowering of the hard-pressed drivers' license fees.

Anna Sewell completed *Black Beauty* in 1877 and sold it to the celebrated Norfolk publisher Jarrolds for £40 – around £3500, $4500 in today's terms. It appeared in bookshops in time for Christmas. Sewell died only five months later, having lived long enough to know that her only novel was a success.

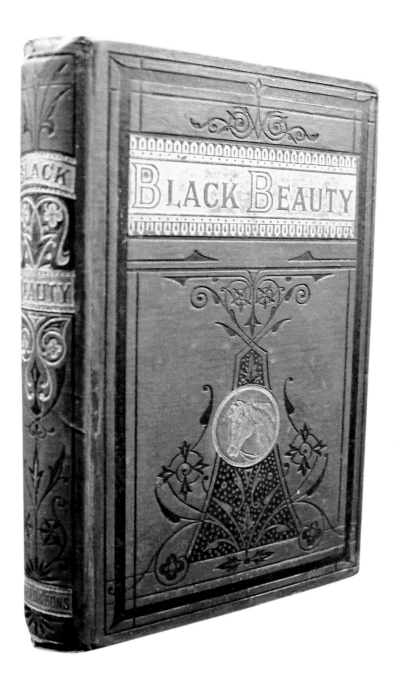

ABOVE: Anna Sewell didn't intend Black Beauty *to be a beloved children's book. It was her vehicle for drawing the world's attention to the everyday cruelty suffered by horses.*
OPPOSITE: The title page declared that it was "translated from the original equine".

LEFT: Heidi *was originally published in two parts, the first part was titled,* Heidi: Her Years of Wandering and Learning *(*Heidis Lehr- und Wanderjahre*) and the slightly awkward second* Heidi: How She Used What She Had Learned *(*Heidi kann brauchen, was es gelernt hat*).*

BELOW: *A German language version sent to Shirley Temple who brought a new audience to the story in the Daryl Zanuck-produced film of 1937. Temple was nine at the time of filming.*

Heidi

(1881)

Johanna Spyri (1827–1901)

A beloved character in an idealised pastoral landscape, *Heidi* is the embodiment of childhood innocence. At a time when books are ever more realistic in their depiction of the trials and tribulations of youth, innocence is still a good starting point for the young reader.

In the film *The Third Man* the black marketeer Harry Lime, played by Orson Welles, famously complains that after 500 years of peace and democracy, all that Switzerland has given the world is the cuckoo clock. It's a deliberately false statement which the film uses to demonstrate Lime's ignorance: in fact, the cuckoo clock is a product of Germany's Black Forest. The Swiss have given us, among other things, cheese and chocolate; a Swiss Guard for the Vatican (because of their centuries-old reputation as fierce fighters); and one of the bestselling children's books of all time, *Heidi*.

Heidi is a twice-abandoned, five-year-old Swiss girl. After the death of her parents she is raised by her aunt Dete; after Dete gets a job in the city Heidi is passed on again to her bitter, isolated grandfather who lives high in the Alps. The pair develop an affection for each other, and Heidi's kindness and happiness make her numerous friends in the nearby village.

When Heidi is eight, Dete finds her work in Frankfurt as paid companion to a young girl named Clara, who cannot walk and is regarded as an invalid. Heidi's inexperience of city life is a source of much humour, and she and Clara become firm friends. But Clara's housekeeper, the mean Miss Rottenmeier, disapproves of Heidi's innocent frivolity and restricts her freedom. Heidi becomes miserably ill and is sent back to the Alps for the good for her health, where she again finds happiness. Clara joins her there one summer and learns to walk again in the pure mountain air.

With its orphaned central character, a wicked housekeeper and the miraculous cure of an invalid at the end of the book, *Heidi* contains many of the elements popular in children's literature of the nineteenth century. It also displays a strong Christian morality. Heidi is encouraged to pray when she is unhappy in Frankfurt,

and later in the book her grandfather sees her return to the Alps as an answer to his prayers, and starts going to church again.

What really distinguishes Johanna Spyri's best-known novel is her evocation of the Swiss landscape and the role it plays in the wellbeing of all her characters. By the time of its publication, Switzerland's reputation as a land of clean air and healthy pursuits was firmly established. *Heidi* tapped into that view with its depiction of a young girl's innocent joy in the open air of the Swiss mountains. Here was a wholesome book for the children of highly moral nineteenth-century parents. *Heidi* was translated into English within a year of its publication.

Johanna Spyri spent most of her life in the Swiss canton of Graubunden, where *Heidi* is set. Born Johanna Heusser, she only began to write after her marriage to lawyer Berhard Spyri. Her first published story, using a pen-name for anonymity, was *A Leaf on Vrony's Grave* (1870), about domestic abuse. She continued to write for adults and children for the rest of her life. *Heidi* has overshadowed all her other works, but several editions of her collected output are still available today. A number of sequels about the adult Heidi were written after Spyri's death by her French translator Charles Tritten, but nothing could ever equal the tale of the nature-loving child of the mountains.

Some other children's books by Johanna Spyri: *Uncle Titus and His Visit to the Country* (1881), *Toni, the Little Woodcarver* (1882), *Gritli's Children* (1883), *Rico and Wiseli* (1885), and *Moni the Goat-Boy* (1886).

Treasure Island

(1883)

Robert Louis Stevenson (1850–1894)

Pirates! Treasure! Fighting! One of the finest adventure stories ever written, *Treasure Island* has all the ingredients to capture a young child's imagination. It was Stevenson's first published novel and brought his genius for storytelling to the attention of all ages, from six to seventy-six.

Stevenson grew up in North Edinburgh on the estuary of the River Forth, near the port of Leith. His father and grandfather were lighthouse builders, and his school holidays were often spent on inspection trips with his father to sites on the coasts and islands of Scotland. Sir Walter Scott had made similar journeys with Stevenson's grandfather which resulted in the 1822 novel *The Pirate*. Now the grandson followed in the great author's footsteps. His observations during sea journeys with his father brought authenticity to his descriptions of the sailing ship the *Hispaniola* in *Treasure Island*, his first full length novel.

Stevenson began to write *Treasure Island* soon after returning from his honeymoon. His new wife, Fanny, had a son, Lloyd Osbourne, from a previous marriage; and Stevenson set out to write a story which his 14-year-old stepson would enjoy. He bounced ideas off Lloyd, and told the story through the eyes of his central character, young Jim Hawkins, a boy of around Lloyd's age. In later life Stevenson and Osbourne would write novels together, including *The Ebb-Tide*, another seafaring tale, published in the last year of Stevenson's life.

Hawkins' adventures follow his discovery of a treasure map. His voyage to the titular island takes him into an adult world where honest men are worthy but dull, and bad men are colourful cutthroats. The battle between good and evil is clearly drawn and frequently fought, hand to hand and to the death, in *Treasure Island*.

The two central characters, young Hawkins and the pirate Long John Silver, move between the two moral extremes. Jim, often disobedient, finds himself among the pirates on several occasions, either as willing eavesdropper or unwilling hostage. And slippery Silver plays both sides against the middle to save his own skin.

Treasure Island was first published in seventeen weekly parts in *Young Folks* magazine. Its popularity there ensured its publication as a book, whose appeal to all ages foreshadowed *Harry Potter*'s similar success a century later. Stevenson's tale has been adapted for the stage more than twenty-five times, and for the large and small screens more than fifty. The public's fascination with the origins of the treasure and the fates of Jim and Silver has also spawned innumerable prequel and sequel novels.

Despite all these reworkings in other media, the original book remains unrivalled in its rich narrative and compelling characterisation. Its impact has been widely acknowledged by storytellers ever since its publication. British Prime Minister William Gladstone, at the age of seventy-six, was so gripped by *Treasure Island* that he read it through the night on his way to visit Queen Victoria in 1886; and children of all ages are still thrilled by the map which Stevenson himself drew, and on which he was the first to use the phrase, "X Marks The Spot".

Other children's books by Stevenson: *Kidnapped* (1886) and *Catriona* (1892).

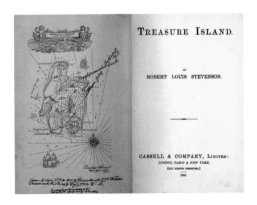

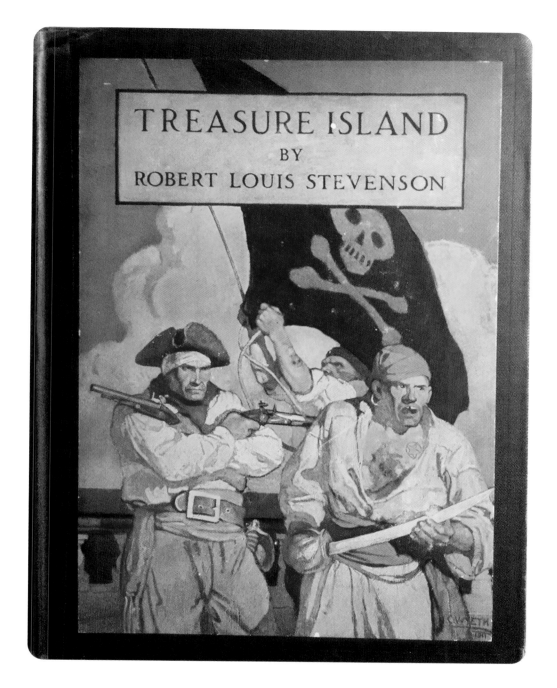

ABOVE: *Stevenson borrowed the real-life pirate Israel Hands as a character for his novel. Hands was part of Blackbeard's crew who was shot in the knee for insubordination.*

OPPOSITE: *Pirate treasure maps were invented by Stevenson. The handy plot device soon became part of pirate folklore.*

ABOVE: The Just So Stories *were written for Josephine "Effie" Kipling, who liked them repeated exactly the same, or "Just so". Sadly only one of Kipling's children, Elsie, lived beyond adolescence.*

OPPOSITE: Kipling's most famous work, The Jungle Book *(1894).*

Just So Stories

(1902)

Rudyard Kipling (1865–1936)

Effie complained if her father did not repeat his bedtime stories to her word for word, "just so". Her father being Rudyard Kipling, the *Just So Stories* were the result. Its "origin" stories are beloved of children and evolutionary biologists alike.

Effie was Kipling's eldest child, oh best beloved, and she used to fall asleep while he told her stories. But if he varied the words and phrases of them she would wake up and correct him. So the *Just So Stories* are full of memorable repetition, as for example in his perpetual way of addressing the reader as "oh best beloved", or his rhythmic description of the "great, grey-green, greasy Limpopo river, all set about with fever trees" in the story "How the Elephant Got His Trunk".

The *Just So Stories* are fanciful tales about the origins of things, mostly attributes acquired by various animal species: "How the Camel Got his Hump", "How the Leopard Got his Spots", and so on. Although they take the form of origin myths, they have a grain of truth in the suggestion that traits are not simply gained, but develop over time. No, the elephant did not get his trunk because a crocodile stretched his nose out of shape, but yes, the elephant developed a trunk in the course of its evolution.

The *Just So Stories* are written lightly and with abundant good humour which makes them perfect for reading aloud at bedtime. But they also introduce the idea of evolution to a young audience. It may not happen as quickly as in the *Just So Stories*, but it does happen.

Rudyard Kipling's collected writings are inextricably linked with the attitudes of the British Empire, which was at its zenith during his lifetime. He became known as the "Poet of the Empire" for poems such as "The White Man's Burden" about the Englishman's duty to serve in the nation's colonies. He was certainly patriotic, but not blindly so; other poems, for example "Recessional", conjure the frailty of it all.

Nor were his works exclusively set in an imperial context. The plot of *Kim* (1901) may revolve around the conflict between Russia and Britain in Asia, but *Stalky and Co* (1899) is (mostly) a set of school stories populated by characters highly cynical toward any notions of patriotism. It may be time for a re-evaluation of the author. His work for children stands apart from any doubts about his views on imperialism. *The Jungle Book* (1894) and its sequel *The Second Jungle Book* (1895) are, despite their title and their animal storylines, essentially fables about human behaviour.

Kipling was born in India to Anglo-Indian parents who conducted their courtship around Rudyard Lake in England – hence their son's name. They sent him to boarding school in England, and Mowgli's abandonment in *The Jungle Book* is said to mirror Kipling's memory of being left to the cruel mercies of his boarding school teachers. The original *Just So* story, about how the tiger got his stripes, appears in *The Second Jungle Book*.

Completing the *Just So Stories* for his editor must have been a bittersweet process for Rudyard Kipling. Although she saw three of them published in a children's magazine, Kipling's eldest daughter Effie died of pneumonia before the book's publication.

Other children's books by Rudyard Kipling: *The Jungle Book* (1894), *The Second Jungle Book* (1895), *Captains Courageous* (1897), *Stalky and Co* (1899), and *Kim* (1901).

The Tale of Peter Rabbit

(1902)

Beatrix Potter (1866–1943)

Beatrix Potter's stories, inspired by her pet rabbits Peter and Benjamin, is one of the bestselling series of all time. It was the product of a lonely childhood, but it has brought joy to millions around the world and its success has helped preserve one of England's most treasured landscapes.

Beatrix Potter's ancestors were wealthy, northern English cotton mill owners, but she grew up in London where her father was a successful lawyer. She and her brother Bertram were educated at home, far away from other relatives and rarely meeting children of their own age. Family holidays were spent in the English Lake District and the Scottish Highlands.

Beatrix, encouraged by her parents, developed a love of rural life and landscape, which she began to draw and paint to pass the time. The family kept several pets including a spaniel called Spot and a rabbit called Peter Piper, who replaced an earlier rabbit called Benjamin. Her interest in nature sparked a thirst for scientific knowledge and she refined her painting skills with accurate botanical studies, especially of fungi.

The family hired a succession of governesses to educate Bertram and Beatrix. The last of them, Anne Moore, was only three years older than Beatrix and became as much a friend and lady's companion to the young author as a teacher. When Anne left to have children, they kept in touch and Beatrix acted as an honorary aunt. She often wrote letters to them, and illustrated these letters with ink sketches in the margins.

In the summer of 1893 Anne's son Noel fell ill and Beatrix, on holiday in Scotland, corresponded with him to keep his spirits up. By the end of the summer she had run out of things to say and wrote instead that "I shall tell you a story about four little rabbits, whose names were Flopsy, Mopsy, Cottontail, and Peter." That, and the

illustrations which accompanied it, were the first draft of *The Tale of Peter Rabbit*.

Anne Moore urged Beatrix to have it published and in 1901, after every publisher had turned her down, she published it herself in a total of 450 impressions – each of them now worth a small fortune. Their success persuaded one publisher, F. Warne & Co, to revise their opinion of the book. In a new, full-colour edition, the first commercial publication of *The Tale of Peter Rabbit* sold 20,000 copies in its first year alone.

It's a charming tale, but its greatest strength lies in Beatrix's illustrations, which draw the reader in irresistibly. They are simple, clear, animated scenes, and – most importantly – drawn at animal level. The result is that we see Peter's adventures from Peter's point of view. He is always nearest in the frame, and his arch enemy Mr McGregor the gardener is beyond him in the distance. There is also real jeopardy when the angry gardener tries to capture the young rabbit with a sieve, and readers can identify the pain and loss he suffers as Peter loses his blue jacket and begins to cry at the trouble he has got himself into.

Miss Potter also brought Peter's predecessor Benjamin to the page in *The Tale of Benjamin Bunny*, and many of her other creations first saw the light in other letters to Noel Moore, including Squirrel Nutkin and the frog Jeremy Fisher. In all there are twenty-three Beatrix Potter *Tales* and their sales allowed her to buy and preserve large areas of her beloved Lake District for future generations.

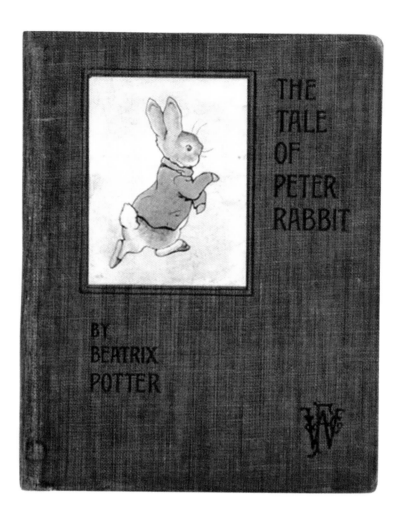

ABOVE: *An early F. Warne & Co. edition of* The Tale of Peter Rabbit. *The company had rejected the book initially because it contained line drawings and Warne had wanted colour illustrations in what they referred to as "the bunny book".*

LEFT: *Beatrix Potter's inspiring illustrated letter to the poorly Noel Moore.*

RIGHT: *Potter had resisted the publisher's request for colour illustrations with the reply that rabbit brown and green were too dull, but the restrained colour palette of the subsequent colour plates has added to their longevity.*

THE RAILWAY CHILDREN

EDITH NESBIT

ILLUSTRATED BY C.E. BROCK

ABOVE: Nesbit's The Railway Children *bears a striking resemblance to Ada Graves'*
The House by the Railway *(1896). At the climax of both books the children have to
warn an approaching engine of danger; Graves has them waving a red jacket, while
Roberta, Peter and Phyllis use the girls' red petticoats.*
OPPOSITE: Five Children and It *has been likened to "ET for the Edwardian era".*

The Railway Children
(1906)

E. Nesbit (1858–1924)

The Railway Children may owe much of its popularity today to the 1970 film adaptation, but it has made stirring reading for the young for seven generations. It owes its success to its author's willingness to place her tenderly drawn characters in realistic jeopardy.

Before Edith Nisbet, popular children's novels included *The Water Babies, Alice in Wonderland* and *Wind in the Willows*, all of them invoking fantastical worlds. Nesbit is sometimes credited with inventing the modern children's story because she was prepared to confront real-life crises from the perspective of the young. Although she was not afraid to invent magical situations, the children in her stories faced real dilemmas and dangers in their own world.

Thus, in *The Railway Children*, a family without a father (who has been wrongly imprisoned for spying) must adapt to their reduced financial circumstances by moving to the country. To save money their mother teaches the children – Roberta, Peter and Phyllis – at home and sells short stories; and to make ends meet Peter steals coal. A landslide threatens to derail the train around which their lives revolve; it is through the train they meet and befriend the wealthy Old Gentleman, and it is the train which delivers their salvation on the last page of the book.

The book refers to contemporary events in the form of the 1904–5 war between Russia and China, and in the person of the left-wing Russian dissident which the family care for. In complementary plotlines, the Russian searches for his family just as the Railway children seek to be reunited with their father. Nesbit was herself a follower of Marxism and in 1884 became one of the founding members of the Fabian Society, the socialist group from which Britain's left-of-centre Labour Party emerged in 1900.

The father's fate may have been inspired by the Dreyfus affair, in which a French army officer was framed for a spying scandal, and only released from Devil's Island, the French penal colony, in the year of *The Railway Children's* publication. Edith Nesbit's own father had died when she was three, and father figures loom large in her writing. In her first children's novel *The Treasure Seekers* (1899) the young family of a widowed father help him to find the family's lost fortune.

The idea of impoverishment, the catalyst for the Railway children's adventures, resurfaces in Nesbit's later novel *The House of Arden* (1908) which also involves its central characters in time travel, something Nesbit first visited in *The Story of the Amulet* (1906). The latter was the third in a trilogy of stories following *Five Children and It* (1902) and *The Phoenix and the Carpet* (1904) which finds Nesbit at her most fantastical. The five children who link the stories stumble across It, a mythical sand-fairy or Psammead who grants them wishes which always go comically wrong.

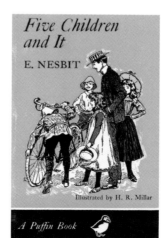

Nesbit's realistic depictions of childhood inspired many who came after her, including Arthur Ransome (*Swallows and Amazons*), P. L. Travers (*Mary Poppins*) and C. S. Lewis (the *Narnia* series). There are no magical elements to *The Railway Children* and no sequels. Its resolution so perfectly makes all its characters (and its readers) happy that there really is no need to know what happens next.

Other children's novels by E. Nesbit: *The Treasure Seekers* (1899) and series, *Five Children and It* (1902) and series, and *The House of Arden* (1908) and series.

Anne of Green Gables

(1908)

L. M. Montgomery (1874–1942)

Canadian author Lucy Maud Montgomery put a lot of her own early life into her first novel. The story, about an orphan growing up on Green Gables Farm in the fictional town of Avonlea on Prince Edward Island in Canada, has been popular ever since its publication.

In the book, Anne Shirley is the eleven-year-old orphan of the title. She is mistakenly sent to Green Gables after its owners, elderly brother and sister Matthew and Marilla Cuthbert, ask the orphanage for a boy to help them manage the farm. Marilla wants to send her back, but Matthew persuades her to let Anne stay. As Anne settles in to her first permanent home, makes new friends at school and shines in class, her lively, if sometimes controversial personality has a positive impact on the community.

At the age of sixteen she trains as a teacher, qualifying in only one year instead of the usual two, before going on to university. When tragedy and financial disaster strike the Cuthbert household, Anne is able to get a job at the school nearest to Green Gables so that she can continue to help Marilla. The position becomes available thanks to the kindness of Gilbert Blythe, against whom Anne has borne a grudge since their schooldays, when he first carried a torch for her. Their friendship blossoms, giving Anne hope for the future. Further novels by Montgomery would continue Anne's story into adulthood, as she experienced first love, marriage and motherhood.

Although not an orphan herself, Lucy Montgomery was dispatched by her father at the age of two to live with her grandparents, after the early death of her mother. She remained with them, in Cavendish on Prince Edward Island, after he moved far away to the country's North-Western Territories when she was seven. Like her orphan Anne, Lucy won a teaching qualification in one year, not two, before continuing to university to study English Literature. After a succession of teaching jobs around P.E.I., she returned to Cavendish to care for her now widowed grandmother, just as Anne did for Marilla.

Lucy had two great passions in life: writing, and nature. Both supplied her with an escape from the often unhappy conditions of her personal life. *Anne of Green Gables* was based on some notes for a possible story which she made many years earlier when she was a young girl.

After the initial success of *Anne of Green Gables*, Montgomery invented a new character, Emily Starr. Emily was another orphan, sent to live on another farm, New Moon; but her personality was much closer to Montgomery's, particularly with regard to her gift for writing.

It was in nature that Lucy, Anne and Emily all felt most alive. During long walks in the P.E.I. countryside Montgomery experienced occasional "flashes", moments of intense spiritual peace, "glimpses of the enchanting realm beyond", when she seemed to connect through her surroundings with something godlike, which she described as "a kingdom of ideal beauty".

Of her twenty novels, nine are about Anne Shirley, while a further two short story collections are about her and the other characters in her fictional community of Avonlea. Emily features in three novels; and Montgomery also wrote two books about a very different young girl, Pat Gardiner (for once *not* an orphan) whose defining characteristics are a stable family life and the love of her home. L. M. Montgomery is the bestselling Canadian author of all time.

Other books by L. M. Montgomery: *Anne of Avonlea* (1909), *Anne's House of Dreams* (1917), *Anne of Windy Poplars* (1936), *Anne of Ingleside* (1939), *Chronicles / Further Chronicles of Avonlea* (1915/1920), *Emily of New Moon* (1923) and sequels, and *Pat of Silver Bush* (1933) and sequel.

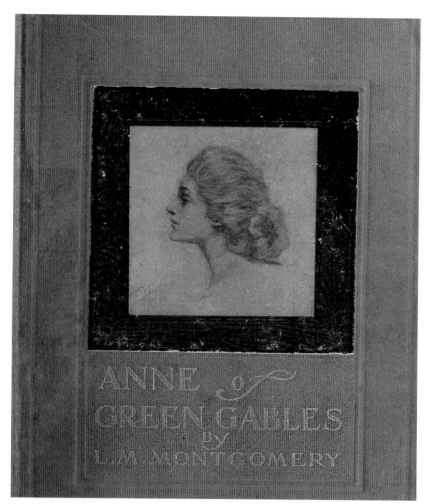

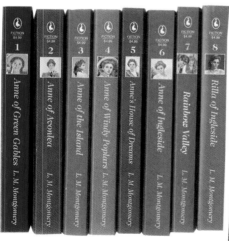

ABOVE: *The first edition of* Anne of Green Gables *pitched the book at an older readership.*

LEFT: *Montgomery's descriptions of nature were reflected in the expressive and animated way Anne experienced the world around her, something for which her character is memorable both to the reader and her fellow townsfolk.*

The Wind in the Willows

(1908)

Kenneth Grahame (1859–1932)

Wise old Badger; cultured, leisurely Ratty; humble, loyal Mole; and of course good-hearted, impulsive, anarchic Toad – Kenneth Grahame's unlikely riverside comrades disappointed critics on publication but have since delighted readers for over a century.

*T*he Wind in the Willows is a book of varying pace. At its heart it is an action adventure which follows Toad's faddish obsessions, his escape from imprisonment for theft and reckless driving, and the liberation of Toad Hall from its occupation by weasels and stoats. But it also includes briefer storylines which intersperse the main narrative.

The varied emotions and characters in these stories illustrate the book's central theme, that – in the words of Badger – "it takes all sorts to make a world." Grahame's protagonists are complex creations with a mixture of admirable and despicable attributes. Toad's carefree generosity, for example, is accompanied by his appalling arrogance and conceit.

These well-rounded inhabitants of the book were the product of Kenneth Grahame's own complicated life. He was born in Edinburgh, Scotland, but after the death of his mother and the subsequent alcoholism of his father he was raised by a grandmother in southern England. There he first experienced the countryside and wildlife of the upper Thames.

Grahame worked in the Bank of England where in 1903 he was shot at three times by a "Socialist lunatic" with a grudge against the bank. All three shots missed, but he may have suffered from post-traumatic stress which forced his early retirement to rural Berkshire in 1908. There he put down on paper the bedtime stories which he had been telling his young son Alastair; and *The Wind in the Willows* was the result. Alastair was born prematurely in 1900 with sight in only one eye and chronically bad health; he took his own life at the age of nineteen.

THE WIND IN THE WILLOWS

The book was originally printed as plain text, but its popularity has attracted many fine illustrated editions since its original publication. Arthur Rackham undertook one such version; and the best known is probably that by E. H. Shepard, illustrator of A. A. Milne's Winnie-the-Pooh stories. By coincidence Milne was also the author, in 1929, of the first stage adaptation of Grahame's *Wind in the Willows*, which he titled *Toad of Toad Hall*.

Grahame's earlier works included *The Golden Age* (1895) and *Dream Days* (1898), collections of reminiscences of childhood both factual and fictional. They were very popular at the time and critics were disappointed not to find more of the same in *The Wind and the Willows*. *Dream Days* is notable for the inclusion of his most famous short story *The Reluctant Dragon*, which broke with tradition in portraying the dragon in question in a sympathetic light.

The Wind in the Willows was Kenneth Grahame's masterpiece, and he never wrote another book. Posthumously however, his story *Bertie's Escapade*, about a pig with ambitions, was published in 1949, once again illustrated by E. H. Shepard. It is a simpler, lighter story than *Wind in the Willows*, although the presence of a human called Mr Grahame and a child called A. G. (possibly his son Alastair Grahame) suggest that it may have been written for private, family consumption. It is a cheerful tale which makes a useful primer for the more chaotic world of Toad and his friends.

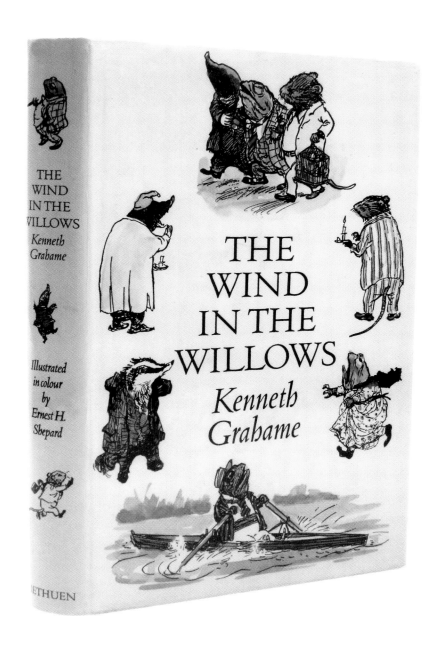

ABOVE: A later edition of The Wind in the Willows *with Ernest Shepard's illustrations to the fore. Grahame grew up around the river Thames, first in Cookham Dean, Berkshire, then at St. Edmunds School in Oxford.*

OPPOSITE: A first edition cover from 1909.

Peter and Wendy

(1911)

J. M. Barrie (1860–1937)

The mark of a truly great fictional character is when it enters the language as a metaphor. Peter Pan, an icon of eternal youth, has captured the public's imagination since his stage debut in London's West End at Christmas in 1904.

The character of Peter Pan made his debut in Barrie's adult novel *The White Bird* (1902), a mixture of social commentary and fantasy about life in and around London's Kensington Gardens. In it, Peter Pan was a baby who fled from home after being taught to fly by fairies. The idea clearly gripped Barrie: what began as a single chapter in *The White Bird* became six, evolving into a much more substantial story-within-a-story.

Not content with that, Barrie wrote a stage play about the character, *Peter Pan, or, The Boy Who Wouldn't Grow Up*, which premiered in the Duke of York's Theatre as a Christmas entertainment on 27 December 1904. His publishers, sensing a good thing, published the Peter Pan chapters of *The White Bird* as a stand-alone novella, *Peter Pan in Kensington Gardens*, in 1905, with pictures by the greatest illustrator of his day, Arthur Rackham.

The plot of the stage play is the story most familiar to us today, and it was this which Barrie expanded and wrote up into a full-length novel, *Peter and Wendy*, first published in 1911. The playscript was finally published in 1928. While Peter remains the central character, the play and book introduce us to Wendy Darling and her brothers John and Michael, the Lost Boys of Neverland, Peter's guardian fairy Tinker Bell, and his arch enemy Captain Hook the pirate.

While there is plenty of fairy dust and swashbuckling adventure in the story, it also raises philosophical questions about the nature of family, childhood and innocence. Magic is possible, it suggests, only if you really, *really* believe in fairies. Mature affection is possible for Wendy, but not for Peter, trapped forever in immaturity, eternally too young, "innocent and heartless", as Barrie described the state.

The character may have had rather melancholy origins. When Barrie was six years old his older brother David drowned in an ice-skating accident. Barrie's mother never recovered from the loss, and she and the young Barrie attempted to preserve their memories of David, forever young, by telling each other stories about him. Barrie took to imitating David by adopting his style of whistling, and even by wearing his clothes. In 1896 he published a biography of his mother, *Margaret Ogilvy: Life is a Long Lesson in Humility*.

Peter Pan continues to intrigue, and a number of unofficial sequels speculate on the futures of the original characters. Barrie himself added a final scene to the play, "When Wendy Grew Up: an Afterthought", which formed the basis of the film *Return to Neverland* (2002).

Peter Pan has become a universal symbol for agelessness. Walt Disney, after making an animated version of the story in 1953, adopted Tinker Bell as a mascot spreading magic in its title sequence. Children's playhouses are still called Wendy Houses, after the accommodation built for Wendy by the Lost Boys. J. M. Barrie bequeathed the royalties from all the works which feature Peter Pan to the Great Ormond Street Hospital for Sick Children in London, a considerable legacy which has benefited the work of the hospital ever since.

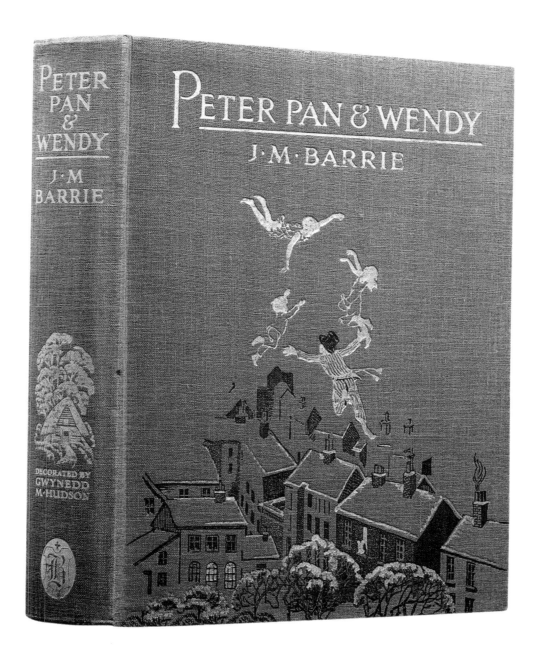

ABOVE: When Peter Pan made his first appearance in Barrie's 1902 novel The Little White Bird, *he was a baby of seven days old who had flown from his nursery to Kensington Gardens.* Peter and Wendy *(1911) was subsequently changed to* Peter Pan and Wendy.

OPPOSITE: A first edition bearing the original title.

THE SECRET GARDEN

FRANCES HODGSON BURNETT

ABOVE: The American first edition, published by Frederick A. Stokes in August of 1911, came with eight colour plates by Charles Robinson.
LEFT: Like so many children's classics, The Secret Garden *has been illustrated by the great and the good of the illustration world – this 1956 edition by E. H. Shepard.*

The Secret Garden
(1911)

Frances Hodgson Burnett (1849–1924)

Now a classic of children's literature, Frances Hodgson Burnett's parable of decline and rejuvenation was largely neglected during her lifetime in favour of other novels and plays from her prolific output. Today the reputation of the book, like the secret garden itself, has been restored.

Revitalisation runs deeply through *The Secret Garden*, as it does through Burnett's life. In the book Mary Lennox, spoiled by servants but neglected by her parents, must learn compassion and empathy during her search for the garden. Her cousin Colin has lost the use of his legs through neglect, having been confined to bed after a spinal injury. He must learn to walk again. The roses of the walled garden, locked up after the death of Colin's mother, have withered. They, like the characters in Burnett's story, can be revived through hard work and loving care. All of them, plants and people, are helped by Dickon, the son of a maid, who has an affinity with nature and is the book's catalyst for recovery.

Burnett's life was similarly a series of setbacks and recoveries. She was born in Manchester, where her father ran a successful hardware store. The family suffered two blows – his sudden death after a stroke, and the damage to the local economy of the cotton famine caused by the American Civil War – which forced them to move into gradually smaller homes. Burnett is known to have mourned the loss of a garden at the time.

The family accepted an invitation to join her uncle in Tennessee, where he ran a thriving dry goods business. But the end of the war which had bolstered his profits meant he could no longer support Frances and her family, who were forced to move out and live in a log cabin. Frances began to write short stories to boost the family's income and for the rest of her life writing became her way of keeping poverty at bay. She was a workaholic, in her own words "a pen-driving machine".

Her first novel, *That Lass o' Lowrie's* (1877) was well reviewed. Following an introduction to Louisa May Alcott in 1879, she began to write for children as well as adults; in 1881 she wrote a stage play, *Esmerelda*, which enjoyed the longest Broadway run of the nineteenth century.

Such a work rate was unsustainable, and she suffered bouts of exhaustion and depression, from which writing was often her escape as well as the cause. Her marriage broke down, and she split her time between the U.S. and England, where for many years she lived in Great Maytham Hall, a large country house with magnificent gardens. Here, following the collapse of a disastrous second marriage, she recovered and wrote the framework of the story which would become *The Secret Garden*.

Frances Hodgson Burnett's greatest literary success during her lifetime was *Little Lord Fauntleroy* (1886), a rags-to-riches story whose central character Cedric was modelled on her son Vivian. Although she had wanted a daughter, Burnett doted on Vivian, dressing him in frilly velvet suits and grooming his long hair into curls. Although the book is rarely read now, the character of Little Lord Fauntleroy has entered the English language as a metaphor for a child of the privileged upper classes.

Burnett's other great children's novel is *A Little Princess* (1905), written during the gestation of *A Secret Garden*. It is a blend of *Secret Garden* and *Fauntleroy* in that the protagonist Sara, like Mary, is a child of a father serving in India. Sara finds herself impoverished in England, and her life, like Cedric's, is transformed by unexpected wealth. *A Secret Garden*, whose resolution relies not on wealth but on redemption through hard work and kindness, has outlasted them all.

Other children's books by Frances Hodgson Burnett: *Little Lord Fauntleroy* (1886), *A Little Princess* (1905), *Queen Silver-Bell* (1906) and series, and *The Lost Prince* (1915).

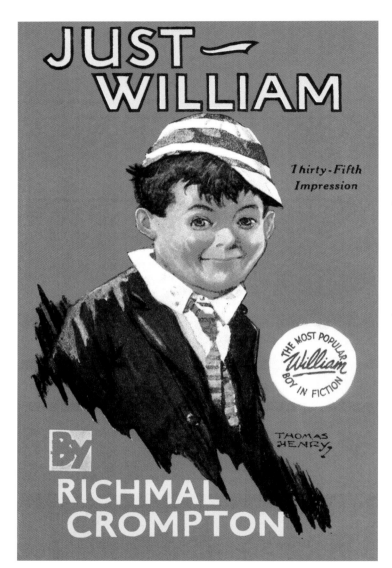

THE MOST POPULAR *William* BOY IN FICTION

LEFT: William Brown made his first public appearance in "Rice Mould Pudding", a short story in Home Magazine *in 1919.*
BELOW: William and the Masked Ranger *was published in 1966. The final book in the William series is* William the Lawless *from 1970.*

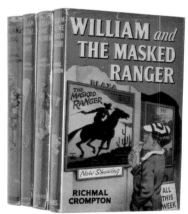

Just – William

(1922)

Richmal Crompton (1890–1969)

William Brown, to give him his full name, is a classic British character – the schoolboy who is always getting into trouble, either through no fault of his own or because he occasionally sidles carefully around the truth. Every real schoolboy knows his world.

School children who get into trouble are popular protagonists in children's stories, central characters that their readers can readily identify with. In American literature the truants Tom Sawyer and Huckleberry Finn spring to mind. In Britain, where the layered class system is reflected in a variety of separate school systems, there are several candidates. Chronologically, wedged between the upper class boarding school antics of Frank Richards' Billy Bunter (created in 1909) and Anthony Buckeridge's Jennings (who appeared in 1950), comes Richmal Crompton's William Brown.

Schoolboy William and his gang of friends; Ginger, Henry and Douglas – the self-styled Outlaws – wreaked a very British form of middle-class havoc in their southern English village community for 48 years. He witnessed the fascism of the 1930s, the evacuated children of World War II, the space race of the 1950s and the emergence of pop music in the 1960s. Yet throughout his 39 books he has never aged a day, perpetually eleven years old.

Making his debut soon after social order had been comprehensively rearranged by the ravages of World War I, William was altogether more populist than his boarding school rivals. He went to an ordinary day school and his adventures revolved around his family home and its locality, not the dormitories and classrooms of the privileged English Public School. One of the adventures in his first collection of short stories, *Just – William*, emphasises this by having William find work as a servant in a grand house, "below stairs".

William, like many small boys, is often forced to do things against his will and nature; and we read in *Just – William* of events surrounding his reluctance to be a page boy at a wedding; to attend a temperance meeting; and to babysit – the latter the occasion of the forming of the Outlaws. William is at an age where girls are becoming interesting and the book also describes his crush on a teacher and his rivalry for the affections of his brother's girlfriend.

One of the great comic creations of any schoolboy series, the spoilt and lisping Violet Elizabeth Bott, does not make her debut until the fifth volume of stories, *Still William* (1928). Her threat to "thcream and thcream and thcream until I'm thick" forces William against his better judgement to include her in many of the Outlaws' exploits.

William is a consistently and believably drawn naughty schoolboy with mud on his face and scratches on his knees. It comes as a surprise to many to discover that William's author, Richmal Crompton, was a woman, and one who herself attended a boarding school for the daughters of the clergy. Perhaps it was through her support of Britain's Women's Suffrage movement that she knew what it meant to be a fighter. She wrote often about the inequality of the sexes, for example in the short story collections *A Monstrous Regiment* (1927) and *Ladies First* (1929).

She became a school teacher, working in girls-only schools until her success as a writer allowed her to retire. It has been suggested that she modelled William on her nephews Jack and Tommy; and that her loss of mobility after contracting polio was the reason that her stories never move far from William's home turf.

Other children's books by Richmal Crompton: *Enter – Patricia* (1927), *Jimmy* (1949), *Jimmy Again* (1951), and *Jimmy the Third* (1965).

The Velveteen Rabbit
(1922)

Margery Williams (1881–1944)

The wishful thinking that a child's favourite toy might come to life inspired many of Margery Williams' books. *The Velveteen Rabbit* was her first children's novel, and has remained an enduring favourite.

The velveteen rabbit of the title is an unfashionable Christmas present given to a boy who would much rather play with the latest mechanical toys. But gradually he comes to love the rabbit. This, as a stuffed toy horse has told the rabbit, is how toys become "real". But when the boy contracts scarlet fever, the doctor orders that all his toys, including the velveteen rabbit, be burnt for the sake of hygiene. The rabbit despairs, until it finds itself crying a real tear; its dream has become a reality, and it scampers away to join the other real rabbits in the wild.

After moving from England to the United States with her family as a young woman, Margery Williams began her writing career with novels for adults, but without great success. She was determined to be published back at home, and took her first novel *The Late Returning* (1902) to a publisher in London. There she met her future husband Francesco, an Italian bookshop manager.

They were visiting Turin in northern Italy in 1914 when World War I broke out, and Francesco patriotically joined the Italian army. Margery returned to London with their two children, through whom she became a great admirer of children's author Walter de la Mare's work. Here, she felt as she read to her family, was a writer who truly understood his readership. De la Mare believed that young children's imagination is not restricted by facts but fed by them. In a sense, he thought, children are both wildly creative with the world as they see it and also detached from it. It is when the so-called real world intrudes on their fantasies that their child-like vision of it "retires like a shocked snail into its shell," to be replaced by a duller, more intellectual, analytical imagination.

After the war, Francesco and Margery were reunited and, thanks to her earlier U.S. residency they were able to return to the United States and escape the privations of post-war Europe. Marjory began to write for children, guided by her spiritual mentor De la Mare, and *The Velveteen Rabbit* was the first result. Its immediate success made her a celebrity.

Other stories about toys followed, including *Poor Cecco: The Wonderful Story of a Wonderful Wooden Dog Who Was the Jolliest Toy in the House Until He Went Out to Explore the World* and *The Little Wooden Doll*, both from 1925. *The Wonderful Wooden Dog* was named after her son; *The Little Wooden Doll* and *The Skin Horse* (1927) were illustrated by her daughter Pamela.

There is often a sense of sadness and loss about Williams' books. When the velveteen rabbit returns as a real rabbit, the boy thinks only that it resembles his old toy, not recognising that it really is. Critics have attributed this to the death of her beloved father when Williams was only seven – he was responsible for introducing her to books and to the joy of descriptive narrative, and she felt his loss keenly. She dealt with it by convincing herself that, as she claimed, "hearts acquire greater humanity through pain and adversity."

In later years Williams wrote with critical success for young adults, often with themes of isolation or alienation. *Winterbound* (1936), for example, throws two teenage girls into the role of parents to their younger siblings when the parents depart suddenly.

Other books by Margery Williams: *Poor Cecco* (1925), *The Little Wooden Doll* (1925), *The Skin Horse* (1927), and *Winterbound* (1936).

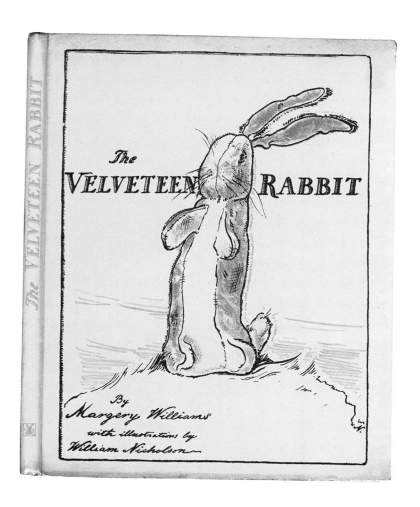

Spring time

ABOVE: *The full title of Margery Williams' book was* The Velveteen Rabbit, or How Toys Become Real.

LEFT: *William Nicholson, whose illustrations define the much-loved rabbit, had a varied artistic career. He designed original stage settings for* Peter Pan *in 1904 and taught art to Winston Churchill in the 1930s.*

ABOVE: A. A. Milne's illustrator, Ernest Shepard, spent a lifetime with Pooh Bear. He first collaborated with Milne on When We Were Very Young *in 1924 and one of his last jobs was* The Pooh Party Book *in 1971 when he was 92.*

Winnie-the-Pooh

(1926)

A. A. Milne (1882–1956)

We each had our own teddy bear as children, but Winnie-the-Pooh speaks for them all. He is a sort of Every-Bear, the best bear that ever lived in the pages of our childhoods. Long before Walt Disney acquired the rights to him, Pooh Bear was the guide and friend in our earliest adventures.

Alan Alexander Milne was a successful author of plays and humorous verse, the latter often published in the British satirical magazine *Punch*. His only child, Christopher Robin Milne, was born in 1920, and it was natural that the new father should turn his hand to writing for the youngest member of his family.

Following an early guest appearance in one of the poems in Milne's 1924 collection of children's verse *When We Were Very Young*, Pooh Bear made his formal debut in the ten stories of *Winnie-the-Pooh* two years later. (Milne always used the hyphens; Disney dropped them and the French had no translation for Pooh and opted for *Winnie l'Ourson*, or Winnie-the-Bear)

The book introduced us not only to Winnie-the-Pooh but to his cuddly toy friends Eeyore the donkey, Piglet, Kanga and Roo, and Hundred Acre Wood, the outdoor world which they explored with its inhabitants Rabbit and Owl. Tigger the toy tiger arrived with the book's sequel *the House at Pooh Corner* (1928).

Hundred Acre Wood is based on Five Hundred Acre Wood, a part of Ashdown Forest in Sussex near the farm on which the Milnes lived. Pooh, Piglet, Tigger, Eeyore, Kanga and Roo were the real toys of the real Christopher Robin (who appears in the books as Pooh's human companion); and all of them except Roo survive to this day, on display in the New York Public Library's Children's Center, having been donated by the book's publishing company in 1987.

The stories in *Winnie-the-Pooh* are memorable – Pooh's efforts to steal honey by disguising himself as a cloud; his getting stuck in Rabbit's doorway after eating too much honey; his attempt with Piglet to trap a Heffalump; their tracking of their own footprints in the search for a Woozle. The game of Poohsticks, still played by children everywhere, is invented in *The House at Pooh Corner*.

Pooh made further appearances in several poems in Milne's collection *Now We Are Six* (1927). The stories are inseparable from the line drawings which illustrated them. The artist E. H. Shepard drew the images for all four books in which Pooh appears. He modelled the woods on Ashdown Forest, and the toy animals on Christopher Robin's own – with the exception of Winnie-the-Pooh himself, which Shepard based on his own son's bear Growler.

Pooh's immediate popularity overshadowed all Milne's other literary successes, much to the author's disappointment. Milne had felt able to turn his pen to many different genres (including a bestselling 1922 detective thriller *The Red House Mystery*); but now all anyone wanted was Pooh. He was also concerned at the unwanted attention shown to his son because of the Pooh books, which strained their relationship for many years.

For the rest of us however, Winnie-the-Pooh, that humming, honey-loving "Bear of Very Little Brain" embodies the innocent joy of being young in a wonderful world, as encapsulated in the last words of *The House at Pooh Corner*, "wherever they go and whatever happens to them on the way … a little Boy and his Bear will always be playing."

Children's books by A. A. Milne: *When We Were Very Young* (1924), *Winnie-the-Pooh* (1926), *Now We Are Six* (1927), and *The House at Pooh Corner* (1928).

Emil and the Detectives
(1928)

Erich Kästner (1899–1974)

Few books by German authors have succeeded in the English-speaking world. Many of Erich Kästner's books were burned in his homeland, thanks to his opposition to Hitler's rise to power. Of his pre-war works, only *Emil and the Detectives* survived the bonfires.

Erich Kästner was a pacifist and an outspoken critic of Hitler's militarism and politics. His opposition came to the attention of Hitler's National Socialist Party. Several times he was arrested and interviewed by the Gestapo, and Hitler's Minister of Propaganda, Joseph Göbbels, included his books in the list of those "un-German" works which should be burned in the Nazi book burnings of May 10, 1933. Kästner witnessed the bonfires in person. Only *Emil and the Detectives* was spared. It was very popular in Germany and had already been adapted into a successful film version in 1931. No doubt Göbbels thought that a ban of such a well-loved story might undermine the politics.

The book broke with the conventional approach to children's literature. It was set in the modern German world, and its subject was real crime – the theft of a month's wages which Emil was given the job of delivering to his grandmother in Berlin. With the assistance of 25 local boys, his detectives, Emil tracks down the thief and exposes a whole gang of bank robbers.

Published just a year before the Great Depression triggered by the Wall Street Crash, here was a children's book confronting very real problems – and they were solved by children. In Britain the first Famous Five book about modern children fighting crime, *Five on a Treasure Island* (1942) was still thirteen years away.

Among Erich Kästner's other "un-German" books, *The 35th of May, or Conrad's Ride to the South Seas* (1931) is a satirical fantasy for children which he began writing before *Emil*. Young Conrad enters a number of extraordinary worlds through his uncle's huge wardrobe, almost twenty years before C. S. Lewis's *The Lion, the Witch and the Wardrobe* (1950), but almost twenty years after E. Nesbit employed the device in her short story *The Aunt and Amabel* (1912).

Kästner returned to Emil in *Emil and the Three Twins* (1933), although – perhaps because of the new political climate – with less inspiration and enthusiasm than before. In the same year he wrote *The Flying Classroom* about a feud between two schools with rival philosophies, a comedy which was no doubt seen by Göbbels as another dig at the political state of one-party Nazi Germany.

For the next decade Kästner wrote uncontroversial children's stories such as *The Missing Miniature* (1935), and light adult comedy romances (often published in neutral Switzerland) like *A Little Border Traffic* (1938), set in Salzburg, Austria, a country which Hitler had just annexed. He avoided the arrival of Russian troops in Berlin in 1945 by inventing a non-existent movie called *The Wrong Face* which, he told the authorities, required him to travel out of the city for location filming. Thus he escaped the worst excesses of the victorious forces in the German capital.

After the war his reputation was restored, his earlier books were rediscovered and his new work appreciated. His 1949 children's book *Lottie and Lisa*, about twins separated at birth who meet for the first time at summer camp, became the Disney classic *The Parent Trap* (1961). The same year, ever a pacifist, he published a satire about the search for peace called *The Animal Congress*, in which the world's animals force the humans to settle their differences peaceably.

His autobiography *When I Was a Little Boy* (1957), intended for children to read as well as adults, won the Hans Christian Andersen Award for a lasting contribution to children's literature in 1960. It covers his childhood in Dresden (whose destruction he mourns in the introduction) and ends in 1914 with the outbreak of World War I. He omits certain memories because,

ABOVE: The 35th of May, or
Conrad's Ride to the South
Seas *was a fantasy featuring
a roller-skating horse. It was
the book Kästner was struggling
to write and set it aside to
write* Emil.

LEFT: Emil and the Detectives
*was regarded as unusual because
it featured an unsanitised world
in which children interacted with
rough-hewn characters. However,
Jim Hawkins and Tom Sawyer
had already passed this way.*

as he writes in the book, "Not everything that children
experience, is meant to be read by children!"

Other children's books by Erich Kästner: *The 35th of May,
or Conrad's Ride to the South Seas* (1931), *Anna Louise and
Anton* (1931), *Emil and the Three Twins* (1933), *The Missing
Miniature* (1935), *Lottie and Lisa* (1949), *When I Was a
Little Boy* (1957), and *The Little Man* (1963).

The Adventures of Tintin series

(1929–1976)

Hergé (1907–1983)

Belgian cartoonist Georges Prosper Remi, known by the pen name Hergé, created an ageless boy reporter who became a veritable icon of children's literature, instantly recognisable to generations of children who have shared his twenty-three adventures.

Tintin made his debut in the Belgian newspaper *Le Vingtième Siècle* (The Twentieth Century) in a serialised comic strip, *Tintin in the Land of the Soviets*. All twenty-three Tintin stories published during Hergé's lifetime began life this way, subsequently in *Le Soir* newspaper and from 1946 in Tintin's own weekly magazine *Le Journal de Tintin*.

The early stories took Tintin's role as journalist seriously, and contained factual reports for the newspaper from the Soviet Union, the Congo and the United States. They were commissioned by Hergé's editor, a highly conservative Roman Catholic priest determined to indoctrinate his young readers, and reflected the often racist, right-wing attitudes of the time. Such attitudes are absent from later tales of Tintin, and Hergé moved away from political commentary towards character-driven stories in order to be able to continue to work during the Nazi occupation of Belgium in World War I.

Tintin is unusual as a central character, highly moral and resourceful but almost devoid of personality. All the colour in his adventures comes from other people. He is based on an earlier strip of Hergé's about a boy scout called Totor, and on Hergé's brother Paul. At first Tintin works alone except for his faithful fox terrier Snowy. Over the nearly fifty years of his drawn existence, however, he gradually accrued a recurring cast of companions and adversaries.

His closest friend Captain Haddock first appears drunk in the ninth book, *the Crab with the Golden Claws* (1941 in book form) but grows into a staunch, vociferous ally in any fight – the perfect antithesis to Tintin's boy-scout practicality. Distracted, hearing-impaired boffin Professor Calculus introduces himself in the twelfth volume, *Red Rackham's Treasure* (1944).

The detective twins Thomson and Thompson, with their hopeless idea of disguising themselves by wearing national costume wherever they go, arrive with orders to arrest Tintin in his fourth adventure, *Cigars of the Pharaoh* (1934), having originally appeared in their own strip. Their slapstick accidents stem from Hergé's love of classic silent movie comedy. When not in national dress they appear in identical suits, bowler hats and walking sticks, a look modelled on two real-life identical twins, Hergé's father and uncle.

Hergé's personal favourite was *Tintin in Tibet* (1960), written during the break-up with his first wife and at a time when he was under great stress to deliver new artwork week in, week out. It is remarkable for its spiritual themes, and features a very personal recurring character in Chang, the young boy who first befriends Tintin in *The Blue Lotus* (1936).

In reality, Zhang Chongren was a student who introduced Hergé to Eastern art and philosophy in 1934. Hergé began to reveal these influences both in his work and his private life, and critics have claimed his output at times is reminiscent of the great Japanese printmakers Hiroshige and Hokusai. From that time too, he began to do much more thorough research for his drawings. If *Tintin in Tibet* is his favourite, *The Blue Lotus* is the first great Tintin story.

When the strips were collated and published as books, Hergé often used the occasion to revise dialogue and even redraw panels which had become outdated or offensive. The notorious *Tintin in the Congo* has proved particularly in need of rehabilitation in its portrayal of imperial Belgium's attitude to its then-colony in Africa. *The Black Island*, set in Scotland, underwent a major reworking at the request of its British publishers, who noted 131 errors about British culture in its images.

LES AVENTURES DE TINTIN

REPORTER DU "PETIT VINGTIEME"

AU PAYS DES SOVIETS

-HERGÉ-

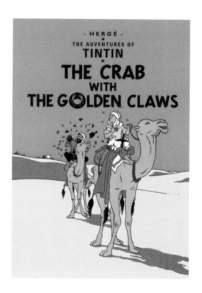

LEFT: One of the few children's books to tackle Joseph Stalin's Bolshevik government policies, Tintin in the Land of the Soviets *was followed up by* Tintin in the Congo.
BELOW: The first sighting of the irascible, whisky-loving Captain Haddock came in The Crab with the Golden Claws *(1941).*

· HERGÉ ·
★
THE ADVENTURES OF
TINTIN
★
THE CRAB
WITH
THE GOLDEN CLAWS

Many of the Tintin books have kept pace with or anticipated developments in the modern world, dealing with subjects such as space travel, television production, propaganda and alcoholism. But Tintin remains constant throughout. Only in the last book completed by Hergé, *Tintin and the Picaros* (1976), does he change at all – by wearing trousers instead of plus fours.

Selected Tintin books by Hergé: *The Blue Lotus* (1936), *The Black Island* (1938), *King Ottokar's Sceptre* (1939), *Red Rackham's Treasure* (1943), *Prisoners of the Sun* (1949), *Destination Moon / Explorers on the Moon* (1952/54), *The Calculus Affair* (1956), and *Tintin in Tibet* (1960).

Swallows and Amazons

(1930) and series

Arthur Ransome (1884–1967)

Arthur Ransome's story about a sailing holiday in the English Lake District is a classic of youthful adventure and make believe. The author became so fed up with the illustrators suggested by his publisher that he eventually took to illustrating the books himself.

Swallows and Amazons relates the summer escapades of the Walkers and the Blacketts, the young crews of two sailing dinghies, the *Swallow* and the *Amazon*. They become friends, join forces against a common enemy (the Blacketts' sullen uncle Jim), play at being pirates and solve a real crime. The success of the novel made it the first of twelve about the characters it introduced, and Ransome was working on a thirteenth at the time of his death.

The book is rooted in Ransome's own childhood. Like the Walkers and Blacketts he spent childhood holidays on a farm in the Lake District; and in the 1920s he settled there as an adult. His observations of rural life were regularly printed in the Country Diary of the *Guardian* newspaper, and contribute to the reality of the world of *Swallows and Amazons*.

The fictional landscape is an amalgam of two lakes, Windermere and Coniston Water, and the mountains that surround them, merged to suit the storyline. Some of the later novels in the series are set in the sailing waters of the Norfolk Broads, to which Ransome had by then relocated.

Ransome was a keen sailor who owned a succession of yachts himself. One of them was named the *Nancy Blackett* after one of the heroes of *Swallows and Amazons*. He made his last long-distance sailing voyage at the impressive age of seventy. The parts of the book which describe the children's journeys under sail are highly convincing, one of the reasons for the series' popularity.

The book was encouraged by a summer during which Ransome taught the children of some friends to sail. Although he owned a dinghy called *Swallow*, his friends' boat was named *Mavis*, not *Amazon* and *Mavis* is preserved to this day in a museum on the shores of Coniston Water. Ransome himself is the model for grumpy Uncle Jim, who in the book resents the children interrupting his efforts to write his memoirs. The children give Jim the nickname Captain Flint, a nod from Ransome to Robert Louis Stevenson's great pirate tale *Treasure Island*.

Arthur Ransome was very protective of his *Swallows and Amazons* series. He rejected the illustrations originally commissioned for the first book by his publishers; grudgingly accepted the publisher's choice of illustrator for a second edition; but began to illustrate later books in the series himself and in time replaced the images in earlier books with his own. He was, it turned out, a fine artist in his own right. When the BBC made a TV adaptation of *Swallows and Amazons* in 1963, Ransome made no secret of his furious dislike of the results.

Before becoming a children's author he had worked as a foreign correspondent in Russia for the Manchester Guardian and became an apologist of the Bolshevik takeover. Though friendly with Lenin and Trotsky – he would go on to marry Trotsky's secretary Evgenia – he also passed sensitive information to the British government

He was also a prolific non-fiction author, particularly on literary criticism and Russian affairs. But he only wrote one novel apart from the *Swallows and Amazons* series. *The Elixir of Life* (1915) is a Gothic novel about eternal youth. In contrast, *Swallows and Amazons* is grounded in a convincing reality of summer holidays, physical activity and make-believe imagination to which children – even in the Age of Technology – can still relate.

Selected other books by Arthur Ransome: *Swallowdale* (1931), *Peter Duck* (1932), *Coot Club* (1934), *Pigeon Post* (1936), and *Secret Water* (1939).

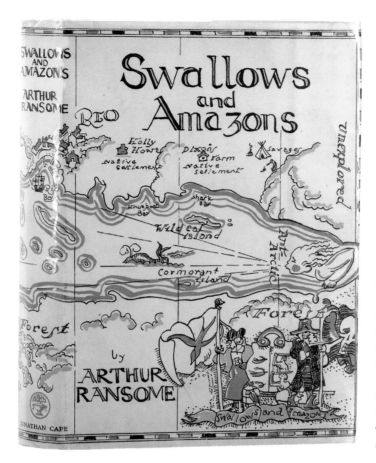

LEFT: Ransome was an exacting author, rejecting the original illustrations commissioned for the book and railing against various aspects of the BBC's 1963 adaptation, which changed the character name of "Titty" to "Kitty".

BELOW: There were twelve completed novels featuring the families of the Swallows and Amazons. After starting in the Lake District the drama moved to the Norfolk Broads, while the final book, Great Northern, *is set in the Outer Hebrides.*

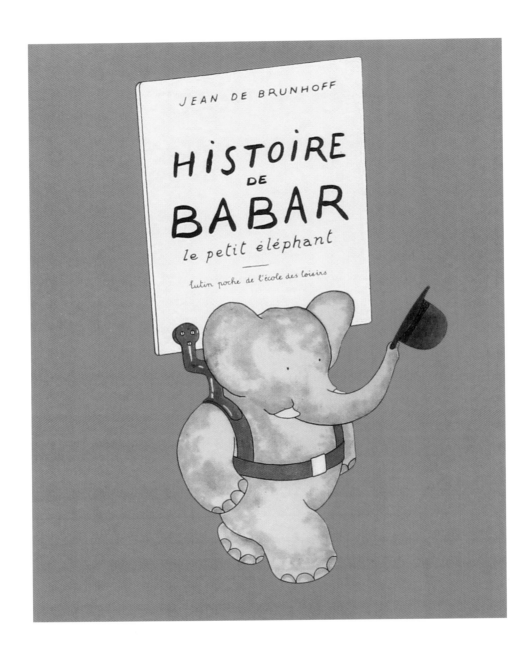

ABOVE: *Jean de Brunhoff managed to complete only seven Babar books before he died from tuberculosis at thirty-seven. His son Laurent continued the series in 1946 and the character continues to be licensed in many spheres. There are Babar stores in Japan.*
OPPOSITE: Le Voyage de Babar *(1932) was the second title in the series.*

The Story of Babar

(1931) and series

Jean de Brunhoff (1899–1937)

A French children's classic written between two global conflicts was conceived in a world very different from today's. But it remains a mind-broadening and charming read for the very young in the twenty-first century.

Jean de Brunhoff died in 1937 after writing seven books about Babar, the green-suited elephant king. While many children's books focus on the intimate situations of childhood – family, friends, homelife – *The Story of Babar* takes us and its characters to new, unimagined places. For the elephant it is urban civilisation; for the reader it's the jungle, the killing of Babar's parents by a big game hunter, parenthood and the notions of palatial monarchy and an ordered society beyond the family home.

The orphaned Babar leaves the jungle and wanders into the city. There he is educated and clothed, before his cousins Arthur and Celeste seek him out and bring him back home. There, his experience of the wider world wins him the crown of the elephant kingdom on the death of the old king. He introduces urban sophistication to the elephants and marries Celeste.

Like many children's characters, Babar began life as a bedtime story, told by Cécille de Brunhoff to her sons. Her husband Jean was an artist and the boys asked him to provide pictures to their mother's tales. When *The Story of Babar* was accepted for publication, she was due to be credited as co-author but modestly asked for her name to be removed.

Babar the elephant shows all the wisdom usually attributed to his species. His character makes quite a journey in the course of the seven books – from the young innocent to benevolent king in the course of the first book; tactical genius in the war with Lord Rataxes of Rhino Land in the second; husband of Celeste and father of his children Pom, Flora and Alexander in the sixth.

De Brunhoff's stories reflect the values of their times. The issue of big game trophy hunting may not have caused a stir back then but may require some explanation today. And his depiction of African natives as blood-thirsty, spear-waving savages in a scene from *Babar's Travels* (1932) now raises eyebrows. Belgian author Hergé has faced similar retrospective examination over his depiction of racial and national stereotypes in the early Tintin stories such as *Tintin in America* and *Tintin in the Congo*.

The Babar stories can be seen as a metaphor for French colonialism in the so-called "dark continent". Babar, an African native, comes to Paris where he is civilised, clothed and educated before returning to spread the benefits of western civilisation among his fellow primitives. Others have interpreted them as an elaborate parody of colonial values; the French Empire was already in the past at the time Jean de Brunhoff was writing. Today, for the most part, we can enjoy the storylines and settings, and the warmth and wisdom of his central character.

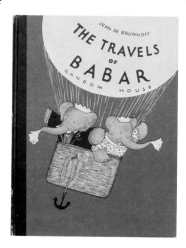

After de Brunhoff's early death his son Laurent picked up his father's pen and has to date added another forty-five Babar books to the canon. They have introduced many new characters to Elephant Land including Babar's grandson Babar II.

Some other Babar books: *Babar the King* (1933), *Babar and Zephir* (1936), and *Babar and His Children* (1938).

The Camels Are Coming
(1932) and series

Captain W. E. Johns (1893–1968)

With a career spanning some fifty years, around a hundred books and well over 250 stories, James Bigglesworth's fictional life is the story of aviation from World War I to the 1960s. That's a lot of derring-do and stiff upper lip from fiction's bestselling air ace.

Biggles made his publishing debut in a short story called *The White Fokker* (1932), printed in *Popular Flying* magazine which his creator W. E. Johns founded. Later the same year the first Biggles book *The Camels Are Coming* appeared, containing *The White Fokker* and sixteen other stories. In them we meet Biggles, his sidekick cousin Algy and 266 Squadron, with which Biggles served in World War I.

Between the wars Biggles flew as a freelance pilot in trouble spots around the world, occasionally on missions for the British Secret Service. At the outbreak of World War II he re-enlisted in the RAF and flew with 666 Squadron, where both he and Captain Johns became acquainted with a new generation of flying machines and jargon. After the war he joined Scotland Yard's specially created Air Police Division and became a flying detective. Biggles was just beginning to think about retirement in 1968 in Johns' last, unfinished Biggles novel, *Biggles Does Some Homework* (1997).

Author Captain William Earl Johns was an RAF pilot in World War I, in the very earliest days of military flying. Aircraft were unreliable and pilots undertrained. Johns joined the Royal Flying Corps, as it was then known, after fighting as an infantryman in Gallipoli and Greece. After only seven months of training he was appointed as a flying instructor, and over the next four months had several brushes with death. In one three-day period he crashed three planes – one into the sea, one into sand dunes, and one into the back door of a fellow officer's lodging.

The risks were high: if you weren't shot down by the enemy you might shoot yourself down. The technology of the time meant that machine guns fired though the path of the spinning propeller. If the synchronisation between bullet and blade failed, you risked reducing your wooden prop to a stub and plummeting earthwards, as Johns did twice. When he was finally posted to active service in August 1918 flying bombers over enemy lines, he was shot down after only six weeks and became a prisoner of war for the last two months of the conflict. Biggles, it must be said, had a better record than his creator.

The early Biggles books contained graphic accounts of war, with deaths a regular occurrence and the strain of combat often relieved by alcohol and cigarettes. Johns' target audience were young adults, who welcomed a certain level of realism. As a younger readership developed a taste for Biggles, Johns began to soften his style accordingly. For example a case of whisky in early editions becomes a crate of lemonade in later ones.

There is little that can be done by editors about the almost complete absence of female characters from the Biggles stories – only the German spy Marie Janis recurs in several stories, the object of Biggles' chaste and unrequited love. But it should be noted that Johns also wrote eleven novels about Flight Officer Joan "Worrals" Worralson, in response to a British Air Ministry request to encourage more women to join the Women's Auxiliary Air Force during World War II. The character was based on his friend, the flying heroine, Amy Johnson.

Other books by Captain W. E. Johns: *Sky High* (1936) and series, about pilot-crimefighter Deeley "Steeley" Montfort Delaroy; *Worrals of the WAAF* (1941) and series, about Flight Officer Joan "Worrals" Worralson; *King of the Commandos* (1943) and series, about Captain "Gimlet" King; and *Kings of Space* (1954) and series, about the sci-fi adventures of retired pilot "Tiger" Clinton.

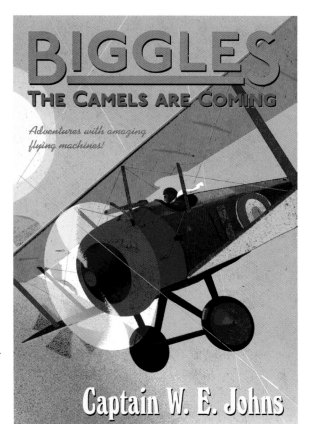

BIGGLES

THE CAMELS ARE COMING

Adventures with amazing flying machines!

Captain W. E. Johns

RIGHT AND BELOW: The Camels Are Coming *was the first of a squadron of ninety-nine Biggles books from 1932 to 1997. Captain William Earl Johns wrote from experience. In World War I he was shot down over enemy lines while piloting a De Havilland DH4. He was taken Prisoner of War, but his rear gunner died. After the war he worked as an RAF recruiting officer in Covent Garden and rejected T. E. Lawrence (of Arabia) from the service, when he tried to join up using a false name.*

The Camel soared up like a bird under the big fuselage.

THE CAMELS ARE COMING

By
W. E. JOHNS
(William Earle)

PUBLISHERS
JOHN HAMILTON, LTD.,
LONDON, W.C.1

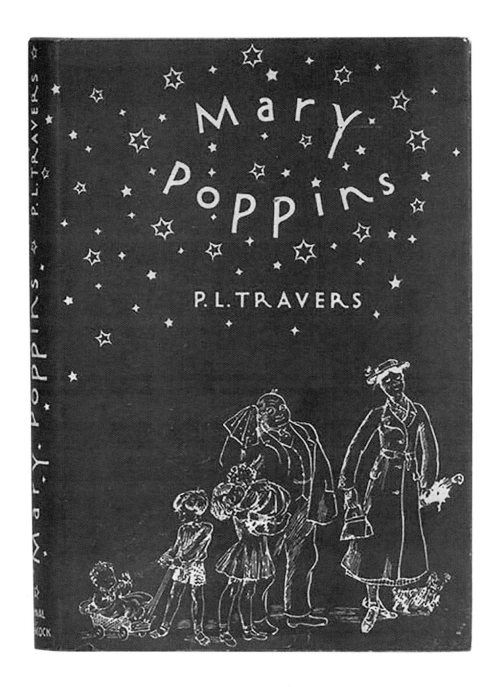

ABOVE: Unlike the film, there were four Banks children in the book; Jane and Michael, and baby twins John and Barbara.

OPPOSITE: There were eight Mary Poppins books in all, Mary Poppins in the Kitchen *(1975) was the last and included recipes.*

66_____ 100 Children's Books That Inspire Our World

Mary Poppins
(1934) and series

P. L. Travers (1899–1996)

It took Walt Disney over twenty years to persuade P. L. Travers to let him film *Mary Poppins*. She didn't believe cinema could do her story justice; and she continued to hold this view after the release of the movie, which she hated with a passion.

It is thanks to Walt Disney that most of us know Mary Poppins, the "practically perfect" nanny to the dysfunctional Banks family at 17 Cherry Tree Lane, London. She arrives on the East Wind with her carpet bag and parrot-handled umbrella; and departs with the West Wind, umbrella aloft, floating away like a parachutist in reverse. While she is with the family, her magic brings joy and order to the children's lives in a series of impossible adventures. They take tea on the ceiling with the irrepressible Mr Wigg, meet the Bird Woman and go Christmas shopping with one of the stars of the constellation Taurus.

Mary Poppins was the first of eight books about the character and the family for whom she cares until it is time to move on. She visits them three times, in the first three books; the other five are collections of adventures which happened during those visits. The last volume, *Mary Poppins and the House Next Door*, was published in 1988, in P. L. Travers' 90th year.

The books differ in some significant respects from the film. There are, eventually, five Banks children, not two, Jane and Michael, who are portrayed in the Disney version. Their adventures are sometimes even more fantastical than those in the film, despite Disney's brilliant use of animation. Dick Van Dyke's on-screen character, the chimney sweep Bert, is an amalgam of several in the original book.

In the books, the children's father Mr Banks is strict and inattentive to the children's needs, largely absent throughout the series. But he softens in heartwarming

fashion during the course of the film. Mr Banks, like Travers' own father, worked in a bank. In the film he is sacked because of the children's behaviour and wins salvation through becoming a better father; in reality Travers' father was demoted from bank manager to clerk because of his alcoholism. Disney saw *Mary Poppins* as P. L. Travers' attempt to rehabilitate her father through the character of Mr Banks, and the story is told in the movie *Saving Mr Banks* (2013).

P. L. Travers' father died of tuberculosis at the age of forty-three when she was only seven; and her aunt, who came to help her mother raise the children, became the model for Mary Poppins. As P. L. Travers first created her she was a much sterner nanny with a strong streak of vanity. Travers thought Julie Andrews too pretty to play her.

She was unhappy about the softening of the Poppins character, strongly objected to the use of animation, and disliked the musical numbers composed for the film by Richard and Robert Sherman. When the film was released, she hated it and refused Disney permission to make any more. And when she negotiated the stage rights with Cameron Mackintosh shortly before her death, she stipulated that no Americans be involved, particularly any with a connection to the Disney production (including the Sherman brothers). Despite her wishes, Disney released a new film, *Mary Poppins Returns* in 2018, with permission from the Travers' estate.

Other books by P. L. Travers: *I Go By Sea, I Go By Land* (1941), *The Fox at the Manger* (1963), *Friend Monkey* (1972), and *Two Pairs of Shoes* (1980).

Ballet Shoes

(1936)

Noel Streatfeild (1895–1986)

Streatfeild's story of dreams and childhood careers came so easily to her that she couldn't believe it was any good. Thousands of dreaming children begged to differ; and it launched her career as a writer for the young.

Writing was not Noel Streatfeild's first choice of occupation. As young women during World War I, she and her older sister Ruth put on plays. Ruth's talent was as an artist, but Noel shone as a performer and pursued a professional career in repertory theatre companies for ten years. When stage work became scarce she turned her hand to writing romantic adult fiction, using the name Susan Scarlett.

The world of theatrical digs and backstage scandal was the setting for several of her novels, and a natural choice when she decided to turn her hand to books for children. The result was *Ballet Shoes*, the story of three adopted sisters and their aspirations. Beautiful Pauline wants to act; spirited Posy loves to dance; only tomboy Petrova has no interest in the performing arts and wants to be an engineer and pilot.

The circumstances of their adoption are unusual. Their adoptive father, Gum, is an eccentric palaeontologist who finds the infants during his travels around the world. Pauline was orphaned by the *Titanic* disaster, Petrova by the death of her parents in Russia; and Posy's ballerina mother had no time for her. A succession of adults guide the girls through their childhoods and toward their dreams. Gum is absent for most of the book, but plays a crucial role in realising the wishes of one of the sisters in the end.

When *Ballet Shoes* was accepted for publication its publishers commissioned an artist, Ruth Gervis, to provide images for it, unaware that Gervis was Noel's sister Ruth, now working under her married name. The sisters were delighted to be working together again. Ruth went on to build a reputation as an illustrator of children's books by many authors, including Mary Treadgold and Enid Blyton.

After *Ballet Shoes*, Streatfeild continued to write her adult novels, but now in tandem with her output for children. Although they are all stand-alone stories, many of them were renamed to capitalise on the success of *Ballet Shoes*, and are sometimes known as the *Shoes* series. *Party Frock* (1946), for example, became *Party Shoes*; *The Bell Family* (1954) was retitled *Family Shoes*.

Several are set in worlds of performance, either in sport – *Tennis Shoes* (1937) and *White Boots / Skating Shoes* (1951) – or in the arts. *Wintle's Wonders / Dancing Shoes* (1957), *Curtain Up / Theatre Shoes* (1944) and *The Circus is Coming / Circus Shoes* (1938). The latter won the Carnegie Medal awarded annually by Britain's Library Association for the best children's book by a British author. It is *Ballet Shoes*, however, the first of her children's novels, for which Streatfeild is best-known and most loved.

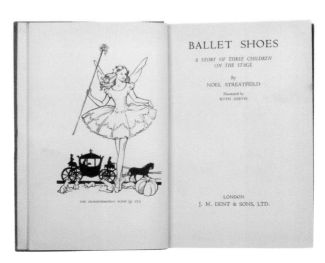

Noel Streatfeild

BALLET SHOES

One shilling and sixpence

A Puffin Story Book

ABOVE: Ballet Shoes *appealed to every budding ballerina. Noel Streatfeild trained at the Royal Academy of Dramatic Art and worked as an actress before turning her hand to fiction. She was the great-granddaughter of prison reformer Elizabeth Fry.*

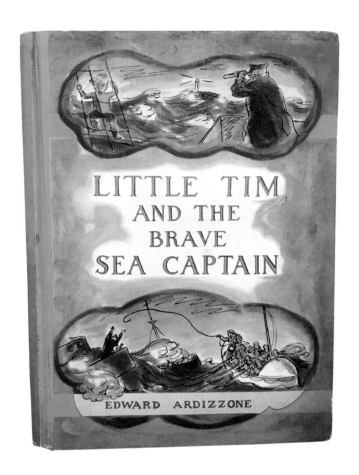

ABOVE AND LEFT: The Little Tim *series of books, published by Oxford University Press, started with Tim stowing away on a steamship after his parents tell him he is too young to become a sailor.*

Little Tim and the Brave Sea Captain

(1936) and series

Edward Ardizzone (1900–1979)

The fine, lively lines and muted colours of illustrator Edward Ardizzone's watercolour paintings have graced many an author's frontispiece. With his own stories about young Tim and his friends, Ardizzone evoked the dream childhood of every boy, full of danger and happy endings.

Born in Vietnam to a French-Italian father and an English mother, Edward Ardizzone was largely raised in eastern England by his maternal grandmother. He showed early promise in art classes and after further training he turned professional at the age of twenty-six.

He found success as a commercial artist providing images for advertisements and magazines – Johnny Walker Whisky was an early client – and the magazine work led naturally to book illustration. His first commission was in 1929 for a new edition of Sheridan Le Fanu's 1872 collection of gothic horror stories, *In a Glass Darkly*.

Little Tim and the Brave Sea Captain was his first book as author, and it launched a long series of young Tim's adventures at sea. Between 1936 and 1977 we were introduced to Tim and his friends Lucy, Charlotte and Ginger in around a dozen titles, such as *Tim and Lucy Go to Sea* (1938), *Tim to the Rescue* (1949), *Tim and Charlotte* (1951) and *Tim in Danger* (1953).

Ardizzone's sketchy style was perfect for animating stormy seas and conjuring up drama. His hand-written speech balloons added impact to the illustrations; and his habit of drawing the lettering for the title on the front cover gave the whole book a sense of personal immediacy, as if the story could not wait to be read.

His naturalistic ink-and-wash drawings gained him a job as a war artist when World War II erupted across Europe. His first mission pitched him into immediate danger as he accompanied the retreating British Expeditionary Force to Dunkirk. He saw further action recording scenes in North Africa, Italy and – in the final months of the war – Germany itself. His two published volumes of war reminiscences, *Baggage to the Enemy* (1941) and *Diary of a War Artist* (1974), are based on over 400 sketches and paintings which he made during his time abroad, all now held by London's Imperial War Museum.

After the war he picked up where he had left off, fulfilling commissions from magazines and advertisers, including Guinness and posters for the films of the famous Ealing Film Studios. When the annual Kate Greenaway Medal for children's illustration was inaugurated in 1956, his latest *Tim* book, *Tim All Alone*, was the first winner.

He was incredibly prolific, and by some estimates he illustrated five times as many books by other authors as by himself. If there is one book cover for which he is best remembered, it is Clive King's *Stig of the Dump* (1963). He also worked with his cousin Christianna Brand, who wrote down the *Nurse Matilda* stories (1964-74) which they had both heard at their grandmother's knee. Their grandmother had in turn heard them from her father, Edward and Christianna's great grandfather. Edward also collaborated with his daughter-in-law Aingelda Ardizzone on two books about abandoned toys, *The Little Girl and the Tiny Doll* (1966) and *The Night Ride* (1973).

Other books written and illustrated by Edward Ardizzone: *Nicholas and the Fast-Moving Diesel* (1947), *John the Clockmaker* (1960), *Diana and her Rhinoceros* (1964), *Sarah and Simon and No Red Paint* (1966), and *The Wrong Side of the Bed* (1970).

The Hobbit

(1937)

J. R. R. Tolkien (1892–1973)

John Ronald Reuel Tolkien's creation of a fantastical world, Middle-earth, was a work of disciplined, painstaking imagination undertaken over decades. Its first appearance came in his first novel, *The Hobbit*, a book which single-handedly revived the fantasy fiction genre for a modern audience.

The poet W. H. Auden, whom Tolkien taught at Oxford University, recalled how his tutor began to write: Tolkien was marking exam papers when, confronted by a blank sheet of paper from one candidate, he was inspired to write, "In a hole in the ground there lived a hobbit." It became the first line of *The Hobbit*.

Bilbo Baggins is the eponymous hobbit, caught up in the search of a band of dwarves for treasure guarded by a dragon called Smaug. Baggins' journey across the Shire is one of self-discovery as he and his companions fight trolls and goblins with the help of the wizard Gandalf.

Tolkien was the Professor of Anglo-Saxon at Oxford between the two World Wars. He was an authority on the Old English narrative poem *Beowulf* and its Scandinavian and Germanic counterparts – epic tales of mythological heroism in the eternal battle between good and evil. He once said that "*Beowulf* is among my most valued sources."

He fought at the bloody Battle of the Somme in World War I, and his traumatic experiences in the trenches may have driven his academic interests. The past is a safer place. These old epics dealt with origin myths from a long-lost world; their battles were over, their story complete, unlike the uncertain present of a modern world torn apart by conflict.

The parallels between those old tales and the brutal war in Europe are obvious, specifically as Tolkien was the first scholar to take *Beowulf* seriously as historical record, not merely a linguistic curiosity of absurd fantasy. *The Hobbit* and its Middle-earth sequel *The Lord of the Rings* rely heavily for their plots on climactic battles and overarching struggles between the dark and the light. Tolkien's descriptions of these battles in *The Lord of the Rings* are vividly frightening.

Tolkien sketched his earliest ideas of Middle-earth in 1914, and made amendments to later editions of *The Hobbit* in the light of Middle-earth events in *The Lord of the Rings*. The stories of those two books are set in a Third Age of Middle-earth, and *The Silmarillion*, published posthumously, includes episodes from the mythical world's earlier history.

Tolkien was not the first modern writer to devise imaginary worlds. He owed much to the author George Macdonald. Tolkien was a devout Christian, and the moral journey of Bilbo Baggins has some roots in John Bunyan's *Pilgrim's Progress*. But his new blend of morality, fantasy and adventure combined with the sustained cohesion of his Middle-earth injected respectability and credibility into a genre which had often been regarded as childish and unsophisticated.

Both Macdonald and Tolkien were influences on C. S. Lewis's *Narnia* series. Lewis and Tolkien were friends, both members of an informal group of Oxford authors known as the Inklings, which also included another great children's author, Roger Lancelyn Green. Lewis also noted the difficulties of writing fantasy, suggesting that its broad acceptance as juvenile literature led many authors to write for children, despite complex concepts that could form an adult work. This was reflected in the Christian parallels of Lewis's *Narnia*, which though not obvious to its younger readers, were unmistakable to its adult audience.

The advent of high fantasy and the popularity of Tolkien's works can be credited with allowing fantasy to enter the mainstream.

The Hobbit has never been out of print, and continues to inspire new generations of readers and writers. Terry Pratchett's Discworld, for example, would not exist without it.

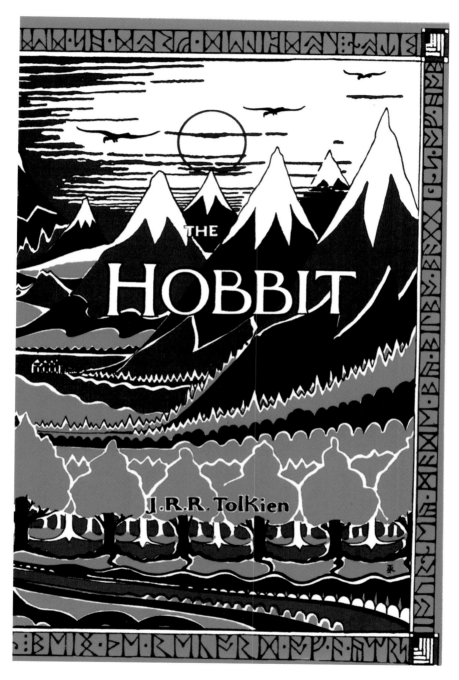

ABOVE: Tolkien finished the story in 1932 and after amassing comments from friends, including C. S. Lewis, gave the manuscript to Allen and Unwin. The initial print run of 1,500 sold out in three months.

ABOVE: Madeline *was first published in 1939 and after its post-war popularity, Bemelmans and (latterly) his grandson John Bemelmans Marciano wrote five sequels between 1953 and 1961. Madeline, of course, is the one at the back turning round.*
OPPOSITE: In Madeline's Rescue *(1953), she falls into the River Seine and is rescued by a dog.*

Madeline

(1939)

Ludwig Bemelmans (1898–1962)

For anyone who knows and loves *Madeline*, these are surely the four most evocative lines of poetry every written:

> In an old house in Paris
> That was covered in vines
> Lived twelve little girls
> In two straight lines.

Each of the six books about the French schoolgirl begins with these words, transporting the reader immediately back to the world introduced in the first volume of the series. There we first meet Madeline, who walks on the parapets of bridges, to the terror of her teacher Miss Clavel; Madeline who teases the tiger at the zoo and sees the shape of a rabbit in a crack in the ceiling; Madeline, whose scar following an appendectomy (in the very first Madeline book) is the envy of all her fascinated friends.

> And all the little girls cried, "Boohoo,
> We want to have our appendix out, too!"

Set in Paris, the story is told in a few short but memorable rhyming couplets and swept along by author Ludwig Bemelmans' swift, movement-filled sketches. Who can forget the sequence of images depicting Miss Clavel, who "afraid of a disaster, … ran fast, and faster"?

Despite the presence of the Eiffel Tower on the cover and in many of the pictures, Bemelmans was not a Frenchman. He was born in a part of the Austro-Hungarian Empire now in Italy, to Belgian and German parents. *Madeline* was written in English after he moved to New York.

The relocation to the United States in 1914 was the result of a troubled childhood. Bemelmans' father was an artist who absconded with another woman when both Ludwig's mother and Ludwig's governess were expecting his child. Ludwig, only six, developed a rebellious attitude to authority and rebelled against the discipline of his new school in Regensburg, Germany. It's easy to see where Madeline gets her bad behaviour from.

Things were no better when instead he was sent to work in his uncle's hotel in Austria, where he behaved so badly that it was a simple choice between reform school and leaving the country. Bemelmans' version of events may not be entirely accurate, but it is colourful. He used to say that the head waiter beat and whipped him to the point where Bemelmans threatened to shoot him if he did it again. The waiter did it again, and Bemelmans shot him, causing serious injury.

In New York, Bemelmans served in the U.S. Army, and then scraped by with several lowly hotel jobs, including one at the Ritz Carlton. Finding himself more or less unemployable for any length of time, he finally gave up and became a fulltime artist like his father, as well as a writer.

His first book, *Hansi* (1934), was for children, but he wrote extensively for adults too. Today, his children's stories are also much loved in Japan, where many of them remain in print.

Some other children's books by Ludwig Bemelmans: *Hansi* (1934), *The Golden Basket* (1936), *Rosebud* (1942), *The Happy Place* (1952), *Parsley* (1955), and *Marina* (1962).

Mike Mulligan and his Steam Shovel

(1939)

Virginia Lee Burton (1909–1968)

A story about a steam-powered mechanical digger may look considerably outdated, but it is the human interest which has made Mike Mulligan and his Steam Shovel *an enduring favourite.*

The steam shovel was invented in 1796 as a device for moving large amounts of earth and minerals quickly. It became an indispensable tool for the great railway builders of the nineteenth century and in the early twentieth century steam shovels dug the Panama Canal. They found a further use in the 1920s when the spread of the motor car led to the rapid expansion of the highway network. But by the 1930s they were being superseded by mechanically simpler, more reliable diesel-powered machines.

This is the situation in which Mike Mulligan and his steam shovel Mary Anne find themselves in Virginia Lee Burton's 1939 story. Obsolescent, they try to outrun the spread of diesels by looking for work in small towns which their new-fangled rivals have not yet reached. When a new town hall is to be built, Mike claims that he can dig the cellars for it in a day. The incredulous town council agrees to let him try, but even Mike has private doubts about the task ahead. Is it the end of the road for him and Mary Anne?

Virginia Lee Burton studied art and dance at the San Francisco Art Institute and used to practice her drawing skills by sketching fellow passengers on the journey to it from her home in Alameda. Her first work was as an illustrator for a Boston evening newspaper, sketching actors, dancers and scenes for the paper's arts reviews. Her theatrical experience resurfaced in her final book, *Life Story* (1962), a history of the world drawn as a stage show.

She published her first book, *Choo Choo*, a forerunner of *Thomas the Tank Engine*, in 1936. An artist first and foremost, her writing process evolved out of her early sketches in charcoal, which inspired the written story, rather than the other way around. In addition she designed every aspect of the book, including the front cover and the lettering.

Choo Choo is, like *Mike Mulligan*, a moral tale about the value of teamwork, willingness to change and a good job well done. The little train is weary of its freight and passenger work and longs to roam free, with disastrous results. Despite the unflashy black and white technique, Burton's images shimmer with speed and life. They are of their time and beautiful.

During World War II Burton founded a textile collective called Folly Cove Designers, guided by the principles of William Morris's Arts and Crafts movement. It produced designs for home furnishings hand-printed with lino blocks and built a strong reputation for its patterns and craftsmanship. It disbanded only after Burton's death.

Burton wrote little more than a book a decade, but her unique style of illustration and the humanity of her stories have endeared her to generations of children.

At the end of the story, Mary Anne completes the phenomenal task of digging the town hall cellar in a day, but Mike has forgotten to dig himself an access ramp. The steam shovel has literally dug itself into a corner, stuck in the basement. Then a child in the watching crowd suggests that Mary Anne could become the boiler for the new town hall, and Mike could be janitor. It was a neat and endearing solution suggested to Lee Burton, by a friend's twelve-year-old son.

Other books by Virginia Lee Burton: *Choo Choo* (1936), *Calico the Wonder Horse, or the Saga of Stewy Stinker* (1941), *The Little House* (1942), *Katy and the Big Snow* (1943), *Maybelle the Cable Car* (1952), and *Life Story* (1962).

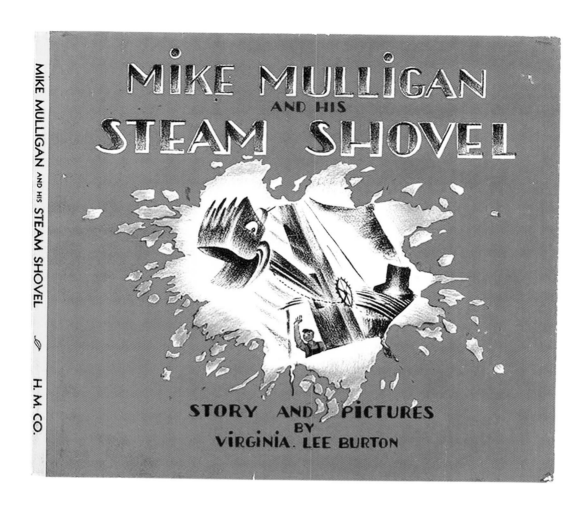

ABOVE AND RIGHT: *One of the reasons for the success of* Mike Mulligan and his Steam Shovel *is the satisfying ending. Virginia Lee Burton credited it to Dick Berkenbush, the twelve-year-old son of a friend who suggested the solution to the plot hole she had dug herself into.*

RIGHT: The debut of the Famous Five with Julian, Dick, Anne and George, who was "as good as a boy" and seemingly drawn like one, too.
BELOW: Three of Blyton's successful series: Old Thatch *(1932),* The Wishing Chair *(1936) and* The Naughtiest Girl *(1948).*

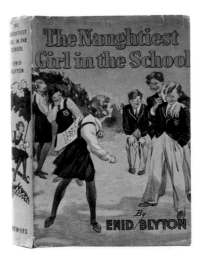

The Famous Five series
(1942–1963)

Enid Blyton (1897–1968)

Only Agatha Christie, Jules Verne and William Shakespeare have been more widely translated than Enid Blyton, whose works have appeared around the world in ninety languages, with global sales of over 600 million copies of over 600 books. At her height in the 1950s, she was writing almost one a week.

While many of the children's authors in these pages drew on incidents from their unhappy childhoods for inspiration, Enid Blyton did no such thing, although there was plenty of material. Her father, whom she adored, left her mother for another woman. Her mother thought her early attempts to write were "a waste of time and money." Blyton did not invite either of them to her first wedding, to a man who became an unfaithful alcoholic; nor did she attend either of their funerals. Only her second marriage, solemnised in 1943 the year after she launched the *Famous Five* series, seems to have been a happy relationship.

None of this appears in her books. She wrote for all age groups of young children, with straightforward stories of good behaviour and innocent fun. In Blyton's books, bad behaviour is always punished. Her first book *Child Whispers* (1922) was a collection of poems, but her career really took off in the 1930s when she started writing the first of her many series, the *Old Thatch* series (from 1934) and the *Wishing-Chair* series (from 1937).

The *Circus*, *Amelia Jane* and *Faraway Tree* series all launched in 1939. Two series set in boarding schools, the *Naughtiest Girl* and *St Clare's*, came out in 1940 and 1941. And in 1942, after writing the first of the *Mary Mouse* series, she published *Five on a Treasure Island*, the first of twenty-one novels about a group of friends who became known to the world as the Famous Five.

The five friends were two boys, Julian and Dick; two girls, Anne and tomboy George (never Georgina); and George's dog Timmy. Theirs is a world of perpetual youth, constant summer and school holidays in the countryside spent cycling, swimming and exploring. Their adventures often involve scheming criminals, secret tunnels and picnics – although, sad to relate, their much quoted taste for "lashings of ginger beer"

never featured in a *Famous Five* story. This idealised childhood is the key to the series' continuing success: nearly eighty years on, it still sells around two million copies a year. Blyton said that she based the character of George on herself.

More new series followed in the 1940s: *the Island of Adventure* (1944) launched the *Adventure* series. By the end of the decade she had introduced new series featuring Mallory Towers School; Barney the schoolboy (and his monkey Miranda); another group of friends, the Secret Seven; and her most famous creations, Noddy and his friend Big Ears. Noddy owes his distinctive appearance to his first illustrator, Dutchman Harmsen van der Beek.

Enid Blyton was an astonishingly prolific author and a shrewd promoter of the Blyton brand. Her many series created a host of fans hungry for the latest instalments, and even writing under a pseudonym on several occasions, her readers were not deceived by the subterfuge. Many of her books included a "personalised message" on the back cover, welcoming the reader to each new volume. And that ubiquitous Enid Blyton signature was a trademark of quality. She once described her writing process:

> "I make my mind a blank and wait – and then, as clearly as I would see real children, my characters stand before me in my mind's eye … The first sentence comes straight into my mind, I don't have to think of it – I don't have to think of anything."

Selected books by Enid Blyton: *The Magic Faraway Tree* (1943) and series, *The Island of Adventure* (1944) and series, *First Term at Mallory Towers* (1946) and series, *Noddy Goes to Toyland* (1949) and series, and *The Secret Seven* (1949) and series.

Le Petit Prince

(1943)

Antoine de Saint-Exupéry (1900–1944)

The Little Prince defies definition. Intended as a book for children, it works on multiple levels and means many things to all ages. In the light of Saint-Exupéry's life and death it has, for some, assumed an almost mystical status.

The tale of the little prince from another planet who comforts a crashed pilot in the desert has beguiled young and old from the moment of its publication. Antoine de Saint-Exupéry wrote and illustrated it, and his gentle watercolour images are as celebrated as the story itself.

Saint-Exupéry was a meticulous wordsmith, a craftsman of language for whom every word was chosen precisely. *The Little Prince* is a reflection of both his writing process and his life. It is a philosophical work written so carefully yet simply that it is often used as an early reader for students of the French language.

The author was a pioneer of French aviation in the early twentieth century. After flying in the French Air Force he took a civilian job devising new airmail routes between France and North Africa, and across South America. He turned his experiences in Argentina into his first major publishing success, *Vol de Nuit* (1931, English *Night Flight*).

His books in turn enhanced his reputation as a pilot, although he had more than his fair share of crash landings. In 1935 a particularly serious crash in the Sahara desert left him and his navigator seriously dehydrated and hallucinating until they were rescued, echoed by the misadventure of Captain Haddock from the *Tintin* series in *The Crab with the Golden Claws* (1941). The episode was recorded in his memoir *Wind, Sand and Stars* (1939) and inspired the premise of *The Little Prince*.

It could be said that Saint-Exupéry was a brilliant but careless pilot. His navigation skills were superb, but he was in the habit of writing, drawing and reading while flying. His mechanics often found screwed-up sketches on the floor of his cockpit after he had landed; on at least one occasion he was reported to have flown around above the landing strip for an hour while he finished the novel he was reading. Being airborne was for him a philosophical experience, giving him the time and perspective to ponder on the world beneath and the universe above.

Following the fall of France to Germany in 1940 Saint-Exupéry fled to North America, where he wrote *The Little Prince* between speaking engagements in support of America's entry into the European war. The inspirations for the character of the prince were two young blonde boys whom he met during his stay – one the son of his friend the philosopher Charles De Koninck, the other the son of the American aviator Charles Lindberg (who, ironically, was campaigning vigorously to keep America out of the war). The rose with which the prince was obsessed on his home planet is assumed to be symbolic of Saint-Exupéry's South American wife Consuelo, with whom he had a passionate but tempestuous relationship.

The patriotic Saint-Exupéry was desperate to fight for the defeated France, and despite officially being eight years too old at the age of forty-three, he was allowed to fly with the Free French Air Force. In re-training he crashed a Lockheed Lightning, but the propaganda value of his presence in the air persuaded the authorities to allow him to continue. On a reconnaissance mission in another Lightning on July 31, 1944, he disappeared without trace over the Mediterranean. The wreckage of his plane was discovered in 2000 off the coast of Marseilles.

He lived long enough to see the publication of *The Little Prince*, of which he was immensely proud. He was in the habit of carrying a copy of it everywhere and reading it to anyone who would listen. In recognition of his early death in the service of his country, the French copyright on the book was extended to 100 years, expiring in 2044.

ANTOINE DE SAINT-EXUPÉRY

Le Petit Prince

Avec des aquarelles de l'auteur

LEFT AND BELOW: The Little Prince *was published posthumously in France in 1945. Saint-Exupéry's books had already been banned by the Vichy government and the author condemned as a defender of Jews.*

ANTOINE DE SAINT-EXUPÉRY

Le Petit Prince

Avec dessins par l'auteur

REYNAL & HITCHCOCK · NEW YORK

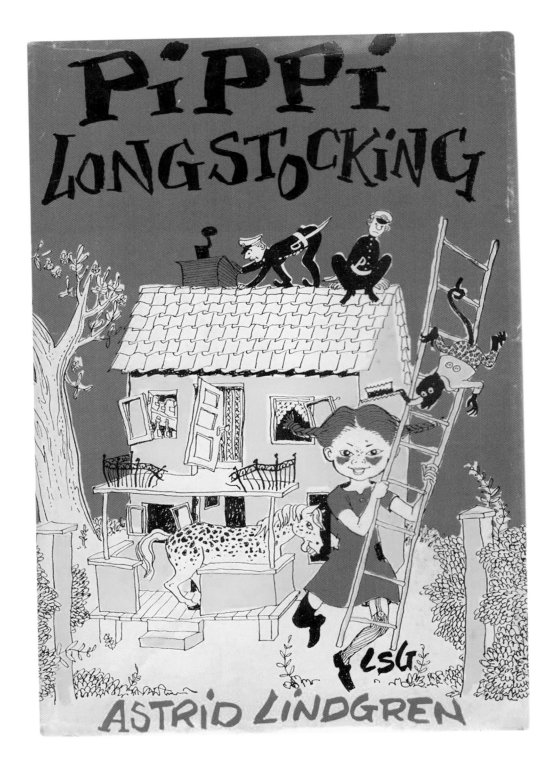

Pippi Longstocking
(1945)

Astrid Lindgren (1907–2002)

One of the most successful and popular children's stories ever written, *Pippi Longstocking* always finds a place on editors' lists of best books for the young. In 2002 the Nobel Institute included it in their list of the top 100 works of world literature for ANY age.

Pippi is a completely original character, a wild child with her pigtails, her suitcase full of gold and her superhuman strength. Like many fictional children, her Swedish creator Astrid Lindgren had contrived to put her in a situation without parents, thereby allowing her behaviour free rein. In Pippi's case, her mother has died, and her father is a sea captain, perpetually out at sea.

Pippi is more than capable of looking after herself, although having been raised at sea, she often gets into trouble when navigating the social conventions of life on land. Having made friends with two other children, she and her pet monkey and horse cause havoc at a tea party, on a visit to the circus, and especially when Pippi starts attending her friend's school – something she only wants to do in order to get the school holidays.

Pippi Longstocking began life, like so many great children's books, as tales which Lindgren told to her daughter during a bout of illness in the early 1940s. The name was her daughter's suggestion. Although Sweden remained neutral during World War II, Pippi's lack of respect for authority may reflect Scandinavian attitudes to Germany's occupation of neighbouring Norway and Denmark at the time. Lindgren's diaries from 1939-1945 were later published under the title *A World Gone Mad* (2016), revealing the author's insight into the horrors and privations of war, even in neutral Sweden.

After *Pippi Longstocking* was rejected by one publisher, Lindgren revised her manuscript by increasing its delight in absurdities. It was a wise decision, and the resulting published version won a national prize in 1946. It was followed by two full-length sequels, *Pippi Goes On Board* (1946) and *Pippi in the South Seas* (1948) , as well as a handful of short stories.

Despite Pippi's nautical background, Lindgren had no seafaring connections. She was born and raised in the town of Vimmerby (twinned with Fargo, North Dakota), some 55km inland from the Swedish coast. She is buried there and the town has become a mecca for fans of her work. It is the location of a theme park based on literary creations, Astrid Lindgren World.

She is the fourth most widely translated children's author in history, surpassed only by fellow Scandinavian Hans Christian Andersen, the Brothers Grimm and Britain's Enid Blyton. Her works have been translated into over ninety other languages; *Pippi Longstocking* alone has been read in over forty of them. Her literary fame made her a national hero in Sweden, and her death was marked by a state funeral in all but name, attended by Sweden's king, queen and prime minister.

Other books by Astrid Lindgren: *Bill Bergson, Master Detective* (1946) and series, *The Children of Noisy Village* (1947) and series, *Mio, My Son* (1954), *Karlson on the Roof* (1955) and series, *The Children on Troublemaker Street* (1956) and series, *Emil and the Great Escape* (1963) and series, *Most Beloved Sister* (1973), and *Ronia the Robber's Daughter* (1981).

OPPOSITE: *Astrid Lindgren was advised to tone down some of the more extreme incidents in the book, such as a full chamber pot being used as a fire extinguisher, and make the dialogue more comprehensible for six- to ten-year-olds.*

Thomas the Tank Engine
(1946)

Reverend Wilbert Awdry (1911–1997)

It is the railway enthusiast's equivalent of the fantasy worlds of J. R. R. Tolkien and C .S. Lewis – Sodor, the imaginary island inhabited by the Fat Controller and his railway engines. At its heart, like a coal-powered hobbit, is Thomas the Tank Engine.

In the years immediately after World War I, Wilbert Awdry lay awake as a child listening to engine movements. His bedroom in the family home was close to the infamous Box Tunnel in southwestern England, where steam engines of the Great Western Railway had to pair up to haul their loads up its steep, 1:100 gradient. Engine drivers had their own system of whistle signals, and it seemed to young Awdry that he could make out individual whistles, and that the engines were talking to each other.

Awdry's son Christopher was born in 1940, and when Christopher was laid up with measles at the age of three, his father tried to cheer him up with bedside stories about three steam engines – Henry, Gordon and Edward. These were the first stories of the *Railway* series, published in 1945 as *The Three Engines*.

Awdry went so far as to make a model of Edward for Christopher, but he did not have enough broom handles for axles to model Gordon, the larger engine, as well. Instead, Awdry built a little tank engine. Steam enthusiasts know that a self-sufficient tank engine carries its own water in tanks, usually either side of the boiler, rather than in a separate trailer or tender. Naturally Christopher wanted stories about this new engine too, and Thomas the Tank Engine made his print debut in 1946, in the second book of the series. Awdry prefaced the book with an open letter to his son:

> "Dear Christopher,
> Here is your friend Thomas, the Tank Engine.
> He wanted to come out of his station-yard and see the world.
> These stories tell you how he did it."

Thomas's appearance was created by the illustrator of the book, Reginald Payne, and revised by a later illustrator of the series, Reginald Dalby. Awdry wrote twenty-six books of the *Railway* series before hanging up his typewriter in 1972. One by one they expanded Sodor's rail network and Thomas's circle of friends with the introduction of engines James, Percy and others; Annie and Clarabel the carriages; and other vehicles such as Terence the tractor, Bertie the bus and Harold the helicopter. Daisy the diesel, in the sixteenth book, was the first female engine.

Christopher Awdry had little choice but to become a railway enthusiast like his father. In 1983 he began, with Awdry senior's blessing, to write new *Railway* stories, now under the series title *Thomas and Friends*. He has added another sixteen books to his father's canon, concluding the last in 2011 with the words "The End", the only one of the books to do so.

Rev. Awdry took the name Sodor from the Diocese of Sodor and Man, which used to encompass the southern islands (Sodor in old Norse) of Scotland and the Isle of Man in the Irish sea. The diocese still exists, even though it no longer covers any Scottish parishes. In 1987, perhaps in an effort to preserve the world of Sodor which he had created, Rev. Awdry wrote with his brother George a comprehensive back-story for the place: *The Island of Sodor: Its People, History and Railways*. In 2005 Christopher amplified that with *Sodor: Reading Between the Lines*, a biographical who's who of the Sodor community.

With the success of the 1989 Brit Allcroft-produced television series, Thomas the Tank engine has become a global phenomenon with the blue engine adorning pyjamas and duvet covers as far afield as China and Japan.

Books about Sodor: The *Railway* series by Rev. Wilbert Awdry (1940–1972, 26 books), the *Thomas and Friends* series by Christopher Awdry (1983–2011, 16 books).

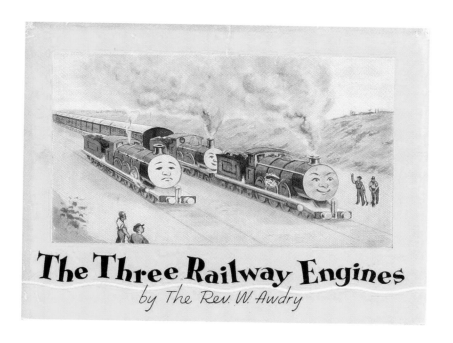

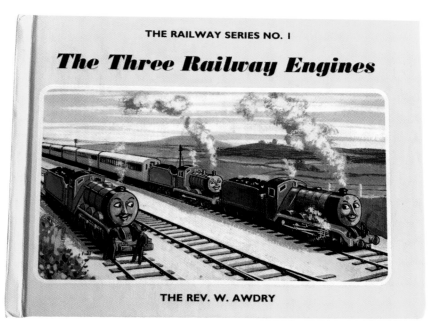

ABOVE: Rudyard Kipling had anthropomorphised railway engines as early as 1897, but the Reverend Awdry created his own locomotive universe. The first book (top) was illustrated by William Middleton, whose work Awdry disliked, and then improved by Reginald Dalby. Awdry would make scale models of the engines but fell out with Dalby when he ignored his model of Percy the Small Engine.

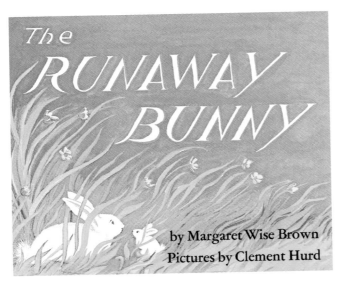

ABOVE: *When Margaret Wise Brown sent illustrator Clement Hurd the manuscript for* Goodnight Moon *she gave her little guidance, but did enclose a copy of Goya's* Boy in Red *for inspiration. The New York Public Library refused to stock it, describing it as "an unbearably sentimental piece of work." They finally relented in 1973.*

LEFT: *Despite writing about rabbits, Margaret Wise Brown had few qualms in hunting them. She also had an equivocal attitude to children. Talking about marriage in 1946 she said, "Well, I don't especially like children, either. At least not as a group. I won't let anybody get away with anything just because he is little."*

Goodnight Moon

(1947)

Margaret Wise Brown (1910–1952)

The perfect night-time book for the very young, to many parents and children, Goodnight Moon is more an end-of-day ritual than a bedtime story. Its author was an unconventional woman and a proponent of radical reform in children's literature and education.

Goodnight Moon is a form of hypnosis for the very young. It introduces us to a bedroom and describes it in rhyming couplets, before saying goodnight to each object in turn and finally "goodnight to noises everywhere." Sleep is ushered in not only by the rhythm and repetition of the words, but by the illustrations of Clement Hurd. The recurring images of the room change slightly in detail with each goodnight, and the room itself gradually fades under a blanket of fog as sleep engulfs the little rabbit in the bed.

The book manifests comfort and stability: everything will still be there in the morning. Sleep is irresistible by the end of *Goodnight Moon*, and more so with each re-reading of it. The book is the second in a loose trilogy of three by Margaret Wise Brown about a young rabbit. It's preceded by *Runaway Bunny* (1942) and followed by *My World* (1949), which is dedicated to Hurd's then newborn son Thacher. Thacher Hurd is now a children's author and illustrator in his own right.

Margaret Wise Brown and Clement Hurd met while teaching at the Bank Street Experimental School in Manhattan. The school advocated a more responsive, child-centred approach to education formulated in the "here and now", not in an inflexible educationalist's boardroom. The school's founder Lucy Sprague Mitchell published *The Here And Now Story Book* in 1921, one of the first children's books to focus on the routines of everyday life rather than fairy tales. She also established the Writers' Lab in Bank Street in 1937, which produced children's books in conjunction with the students of Bank Street's training institution the Cooperative School for Teachers. Brown and Clement's wife Edith Thacher Hurd were among the Lab's early members, and Brown published her first book, *When the Wind Blew*, in the same year, 1937.

The father of one of the children attending Bank Street Experimental School was William Rufus Scott. He was so impressed by *When the Wind Blew* that he hired Brown as editor of his new publishing house in 1938. Brown's job was to persuade leading contemporary authors to write books for children. She had notable success with Gertrude Stein, whose book *The World is Round* (1939) was illustrated by Clement Hurd. Hurd also provided pictures for Brown's debut with W. R. Scott, *Bumble Bugs and Elephants: A Big and Little Book* (1938). Brown introduced Edith Hurd to Scott, and he published Edith's first book, *Hurry Hurry* (1938).

Margaret Wise Brown saw no contradiction between her anthropomorphism of rabbits and her lifelong enthusiasm for hunting them with packs of beagle hounds. Traditionally, hunters follow the beagles on foot, and Brown was noted for her fleetness and agility in keeping up with the pack. She was proud of her fitness, a pride which was her undoing. After some emergency surgery for an ovarian cyst in the French coastal resort of Nice in 1952, she was showing off to the nurses by giving a high kick. Unwittingly, she dislodged a blood clot in the leg which was then able to travel to her heart. A few days later she died of the resulting embolism.

Her personal life was full of unconventional relationships, not least that with nine-year-old Albert Clarke, the son of a friend. In her will she left Albert the royalties for most of her published work, to be payable once he had reached the age of twenty-one. Unfortunately, long before Albert came into his inheritance, he went off the rails. Juvenile delinquency led to a life of crime, and he squandered the millions of dollars he subsequently received from Brown's publishers on bail, easy living and bad financial decisions – a case of "Goodnight, money."

The Diary of a Young Girl
(1947)

Anne Frank (1929–1945)

An adolescent girl's innermost thoughts are given terrible poignancy by the reader knowing what she could not know when she wrote them down – that she would never reach the adulthood of which she dreamt.

Anne Frank was given a diary on her thirteenth birthday, June 12th 1942. For a little over two years she filled it with everything that concerns a girl of that age – the questioning of her mother's authority, the irritation about near neighbours, the lack of privacy, boys, and the stirring of ambition. Anne loved to write and wanted to be a journalist, more than ever after she heard a radio broadcast urging people to preserve their diaries as records of the time through which they were living. Anne herself would edit her writing, removing some sections and rewriting others.

They were dark times. Anne was a German Jew, living in Amsterdam where her family had fled in 1933 (when she was just three) after Hitler gained power in her home country. After Germany invaded the Netherlands the lives of the Frank family were in danger once again. With the help of sympathetic workers in her father Otto Frank's Amsterdam food company, they were hidden in an annex to the company's canal-side offices, with a secret entrance concealed behind a bookcase.

For almost twenty-six months they lived there, their ranks swelled to eight by further refugees from the Nazis. Anne's last diary entry is dated August 1, 1944. On August 4 German police led by an SS officer raided the premises. No one knows whether the Franks and their companions were betrayed by a Nazi sympathiser, the daughter of one of their helpers; or discovered accidentally during an investigation into possible rationing abuses.

Another of their helpers found Anne's diaries in their hiding place after their capture and kept them safe to return them to her after the war. But only her father Otto lived to receive them. Of the 1019 Jews on the train which took the family to Auschwitz, 549 were sent to the gas chambers immediately. Anne, her sister, her mother and all the other Jews in the secret annex died in concentration camps in the following months. Anne died during an outbreak of typhus in Belsen which killed 17,000 prisoners. Only 5,000 of the 107,000 Jews deported from the Netherlands during the war survived.

None of this is in Anne's diaries, although she does record the restrictions being placed on Dutch Jews before and after they went into hiding. Anne's unique record of her times has made her, posthumously, the journalist she wanted to become. Otto Frank was determined to publish them and they appeared in print in 1947, originally entitled *The Secret Annex*. The first version published was censored by Otto, with certain passages removed such as criticisms of her parents (especially her mother), and sections that discussed her burgeoning sexuality. Later editions have restored these diary entries.

The first English translation was published in 1952. It aroused little interest at first in the U.K. where it was already out of print by 1953. In the U.S. however, where its first edition contained a foreword by Eleanor Roosevelt, it caused a sensation. Perhaps Britain was just too close to the horrors embodied in it.

Part eye-witness report, part private journal, it is a must-read for young adults whom it awakens "to the folly of indifference and the terrible toll it takes on our young", as Hilary Clinton described it. Even Nelson Mandela drew comfort from it during his imprisonment. In her diaries, Anne Frank is both entirely herself and an everyman for all those innocent victims of war.

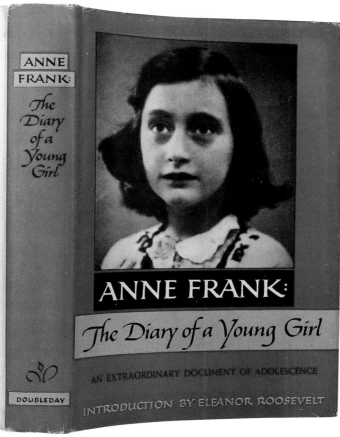

THIS IS A PAGE FROM
THE DIARY OF ANNE FRANK

ABOVE: The Diary of a Young Girl was first published in Holland. Anne started writing her diary in September 1942. Then, following a broadcast from London in March 1944 by the exiled Dutch Minister for Education calling for the preservation of "ordinary documents, a diary, letters", she started redrafting it for the benefit of future readers.

LEFT: Anne Frank in 1940.

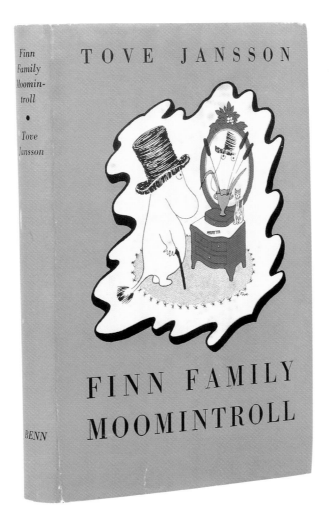

ABOVE: The English edition of the novel appeared as Finn Family Moomintroll.

LEFT: A first edition of Trollkarlens Hatt *(Magician's Hat), with what the second-hand book trade might describe as "a little light rubbing".*

Finn Family Moomintroll

(1948) and series

Tove Jansson (1914–2001)

The first Moomin book to be published in English (in 1950), Finn Family Moomintroll was actually the third in a series which eventually ran to nine reading books and five picture books, as well as a long-running comic strip.

Tove Jansson was born in a Swedish-speaking part of Finland, which was then ruled by the pre-revolutionary Russian Empire. She trained in art in Helsinki, Stockholm and Paris, and travelled widely in Europe. During World War II she drew satirical cartoons, including a famous image of Hitler as a baby in a nappy throwing a tantrum.

But the upheavals of the European conflict brought on depression, and it was a longing for a happier, more innocent world that drove her to conjure up the Moomins – gentle, hippo-like creatures with strong, happy family ties and simple adventures in a world of their own, Moominvalley. Tove Jansson's self-contained Moominworld is perfect for exploration by the colourful imaginations of the very young.

Finn Family Moomintroll was the first Moomin title to be written in peacetime after the war. It was originally published in Swedish as *The Magician's Hat*, though the name was changed to introduce the series to an English-speaking audience.

It tells the story of Moomintroll, child of Moominmamma and Moominpappa, who discovers a hobgoblin's top hat on a mountain. The hat has the power to change whatever is placed inside it. Eggshells become clouds, flowers become a jungle, and even Moomintroll is transformed when he conceals himself in the hat during a game of hide-and-seek. After many adventures the hat's owner arrives and grants everyone a wish.

The book is about the joy of family and friends, and also serves as an introduction to the often-difficult binary of right and wrong for very young children. Two characters, Thingumy and Bob, steal things – a precious ruby and Moominmamma's handbag. They are put on trial for the ruby, and they later show remorse

by returning the handbag to its distressed owner. *Finn Family Moomintroll* has plenty of anarchic mayhem for its young audience, but a clear moral line to satisfy the audience's parents.

It was with this third book in the series that Jansson and the Moomins broke through to international success. Although Jansson spent less time on the series after 1970, it is now firmly established as a children's favourite. A theme park, Moomin's World, opened in southern Finland in 1993, attracting criticism of the perceived Disneyfication of the brand. But the Jansson family, who still control Tove's legacy, have rejected advances from Disney Studios.

Nevertheless there have been many European film and TV adaptations and extensions of the Moomin books, as well as stage productions. In Jansson's imagination, Moominvalley is a musical place, and she worked with Finnish composer Erma Tauro to make the Moomin songs a reality. They were collected together on CD for the first time in 2003 as a tribute after her death.

Tove Jansson was awarded the Hans Christian Andersen Medal in 1966 for her lasting contribution to children's literature. More than fifty years later her contribution still persists in the world of playful happiness where the Moomins live.

Selected other Moominbooks: *The Moomins and the Great Flood* (1945), *Comet in Moominland* (1946), *Finn Family Moomintroll* (1948), *The Book about Moomin, Mymble and Little My* (1952), *Moominsummer Madness* (1954), *Tales from Moominvalley* (1962), *Moominvalley in November* (1970) and *Songs From Moominvalley* (1993).

I Capture the Castle
(1949)

Dodie Smith (1896–1990)

A delightful coming-of-age story, set in a romantic pre-war English country landscape, could have been a lost Jane Austen novel except for some surprising modern twists.

The Mortmain family live in genteel poverty in a dilapidated castle owned by nearby Scoatney Hall. They are behind with their rent because father James has had writer's block since the publication of his first book twelve years ago. Beautiful Rose and wise Cassandra are his daughters, Stephen the son of their deceased maid. Scoatney is inherited by the Cotton family, wealthy Americans who arrive with their handsome sons Simon and Neil.

Intrigue ensues worthy of a modern soap opera. Stephen is in love with Cassandra. Rose decides to marry Simon for his money. Simon falls in love with Rose. Simon and Rose become engaged. So far so good. But Cassandra secretly kisses Simon. Rose and Neil secretly fall in love and elope. Simon is heartbroken. Stephen leaves. Simon leaves. Cassandra lives in hope. The end.

The whole story is told through the eyes and journal-writing of seventeen-year-old Cassandra. Through this summer of love, unrequited or uninvited, she matures; a girl at the beginning, she is a young woman by the end, setting out on a career with her adult heart awakened. The modern twists are provided by the willingness of Cassandra's father's second wife to sunbathe in the nude and by the distinct lack of a happy ending. There are no double weddings here, but there is hope. Simon has told Cassandra he will return, and her father has overcome his writer's block. With the Cottons' help the family has begun to improve their circumstances. It is, ultimately, an optimistic story.

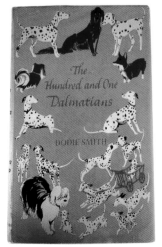

It was written during World War II when British-born Dodie Smith and her husband, a conscientious objector, were living in exile in the United States. Smith missed England, and wrote *I Capture the Castle* partly as a way of evoking happier times. It was her first novel, but not by any means her first published work. Before the war she had a string of plays performed in London by stars of the day, including Fay Compton, Raymond Massey and John Gielgud. She had been an actor before that, and she revisited her theatrical past in her novel *The Town in Bloom* (1965) about a young woman determined to make it on the stage.

She resumed her role as playwright when she returned to England after the war, one of her productions being a stage adaptation of *I Capture the Castle* (1954). She is perhaps best remembered for her second novel, *The Hundred and One Dalmatians* (1956), which was prompted by a remark from a friend about Smith's own Dalmatians, "Those dogs would make a lovely fur coat." One of her dogs was called Pongo, the name she gave to her canine protagonist in *The Hundred and One Dalmatians.* After the Disney film of the book brought it to the world's attention in 1961, she wrote a sequel, *The Starlight Barking* (1967).

Other children's books by Dodie Smith: *The Hundred and One Dalmatians* (1956), *The Town in Bloom* (1965), *The Starlight Barking* (1967), and *The Midnight Kittens* (1978).

ABOVE: *Though her best-known work is* The Hundred and One Dalmatians, *Dodie Smith's best-loved book is* I Capture the Castle. *Disney bought the film rights to both, but only made the first. After her death in 1990, her literary executor, novelist Julian Barnes, retrieved the film rights paving the way for the 2003 screen adaptation.*

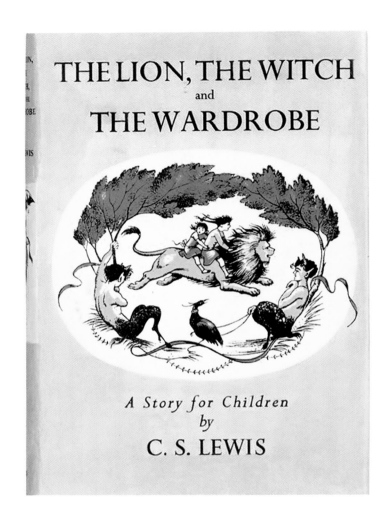

THE LION, THE WITCH
and
THE WARDROBE

A Story for Children
by
C. S. LEWIS

ABOVE: C. S. Lewis recalled that his inspiration for Lion *had been a picture in his mind of a faun carrying an umbrella and parcels in a snowy wood, a vision he'd carried since the age of sixteen.*

LEFT: The seven Chronicles of Narnia *books were written in quick succession between 1949 and 1954.*

The Lion, the Witch and the Wardrobe

(1950)

C. S. Lewis (1898–1963)

A paradoxical novel, both an allegory of Christianity and a fantasy inspired by pagan tales, The Lion, the Witch and the Wardrobe has been the subject of much academic analysis. For the young, however, it's an old-fashioned battle between good and evil.

Peter, Susan, Edmund and Lucy, four children, discover the land of Narnia through the back of an old wardrobe in their new home. There they encounter the White Witch, who keeps Narnia in perpetual winter. Aslan the lion, the rightful ruler of Narnia, returns from exile, bringing spring. When Edmund betrays him and is captured by the White Witch, Aslan gives his life to save the boy; but he is resurrected and joins the children and the people of Narnia to defeat the Witch. The Narnians place the children on the four thrones of Narnia in fulfilment of an ancient prophecy.

C. S. Lewis was born and raised in Northern Ireland where he acquired a love of legend – Irish, naturally, then Scandinavian, and thanks to a private tutor, the myths of ancient Greece. Later, as a tutor at Oxford University, his friendship with J. R. R. Tolkien, author of *The Lord of the Rings*, grew out of that shared interest; and from that friendship began his renewed Christian faith, which he had abandoned as a teenager.

The parallels with Christianity, at least with the death and resurrection of Jesus, are clear – Aslan's self-sacrifice to save the boy who betrayed him resembles Christ dying for the sake of all sinners. When the stone table is found broken the morning after Aslan has been put to death on it, it is like the stone cover being rolled away from Jesus' tomb after his crucifixion. In both cases, the dead have risen. Lewis always insisted that he had not set out to write a Christian allegory. But as a devout born-again believer he must have been aware of the turns his story was taking; and he was pleased if it led its readers to Christianity in later life.

Other elements of *The Lion, the Witch and the Wardrobe* were inspired by events in Lewis's life. The fictional children's arrival in a new home is the result of their evacuation from London at the start of World War II. Such evacuations did indeed take place, and Lewis accommodated several evacuees in his Oxford home. Their exploration of the large empty house, which leads them to the wardrobe, mirrored Lewis's memories of moving into a new home as a child. Lewis has also expressed his debt to children's author E. Nesbit, in one of whose short stories a wardrobe serves as the entry point to a world of magic.

The landscape of Narnia was evoked by the granite Mourne Mountains, close to Lewis's early Northern Irish homes. The same peaks have also been locations in the filming of *Game of Thrones*. Lewis chose the name Narnia just because he liked the sound of it, after seeing it on a map of Ancient Rome – Narnia is the Latin version of Narni, a city between Rome and Assisi.

Lewis subsequently wrote five sequels and a prequel to *The Lion, the Witch and the Wardrobe*. The success of the *Chronicles of Narnia* have overshadowed his other work. *The Screwtape Letters* (1942) is a delightful, imaginary correspondence between senior demon Screwtape and his nephew Wormwood, a junior tempter. It's a witty examination of the nature of temptation, at which Wormwood is a bit of a failure. Lewis was also the author of an uncharacteristic series of science-fiction novels beginning with *Out of the Silent Planet* (1938), the result of a bet he had with Tolkien.

Selected other books by C. S. Lewis: *The Space Trilogy – Out of the Silent Planet* (1938), *Perelandra (aka Voyage to Venus)* (1943) and *That Hideous Strength* (1945); and *The Screwtape Letters* (1942).

Charlotte's Web

(1952)

E. B. White (1899–1985)

For over fifty years E. B. White was a staff writer at the literary magazine *The New Yorker*. He wrote only three major works of children's fiction, all in the second half of his long career, but he was twice nominated for the prestigious Hans Christian Andersen Award for a lasting contribution to the genre.

The unlikely friendship between a pig and a spider is the warm heart of E. B. White's most famous work. It captures one of the central themes of the book – individuality. We are all different and follow our own paths, but that doesn't mean we can't forge the greatest of bonds with each other. All friendships are different too – Wilbur the pig is first befriended by Fern, a human.

All three of the main protagonists – Wilbur, Fern and Charlotte the spider – change in the course of the story. Wilbur and Fern grow up and move from innocence to wisdom. Charlotte undergoes further rites of passage when she becomes a mother and subsequently reaches the end of her life. White sets these mental and physical transformations against the background of seasonal farm work. The cycle of the seasons and of life itself make up the landscape on which the drama of *Charlotte's Web* is played out.

Nothing illustrates the cycle of life so much as death, a constant presence in the book. Its first line, "Where's papa going with that axe?", introduces the fate that even newborn Wilbur, the runt of the litter, faces. Fern, the farmer's daughter, successfully pleads for the young pig's life, delaying his death. Under new ownership, Wilbur's life is again threatened – and again saved, this time by the words which his new friend Charlotte weaves into her web.

Wilbur's subsequent celebrity and indeed his continuous existence are thanks to the interventions of

Fern and Charlotte. His life is prolonged and enhanced by his friendships – but although death may be postponed, it is inevitable. Charlotte's quiet passing after laying her 514 eggs is the emotional climax of White's novel, but the hatching of her offspring is its optimistic conclusion. A new cycle of life has begun.

White never discussed the inspiration for his work. But a year before he began to write *Charlotte's Web*, he published an article called *The Death of a Pig* which described his own failure to save the life of a pig in poor health. *Charlotte's Web* has been seen as an attempt to atone for that pig's death.

He wrote about weighty themes – individuality, change and death – with gentle, understated sensitivity for a young audience which might easily have been distressed by them. In so doing, White created one of the most popular and successful children's books of all time.

With global sales approaching fifty million in over twenty languages, *Charlotte's Web* is his crowning achievement and has captured the hearts of children around the world for five generations.

Best-known works: *Stuart Little* (1945), *Charlotte's Web* (1952), and *The Trumpet of the Swan* (1970).

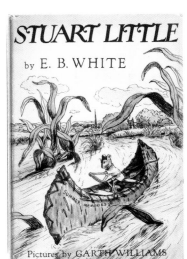

LEFT: Stuart Little *featured the adventures of a mouse in New York.*

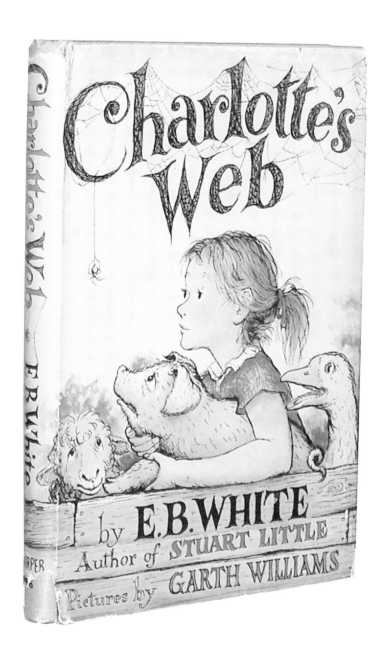

ABOVE: E. B. White – or as he was known from his Cornell University days, "Andy" – had a farmhouse in Maine. Like Robert the Bruce before him he was inspired by watching a spider, in this case spinning an egg sac in one of the barns.

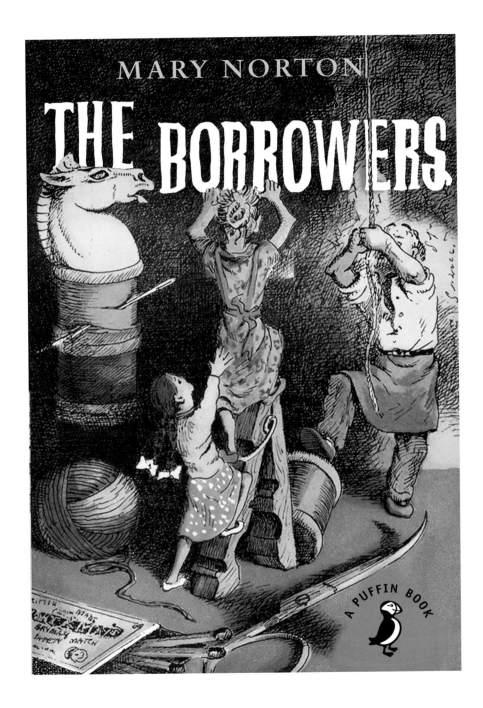

ABOVE: The first Borrowers novel was published in 1952; the final book of five, The Borrowers Avenged, *came out in 1982. For Borrowers fans there was a whopping twenty-one years between the fourth and fifth books.*

The Borrowers

(1952) and series

Mary Norton (1903–1992)

Children are fascinated by miniature worlds. They form the basis for most toys, from doll's houses to model railways. So Mary Norton's series about a race of tiny people living under the floorboards of a full-sized human home makes irresistible reading.

The borrowers are tiny people who steal, or "borrow", what they need from the big people whom they call "human beans". To borrowers, food scraps are a meal; needle and thread a lance and a rope. They even borrow their names from their full-scale habitats – so a borrower who lives in the cutlery drawer may be called Stainless, while other borrower families are known as the Boot-Racks, the Overmantels and the Rain-Pipes (the Rain-Pipes moved up in the world when one of them married a Harpsichord.)

Norton wrote five novels about the Clock family of borrowers, whose teenage daughter is forever getting them into difficulty and danger. In the first novel she befriends a human boy, a relationship which leads to the discovery of the borrowers by the household's horrified cook. Treating them like vermin, she hires a rat catcher to get rid of them. The Clocks must hurriedly evacuate their home or face extermination.

At the end of the first book the reader is unsure whether they have survived at all; the whole story is framed by an elderly human aunt, the now aged sister of the boy, who is telling the story to her niece. The only evidence of the borrowers' existence is a memoir written by the boy: was it all an invention of his imagination? The first readers of *The Borrowers* had to wait until the first sequel, *The Borrowers Afield* (1955), to find out.

Mary Norton was the daughter of a doctor in the English town of Leighton Buzzard. She grew up in a fine stone-built Georgian house called The Cedars, which was the model for the borrowers' original home. In a nice twist of history, it is now occupied by another race of (not-quite-so) tiny people, the pupils of Leighton Middle School.

During World War II she worked for a government agency called the British Purchasing Commission, which was based in New York and procured arms and airplanes for the British war effort. It was at that time that she began writing, and her first book, *The Magic Bedknob, or, How to Become a Witch in Ten Easy Lessons* (1943), was published in the U.S. two years before it appeared in Britain.

The Magic Bedknob has suffered at the hands of unscrupulous editors. Originally set firmly against the backdrop of World War II, later editions have expunged all references to the war for the sake of spurious "timelessness". Subsequent books by other writers, notably Michael Morpurgo's *War Horse*, have proved that children are perfectly capable of reading historical novels.

Bedknob's sequel, *Bonfires and Broomsticks* appeared in 1947. In 1957 they were printed in an omnibus edition with a composite title, *Bedknob and Broomsticks*, which caught the eye of Walt Disney. During Disney's protracted negotiations with P. L. Travers for the film rights to her *Mary Poppins*, he considered Mary Norton's books as an alternative project and assigned many of the *Mary Poppins* creative team to it. The Sherman brothers wrote songs for it, David Tomlinson who played the father in *Mary Poppins*, was cast as Professor Emelius Browne, and Julie Andrews was originally slated for the part of the incompetent witch Miss Price. When *Mary Poppins* finally got the go-ahead in 1961, the slightly retitled *Bedknobs and Broomsticks* was shelved for being too similar to *Poppins*. It was finally finished and in 1969.

Other books by Mary Norton: *The Magic Bed Knob* (1945), *Bonfires and Broomsticks* (1947), *The Borrowers Afield* (1955), *The Borrowers Afloat* (1959), *The Borrowers Aloft* (1961), *Are All the Giants Dead?* (1975), and *The Borrowers Avenged* (1982).

Miffy
(1955) and series

Dick Bruna (1927–2017)

Miffy the white rabbit first came to children's bookshelves back in 1955. Today there are over thirty Miffy stories in Dick Bruna's stylish, bold, bright colour illustrations, and another eighty about her many friends.

Dick Bruna, the son of a Dutch publisher, created Miffy for his own son after they watched a real rabbit playing in the sand dunes during a family holiday in 1955. Bruna, who by his own admission could not draw perspective, tried to sketch the rabbit, and Miffy was born. Her original Dutch name is Nijntje (pronounced Nine-t-yeh), meaning "Little Rabbit".

Miffy's image took shape gradually. She was originally a boy rabbit, but Bruna decided that she looked better in a skirt than in trousers. In the early books she had floppy ears and looked more like a cuddly toy, but by 1963 she had become the familiar figure we know and love.

From the beginning Bruna chose to use only a limited palette of paintbox colours – black, white, red, yellow, blue, green, orange and brown – and no shading. This eye-catching colour scheme is perfect for the very young, and owes something to the Walt Disney cartoons of Bruna's youth and his love of art. Growing up he admired the strong lines and bold colours of the post-impressionists, especially Henri Matisse of France and Vincent van Gogh of Bruna's native Holland.

Miffy also reflects the simplified visual compositions of the early-twentieth-century art movement De Stijl, whose adherents included artist Piet Mondrian and architect Gerrit Rietveld. Bruna was too young to have been part of the first wave of De Stijl, but he was almost certainly taught at art school by its admirers. His picture book *Round, Square, Triangle* (1984) pays tribute to De Stijl's contemporary equivalent in Germany, the Bauhaus.

Bruna worked for his father's publishing house, which was renamed A. W. Bruna & Son. There he designed over 2000 covers for the firm's output, including editions of Shakespeare and a wide range of detective novels. Dick Bruna's artwork launched Dutch editions of Georges Simenon's Maigret novels, Leslie Charteris's The Saint, Raymond Chandler's Marlowe and Ian Fleming's Bond.

His own creation, Miffy, is especially popular in Japan, and the Japanese cartoon character Hello Kitty, launched in 1974, bears a striking similarity to her. Bruna successfully sued Hello Kitty's creator Sanrio in 2010 over the almost identical character of Cathy, a rabbit friend of Kitty. In 2011 both parties donated their legal fees to a fund for the survivors of that year's devastating Japanese earthquake.

Like many successful children's characters Miffy has made the transition to TV and film. She and her friends have made three television series, and a full-length feature film that came out in 2013. She has also given her name to a new species of booklouse discovered in Peru in 2008. Booklice feed on the glue used in old books, and this particular species, *Trichadenotecnum miffy*, gained its name from its tail-like appendage shaped like a rabbit. Perhaps the greatest tribute to Miffy, however, has been the naming of a square in Bruna's home town of Utrecht. A small statue of Miffy now graces the Nijntjepleintje – it rhymes in Dutch, and might very loosely be translated "the little hare square".

Some other books by Dick Bruna: *Snuffy* (1969) and series), *I Can Count* (1975), *The School* (1979), *When I'm Big* (1981), *In My Toy Cupboard* (1988), *Dear Grandma* (1997), and *Round, Square, Triangle* (2012).

OPPOSITE: *The first book introducing Miffy to the world, along with three subsequent titles in the series. Nijntje is how she is known in her native Netherlands.*

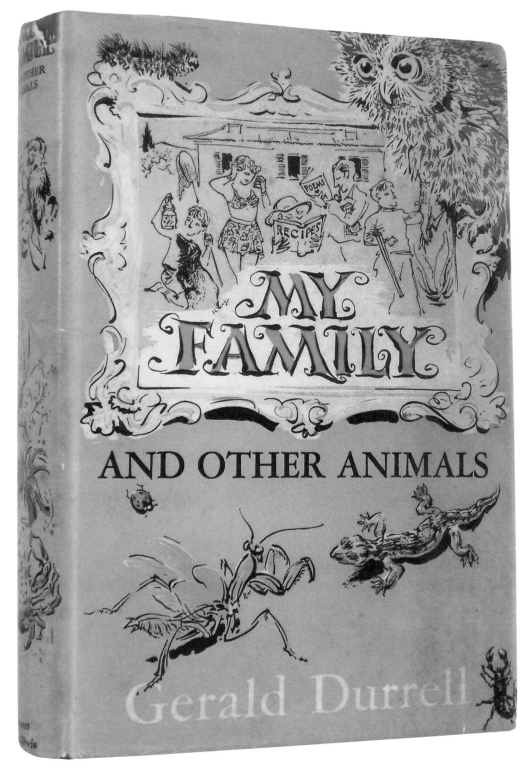

My Family and Other Animals

(1956)

Gerald Durrell (1925–1995)

The autobiography of naturalist Gerald Durrell's teenage years is written in the spirit by which he lived his life – exaggerated, irreverent and good-humoured. It charts his first steps in zoology on the island of Corfu.

Durrell traced his fascination with animals to an early visit to a zoo in India, where his father was working as an engineer at the time of his birth. Following the death of his father the Durrell family moved in 1935 to the Greek island of Corfu, where Gerald's older brother, the novelist Lawrence Durrell, was already living. They returned to England in 1939 at the outbreak of World War II.

For those four years on Corfu Gerald was schooled at home. Outside school hours, however, he roamed the island studying its animal life, guided by Theodore Stephanides, a friend of one of his tutors. Together they captured various species for study, keeping them in the Durrell family home as best they could, in any suitable enclosure, from a test tube to the family bathtub. At this early stage in his life there was no doubt about Durrell's future career path.

He was already a naturalist, but he was still a boy, the youngest member of his family. Written when Durrell was thirty, *My Family and Other Animals* has the perspective of his younger self, poking fun at his elders and betters. It also has his elder brother Lawrence's ear for a good plot – Gerald was not afraid to forget some details and misremember others if it made for a more enjoyable story. What it lacks in objective accuracy it more than makes up for with irreverent wit. It forms the first part of the so-called *Corfu* Trilogy, which he completed with *Birds, Beasts, and Relatives* (1969) and *The Garden of the Gods* (1978).

Despite his entertaining writing style, Durrell always maintained that he wrote only in order to raise funds for his wildlife expeditions. He was passionate about conservation, and founded a zoo on the island of Jersey which housed only endangered species. He profoundly disapproved of zoos which served merely as exhibition

spaces for the weird and the wonderful, and believed that animals should be in zoos only after all efforts to save them in the wild had failed.

It was a controversial view in his time, resisted by many zoos including London Zoo, where Durrell worked for a period. Durrell championed it almost single-handedly and by sheer force of personality. It is in part thanks to him that the principle of captive breeding is widely accepted now. Thanks to Durrell, diet and habitat in zoos more closely reflects those of the animal in the wild than the traditional caged enclosures of the past.

My Family and Other Animals was an instant success. Its infectious enthusiasm for the natural world makes it a great book for the young animal lover, and its affectionate mocking of the humans in Durrell's teenage world – captured in the book's title – delights those readers feeling the first stirrings of adolescent frustration and rebellion.

Some other books by Gerald Durrell: *The Overloaded Ark* (1953), *The Bafut Beagles* (1954), *A Zoo in My Luggage* (1960), *Menagerie Manor* (1964), *Birds, Beasts, and Relatives* (1969), *The Garden of the Gods* (1978), and *The Aye-Aye and I* (1992).

OPPOSITE: Though written in autobiographical form, there are significant omissions in My Family. *Brother Larry (the author Lawrence Durrell) moved to the island with his wife Nancy and the couple didn't live at the Villa Anemoyanni more than a few months before moving to their own cottage. Nancy is not mentioned in the book.*

The Red Balloon

(1957)

Albert Lamorisse (1922–1970)

The Red Balloon is a rare example of a hugely successful children's book which began life as a film, instead of via the more conventional route, from book to film. Both the film and the book have won major awards.

The story was written by French film director Albert Lamorisse as a script for a thirty-five-minute short film in 1956. It's about a boy (played by Lamorisse's young son, Pascal) who finds a big red helium-filled balloon. The balloon seems to have a mind of its own and follows him everywhere – to home, to school, to church – with often comical disapproval from the adults concerned. In the end some mean older boys destroy the balloon on a bare hilltop – but the boy is comforted when all the other helium balloons in Paris gather round him and lift him up into the sky.

The film was a big hit in its day, winning the Palme d'Or at Cannes for Best Short Film, and the Oscar for Best Original Screenplay, the only short film ever to do so. In the bleak, ruined cityscape of a Paris not yet reconstructed after World War II, the bright red balloon was a symbol of hope. Much of the film was shot in the run-down neighbourhood Belleville, where most of the locations have since been demolished, with the exception of the church featured in the film.

It's hard to escape the religious spirit of the film – the infectious, uplifting impact of the balloon on the boy; its rejection by the establishment figures of parents, teachers and clerics; its death on a barren hill; and the universality of its spirit, reborn in the other balloons to lift the boy heavenwards. The story draws on a very deep human need.

A book of the film was published in 1957, with a simple text by Lamorisse illustrated with black and white photographic stills from his film – but the balloon always overprinted in red. It became a firm favourite with early readers in the mid-twentieth century and remains in print today. In its original year of publication it won the *New York Times* award for Best Illustrated Children's Book of the Year.

The Red Balloon was not Albert Lamorisse's first critical success. In 1953 he had directed another short film, *White Mane*, based on a novel by the great French children's author René Guillot (some of whose books found their way into English in the 1960s thanks to the Oxford Children's Press). The films of *White Mane* and *The Red Balloon* are now available again together on DVD.

In 1960 Lamorisse made a sort of sequel to *The Red Balloon*, a full-length feature called *Stowaway in the Sky* (in French, *Le Voyage en Ballon*) in which a young boy (Pascal Lamorisse again) takes to the skies with his grandfather in a home-made balloon which is not as controllable as the grandfather imagined. It's a delightful family adventure across France, from Brittany to the French Alps, and won an award at the Venice Film Festival. The English version was narrated by Jack Lemmon, who liked the film so much that he bought the American rights to it.

Lamorisse never wrote another children's book, and his life was cut short when he died in a helicopter crash during the filming of a documentary in Iran. Apart from his legacy as a film director and *auteur*, he is best remembered for his invention of the perennially popular board game Risk.

Other films for children by Albert Lamorisse: *White Mane* (1953), *Stowaway in the Sky* (1960), and *Circus Angel* (1965).

OPPOSITE: *The film and book starred Albert Lamorisse's son, Pascal.*

ABOVE: *Paddington on the cover of the first edition. Many British children became aware of Paddington in the 1970s through the BBC's storytelling programme* Jackanory. *For a generation of children the whimsical delivery of playwright Alan Bennett, who narrated the stories, will be associated with Paddington Bear. When Michael Bond passed away in 2017, people left jars of marmalade by Paddington's statue at the station.*

OPPOSITE: *Paddington now installed in his familiar duffel coat in* Paddington Marches On *(1964).*

A Bear Called Paddington

(1958) and series

Michael Bond (1926–2017)

Cuddly toys have always been an obvious choice as characters in stories for the young. Two bears tower over all others in children's literature – Winnie-the-Pooh, and Paddington. Though only one of them has a statue at a mainline London railway station …

Twenty-seven books in sixty years and two recent high-grossing films are evidence of the enduring appeal of Paddington Bear. Four generations of young readers have enjoyed the exploits of the famous marmalade-loving, duffel-coat-wearing bear from Peru.

Paddington is named after one of London's mainline railway stations. It was near Paddington Station that Michael Bond bought his wife a teddy bear as a present for Christmas in 1956. The first story about it appeared two years later. The circle was completed in 1972 when the first Paddington Bear cuddly toy was produced by Shirley and Eddie Clarkson. They gave the prototype bear to their son, young Jeremy Clarkson of future *Top Gear* and *Grand Tour* fame.

Paddington Bear is invariably polite, with a talent for misunderstanding situations and getting into trouble as he tries to put things right. He is an orphan, and his appearance in a railway station – carrying a suitcase and sporting a luggage tag imploring "Please look after this bear" – was inspired by Michael Bond's memories of wartime evacuations. During World War II children from Britain's cities were sent with a few possessions and an identifying label to foster families in the countryside, where they would be less vulnerable to German air raids.

Bond's own childhood was disrupted by the war. Unhappy at school, he abandoned his education in 1942 at the age of fourteen and got a job in a solicitor's office. In 1943 the building in which he was employed was hit by a bomb. Bond, working on

an upper floor, survived; but forty-one others lost their lives in the collapse of the floors and walls.

After the war he worked as an engineer and cameraman at the BBC, assigned latterly to the long-running children's magazine series *Blue Peter*. Several early Paddington stories, including a chaotic adventure in a television studio, were first published in *Blue Peter* annuals. The Paddington stories have been adapted for television and two hugely successful big-screen films, *Paddington* and *Paddington 2* were released in 2014 and 2017. Paddington was voiced by Ben Wishaw, who has also reprised the role for a TV series of Paddington shorts.

Bond wrote another popular series of children's books featuring the Bond family pet, a guinea pig called Olga da Polga. And before Paddington migrated to television Bond wrote a popular British animated children's series called *The Herbs*, and its spin-off *Parsley the Lion*. For adults he created Monsieur Pamplemousse,

a bumbling gastronomic detective who appeared in seventeen books accompanied by his faithful bloodhound Pommes Frites. The gentle dry humour of Parsley, Pamplemousse and Paddington appeals across a broad age range. Paddington's innocence continues to charm children and their adults over sixty years after his first appearance.

Books by Michael Bond: *Paddington* series (27 books, 1958–2018), *Olga da Polga* series (14 books, 1971–2002), and *Monsieur Pamplemousse* series (17 books, 1983–2014).

Green Eggs and Ham

(1960)

Dr. Seuss (1904–1991)

It's a challenge that all writers would do well to attempt at some point in their careers. "Can you write a story using no more than fifty different words?" Not many of them would execute it with as much humour and excitement as Dr. Seuss did with Green Eggs and Ham.

Dr. Seuss (real name Theodor Geisel) was already a successful author when his publisher issued the fifty-words challenge in 1960. His first children's book was *And to Think I Saw It All on Mulberry Street* (1937). Horton the elephant made his first appearance in *Horton Hatches an Egg* in 1940 and both the Cat in the Hat and the Grinch appeared in 1957.

He first adopted the penname Seuss (his mother's maiden name) when he was sacked from his position as editor-in-chief of a student magazine for drinking gin during the Prohibition era. Always a staunch liberal in his political views, he considered his children's books to be a revolt against authority, and stating that he was "subversive as hell."

Green Eggs and Ham concerns an unnamed narrator who does not like the titular meal; and a creature called Sam-I-am who urges him to try it in a variety of ways; but, as the narrator insists, in a list which lengthens with each of Sam-I-am's suggestions,

> I would not eat them here or there.
> I would not eat them anywhere.
> I would not eat green eggs and ham.
> I do not like them, Sam-I-am.

The constraint of the challenge actually strengthens the book, which was intended for early readers. By having so few words to play with, Seuss was forced into repetition. By the time Sam-I-am has proposed a boat, a goat, the rain, a train, the dark, a tree, a car, a box, a fox, a house and a mouse as possible eating companions or locations, the narrator's repeated refusals have become hilariously exasperated; and his final agreement to taste green eggs and ham is all the more unexpected. The book is as much fun for a parent to read aloud as for a child to read to themselves. *The Cat in the Hat*, by comparison, has 236 words.

The strict rhythm of Seuss's verse is a perfect foil to his work's most anarchic characters – the Cat in the Hat, Thing 1 and Thing 2, the Grinch and of course Sam-I-am. Seuss's illustrations capture the loose, chaotic movement of his stories. They are all curves, no straight lines, even for objects which should have them. A word often applied to his drawing is "droopy".

The shorter length of Seuss's books has meant that many of their feature film adaptions have been criticised for taking too many liberties with additions and changes made to the original stories. This includes the live-action remakes of both *The Cat in the Hat* (2003), and *How the Grinch Stole Christmas* (2000). Though the films have their critics, they have their equal share of fans, and *Grinch* is a beloved family Christmas movie. It is Seuss's ability to combine whimsical storytelling with thoughtful messages about society and the human condition that make his tales so beloved by children and adults alike.

Selected other books by Dr. Seuss: *If I Ran the Zoo* (1950), *Horton Hears a Who!* (1954), *The Cat in the Hat* (1957), *How the Grinch Stole Christmas!* (1957), *One Fish Two Fish Red Fish Blue Fish* (1960), *The Lorax* (1971), and *The Butter Battle Book* (1984).

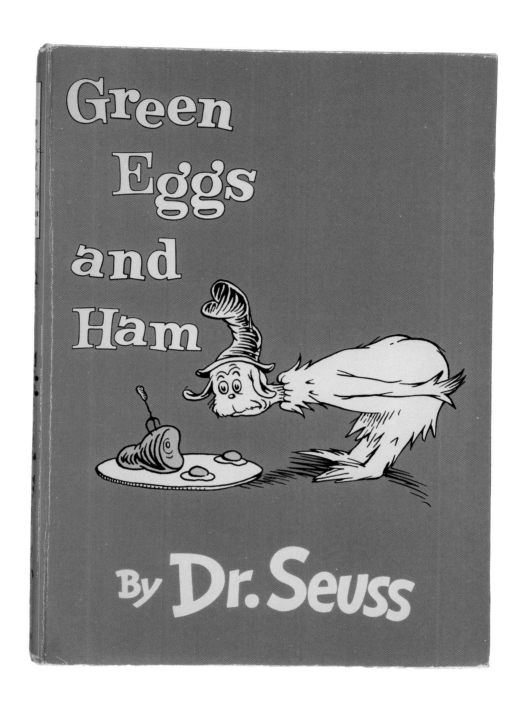

ABOVE: *Dr. Seuss's books have sold an estimated 600 million copies worldwide and been translated into twenty languages. Gourmands will be reassured that there is a* Green Eggs and Ham Cookbook *available.*

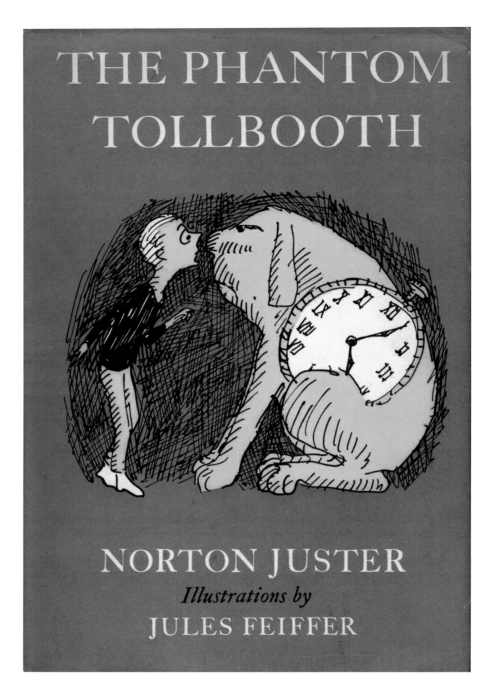

THE PHANTOM TOLLBOOTH

NORTON JUSTER

Illustrations by
JULES FEIFFER

ABOVE: Some of the staff at publisher Random House, who had bought the book, considered the text too advanced. Children's literature wasn't supposed to include words that the target readership didn't already know.

The Phantom Tollbooth

(1961)

Norton Juster (born 1929)

A parable in praise of education. *The Phantom Tollbooth* delights in wordplay inspired by the puns of the Marx Brothers and the sound of talk radio where, as they say, the pictures are better. It defies the convention that says children should not be given difficult words and ideas to read.

A little boy called Milo doesn't see the point of school. He is given an anonymous gift, a toy tollbooth. When he drives his toy car through it, he is mysteriously transported to the Kingdom of Wisdom. As he travels through Wisdom he is befriended by a dog with alarm clocks on each side of it, a watch dog called Tock. He meets the Whether Man and the Which, and Wisdom's twin rulers: King Azaz the Unabridged and his brother the Mathemagician. They have banished their daughters Rhyme and Reason to the Castle in the Air beyond the Mountains of Ignorance – and without Rhyme and Reason, Wisdom is in chaos. It's up to Milo and Tock to rescue the princesses and reunite the brothers and their kingdom. Along the way, Milo discovers that learning is useful and enjoyable, and that it's okay to make mistakes as long as you learn by them.

The Phantom Tollbooth defies classification. Its absurdities have led to comparisons with *Alice in Wonderland*, although Juster had not read the latter when he wrote the former. As a child Norton had synaesthesia, a condition which links sound, colour and meaning in the mind of the synaesthete. One effect on Juster was to understand words very literally. For example, when a character in the *Lone Ranger* cowboy radio serial shouted, "Here come the Injuns!" he pictured a host of little railway engines swarming across the plain.

Examples of this sort of thinking abound in *The Phantom Tollbooth* – Milo at one point jumps to Conclusions, Conclusions being an island in Wisdom. At another, he speculates aloud on how they will manage to get a wagon moving; he is told to be quiet, because "it goes without saying."

Juster's wordplay and jokes fly as thick and fast as any Marx Brothers sketch. Norton Juster was a big fan, as was his father who used to quote long passages from their routines to his young son. Juster listened to their wise-cracking comedy on the radio, and his synaesthesia responded to their *double entendres* and puns by creating fantastically literal images. This is what lies behind the Land of Wisdom.

Norton Juster, most of whose adult life was spent as an architect, was an inveterate practical joker as a young man. While serving in the U.S. Navy he invented a fake journal called the *Naval News Service* so that he could meet women on the pretext of interviewing them for the magazine. Inspired by Groucho Marx whose maxim was, "I don't want to join any club that would admit me as a member", he created the Garibaldi Society. Its sole purpose was to reject all applications for membership.

The first edition of *The Phantom Tollbooth* was illustrated by the celebrated satirical cartoonist Jules Feiffer, Juster's neighbour, who was drawing the pictures even as Juster was writing the words. The two were great friends and would often play tricks on each other. Feiffer drew the Whether Man in Juster's story, and Juster tried to catch Feiffer out by writing the undrawable – for example in his description of the Triple Demons of Compromise: "one short and fat, one tall and thin, and the third exactly like the first two."

Other books by Norton Juster: *The Dot and the Line: A Romance in Lower Mathematics* (1963), *Otter Nonsense* (1982), *The Hello, Goodbye Window* (2005) and sequel, *The Odious Ogre* (2010), and *Neville* (2011).

The Wolves of Willoughby Chase

(1962)

Joan Aiken (1924–2004)

Joan Aiken was educated at home and never went to university. But writing was in her blood, and she wrote her first (unpublished) novel at the age of sixteen. At seventeen her first short story was accepted for publication. *The Wolves of Willoughby Chase* (1962) was her first published novel.

Opinion is much divided on the effectiveness of home-schooling children. In Aiken's case, the proof was in the pudding, and all three of the home-educated Aiken children became successful authors – one as a research chemist, two as novelists. Joan was always going to be a writer. Before she was eighteen she had seen one short story published in a magazine and another broadcast on the BBC's Home Service radio programme *Children's Hour*. Their father, a Pulitzer Prize-winning poet, left when Joan was five; so the credit for their way with words must go to their mother.

During and after World War II she worked for the United Nations Information Unit (UNIC), which was set up in the wake of the Allies' "Declaration of United Nations" in 1942. Following the death of her first husband, a fellow UNIC worker, in 1955 she returned to writing. She subsidised her authorship with work at the literary magazine *Argosy*, which published many of her short stories. At the same time she was working on a new novel, called *Bonnie Green* after its central character. It would take her seven years and a change of title to complete it, before it was finally published in 1962 as *The Wolves of Willoughby Chase*.

Joan Aiken's gothic horror series, known collectively as *The Wolves Chronicles*, runs to a dozen novels. It is set in the nineteenth century of an alternative British history, where the Stuart King James III reigns and Hanoverians are the interlopers. In the opening volume, wolves have swarmed into Britain through a newly constructed tunnel under the English

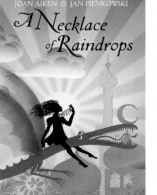

Channel, making life in the countryside a hazardous one. At the same time wolves in sheep's clothing are infesting the life of Bonnie Green, daughter of Sir Willoughby and Lady Green of Willoughby Chase. While her parents are undertaking a trip to warmer climates for their health, three scheming adults – her distant relative Miss Sighcarp, Mr Grimshaw and cruel Mrs Brisket – are plotting to usurp the family estate, incarcerating Bonnie and her cousin Sylvia in Mrs Brisket's orphanage. Danger lurks both inside and outside Willoughby Chase.

It is a classic children's novel in which the young protagonists, left without parents, must fend for themselves, relying on their wit and bravery to right the wrongs that confront them. The success of this, her first published novel, allowed Joan Aiken to become a full-time author. Her retelling of eastern European folk tales, *The Kingdom under the Sea, and Other Stories* (1971) won the Kate Greenaway Medal for its illustrator Jan Pieńkowski. Her *Arabel and Mortimer* series of thirteen novels for younger readers, beginning with *Arabel's Raven* (1972), were illustrated by Quentin Blake. Aiken's abundant creativity enabled her to write over one hundred novels and short-story collections for all ages during her lifetime.

Other children's books by Joan Aiken: *A Necklace of Raindrops, and Other Stories* (1968), *The Kingdom under the Sea, and Other Stories* (1971), *Arabel's Raven* (1972) and series, *The Cocaktrice Boys* (1993), and *In Thunder's Pocket* (2000) and series.

ABOVE: The Wolves of Willoughby Chase *is the first of the twelve* Wolves Chronicles *books. It was followed by* Black Hearts in Battersea *(1964),* Nightbirds in Nantucket *(1966) and a prequel,* The Whispering Mountain *in 1968.*

CLIVE KING

STIG OF THE DUMP

A PUFFIN BOOK

Illustrated by Edward Ardizonne

*ABOVE AND OPPOSITE: Stig of the Dump was adapted for schools radio by the BBC in
1964, but it took a quantum leap of popularity when it was serialised on the children's
magazine programme Blue Peter.*

Stig of the Dump

(1963)

Clive King (1924–2018)

Clive King's strikingly original tale was an immediate hit when it was published at the start of Beatlemania. Whether it was the long hair and untidy appearance, or the alien sounds of its titular character which caught readers' imaginations ...

*S*tig of the Dump is a sort of anti-fantasy. The meeting between prehistoric caveman Stig and present-day boy Barney spans the ages; but this is not a tale of time portals. Few other characters in the book have seen Stig or believe that he is real, but he is; this is not a story of magical comings and goings. It all takes place not as many children's stories do in some gothic fairy kingdom but in a dump, a disused quarry full of the very modern discarded affluence of the western world.

At its heart is a story of new friendship, not across time but across generations. King used to say that Stig was 10,000 years old; but although he is an adult, he is in a sense a child in his unfamiliarity with the modern world in which he finds himself. So Stig and Barney hang out together, repairing Stig's den by repurposing the rubbish from the dump. Without a shared language they find other ways to communicate; and without labouring these points King advocates tolerance – and recycling. The story's conclusion, in which Barney and his sister Lou participate for once in Stig's world, is all the more magical for the absence of magic. If it's "just a dream", it's a shared one.

Clive King's novels are all very different. He attributed this to his service in the British Navy and his employment in the British Council, the body which promotes British language, culture and education overseas. Through those careers King travelled all over the world, and many of his works are centred on places where he was based.

In *Hamid of Aleppo* (1958), for example, he tells the story of a

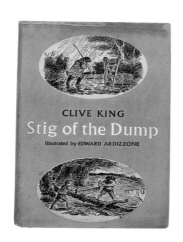

Syrian Golden Hamster who unearths antiquities while tunnelling in that city. *The Twenty-Two Letters* (1966) is set 2,500 years previously in the Eastern Mediterranean, the cradle of civilisation, where three brothers save their home town from attack with the help of three new discoveries: astronomy, literacy and horses. *The Night the Water Came* (1973), set during the aftermath of a cyclone in Bangladesh, contrasts the sort of aid offered by rescue workers with a boy's desire just to get back to life as it was.

In *Snakes and Snakes* (1975) a young Sri Lankan boy wants to know if a rare snake he has found is worth any money. King was posted to Ceylon, as Sri Lanka was then known, for a time during World War II. The story later became *Good Snakes, Bad Snakes* (1977), a BBC play for children for the occasional series "Stories Round the World."

King wrote four plays and over twenty novels, including a mystery series called *The Inner Ring*. If he is today known almost exclusively for *Stig of the Dump*, it is because in Barney and Stig he created a magical relationship without the use of magic; a world of wonder in an everyday setting; a jewel in a waste pit.

Other books by Clive King: *Hamid of Aleppo* (1958), *The Town That Went South* (1959), *The Night the Water Came* (1973), *Snakes and Snakes* (1975), *The Accident* (1976) and *Inner Ring* series, and *The Seashore People* (1987).

Where the Wild Things Are

(1963)

Maurice Sendak (1928–2012)

In any children's book list, whether it's of ten or a hundred, *Where the Wild Things Are* regularly comes out on top in polls of the greatest children's picture books ever written and drawn. For its existence, we must all be grateful that Maurice Sendak couldn't draw horses.

Maurice Sendak was born in Brooklyn, New York to a family of Polish Jews. Confronted as a child by regular large gatherings of members of his extended family, he took to drawing caricatures of his more grotesque aunts and uncles. Sendak's artistic aspirations became more serious when after seeing Walt Disney's ground-breaking *Fantasia* animation, he decided that he wanted to become an illustrator. After World War II he began to get commissions and received a run of awards in the 1950s for his artwork in children's books. Among the authors for whom he created images was his older brother Jack Sendak.

Maurice Sendak made his debut as a writer with *Kenny's Window* (1956), and had begun work on another, *The Land of Wild Horses*. In the story, a badly behaved boy is sent to his room in punishment, where he imagines running away to the land in question. Only when Sendak began drafting the illustrations did he realise that he couldn't draw horses to save his life. His editor suggested that he change it to a land of wild *things*, which would give him more room for manoeuvre. The Yiddish expression for uncontrollable children is "vilde chaya", literally "wild animals."

While broadly sticking to his original storyline, Sendak turned to his pre-war caricatures of relatives for new inspiration. The result was *Where the Wild Things Are*, in which young boy Max, wearing a wolf costume, gets over-excited, causes chaos and is sent to his bedroom without his evening meal. The room starts to turn into a jungle from which Max sails to a land Where the Wild Things Are. These creatures with horns and snouts and hairy bodies are respectfully fearful of Max's wolflike appearance, and among these wild equals Max is free to play as boisterously as he likes. But he misses his home and eventually returns, to find his supper still hot and waiting for him.

The book was not at first well received. Librarians felt that it gave children a license to behave badly. But children themselves loved it, and critics now see it as a beautifully illustrated story of a growing boy coming to terms with unfamiliar and powerful emotions. As Sendak himself commented, this and two other of his books *In the Night Kitchen* (1970) and *Outside Over There* (1981) share a common theme: "how children master various feelings – danger, boredom, fear, frustration, jealousy – and manage to come to grips with the realities of their lives."

Despite its enormous success, Sendak refused to revive its characters in any sequels, although he was involved in some of its adaptations. For a 1983 opera version of *Where the Wild Things Are* he named five previously unnamed Wild Things after five of his relatives: Tzippy, Moishe, Aaron, Emile and Bernard.

President Barack Obama's choice of the book to read to children each year on the White House lawn has guaranteed its place in the pantheon of children's classics. Though there was never a chance he would read out *The Story of the Little Mole* …

Selected other books written and illustrated by Maurice Sendak: *Kenny's Window (1956)*, *In the Night Kitchen* (1970), *Seven Little Monsters* (1977), *Outside Over There* (1981) and *Bumble Ardy* (2011). Selected other books illustrated by Maurice Sendak: *A Very Special House* by Ruth Krauss (1953), *Hurry Home, Candy* by Meindert DeJong (1953), *Circus Girl* by Jack Sendak (1957), and *Little Bear* by Else Holmelund Minarik (1957) and series.

WHERE THE WILD THINGS ARE

STORY AND PICTURES BY MAURICE SENDAK

ABOVE: Unusually for a children's book of the 1960s, the cover of Wild Things hasn't changed in nearly sixty years. *LEFT:* Michelle and Barack Obama reading from Maurice Sendak's book during the annual Easter Egg Roll on the White House Lawn. The event held on Easter Monday was started up by President Rutherford B. Hayes in 1878. The Obamas made the reading of this particular book a yearly tradition.

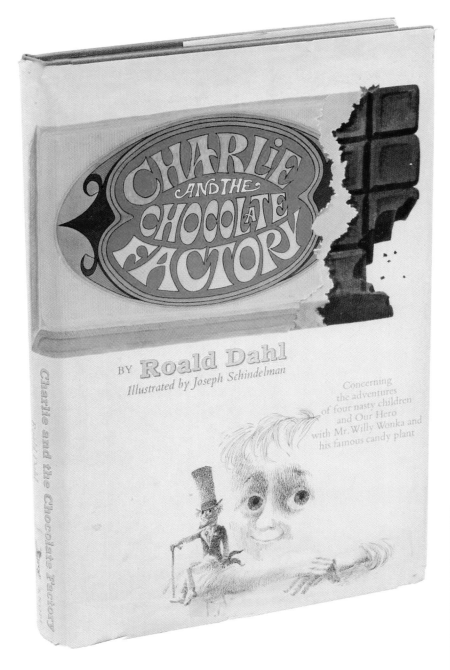

LEFT: The original cover of Charlie and the Chocolate Factory.

BELOW: Illustrator Quentin Blake's work has long been associated with Dahl. Their first book together was The Enormous Crocodile *in 1978. Dr. Seuss trusted Blake to illustrate the first book he did not illustrate himself,* Great Day for Up! *(1974) and he has subsequently worked with Joan Aiken and David Walliams, as well as producing his own books.*

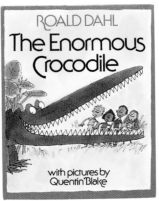

Charlie and the Chocolate Factory

(1964)

Roald Dahl (1916–1990)

The best-known book by Roald Dahl has all the master storyteller's hallmarks: grotesque wickedness, punishment to fit the crime, and good triumphing over evil. Dahl's wild imagination was fired by his parents' Scandinavian heritage and his own schooldays.

As a small boy, Roald Dahl was sent to board at Repton School in Derbyshire, one of several used by chocolate manufacturer Cadbury to test new products. It was one of few highlights of his time in an educational institution which legitimised beatings by teachers and bullying by senior pupils. That English public school cruelty inspired many of his stories' villains. By contrast the embodiment of goodness and innocence in his books are always children, as exemplified by Charlie Bucket in *Charlie and the Chocolate Factory.*

Which child hasn't dreamed of being the proverbial "kid in a sweet shop"? But in *Charlie and the Chocolate Factory*, Dahl takes and then subverts that childhood fantasy. Five children get to live the dream when they find golden tickets in Willy Wonka's chocolate bars. They have won the tour of a lifetime round his confectionery factory.

But the dream turns bitter for four of the five who reveal their thoroughly unpleasant sides during the tour. Only sweet little Charlie Bucket, in the company of his grandpa Joe, behaves impeccably throughout and wins a prize beyond his wildest dreams. Between the badly behaved children and virtuous Charlie, Willy Wonka rules his sugary world like an amoral god, a distinctly ambiguous and rather menacing character.

Inseparable from the words of Roald Dahl's stories are the illustrations that accompany them, especially those by Quentin Blake. From 1978 to 1990 Blake illustrated the first editions of eleven Dahl titles including *George's Marvellous Medicine* (1981) and Dahl's last, *Esio Trot* (1990). Since the author's death Blake has,

to date, illustrated new editions of a further thirteen including *Charlie and the Chocolate Factory*, which was first illustrated in the U.S. by Joseph Schindelman and in the U.K. by Faith Jaques. Blake's chaotic, loose style of caricature suits Dahl's anarchic imagination perfectly.

Charlie and the Chocolate Factory is by no means a straightforward good-versus-evil fairy tale. Children and adults can be good or bad, just like the giants in Dahl's *The BFG*. Dahl's imagination was fuelled by his Norwegian parents, whose heritage of Scandinavian folk tales with their trolls, goblins and water spirits was generally darker than the British equivalent. Hence Dahl's depiction of the National Society for the Prevention of Cruelty to Children as a front for a gathering of evil in *The Witches* for example, which is set in both Norway and England.

Those Norse legends may also have given rise to Dahl's wicked sense of humour. At the age of eight he hid a dead mouse in a jar of gobstoppers because he disliked the keeper of his local sweetshop. There are echoes of this episode in the Everlasting Gobstopper which Willy Wonka shows the children. For young readers ready to move on from the black-and-white morality of their early books, *Charlie and the Chocolate Factory* contains a delightful blend of unconventional mischief. Life, they can start to discover through Roald Dahl, is rarely straightforward.

Selected works: *James and the Giant Peach* (1961), *Fantastic Mr Fox* (1970), *The Twits* (1980), *The BFG* (1982), *The Witches* (1983) and *Matilda* (1988).

The Tiger Who Came to Tea

(1968)

Judith Kerr (1923–2019)

The strange notion of sitting down to tea with a ferocious animal made Judith Kerr's first story an immediate hit with young children. Like so many of the successful stories in this collection, it began life as a bedtime story for her family.

The Tiger Who Came to Tea was a story that Judith Kerr began telling her infant children after a day out at the zoo. They loved it, and she refined it in repeated tellings. When they were old enough to read, it was an obvious step to write it down for them. Kerr, who studied art at the Central School of Arts and Crafts in London, also illustrated the tiger's tale.

In the story, a tiger unexpectedly joins young Sophie and her mother while they are having tea. It eats them out of house and home, then leaves. When Sophie's father gets home he takes them out to a café. They go shopping for more food including some for the tiger; but the animal does not return.

If a trip to the zoo and bedtime stories seem very unremarkable, Kerr's own childhood was far from peaceful or conventional. Her parents were German Jews. Nazis burned books written by her father, originally called Alfred Kempner, because he was critical of Hitler's rise to power.

Alfred was on a Nazi death list, and in 1933 the Kerrs fled Germany, travelling to Switzerland and France before settling in England in 1936. Although Judith always insisted that her tiger was just a tiger, it is tempting to speculate, as children's author Michael Rosen has done, that it represents the potential danger from any unexpected visitor to her childhood home in Berlin. By creating a tiger which does NOT destroy the family home and kill all its inhabitants, perhaps she was subconsciously disempowering the Nazi tiger in her memory. When in the book the tiger does not return for second helpings, perhaps it is just as well.

It took Kerr a year to write and draw The Tiger Who Came to Tea. Its immediate success launched her on a writing career of which she had always dreamt. Besides The Tiger, she is also the author of the seventeen books of the Mog series, not to be confused with the Meg and Mog series, about an altogether more domesticated cat called Mog and the family with whom she lives. In a surprising plot for a young children's series, the final instalment of Mog's adventures, Goodbye, Mog (2002), sees the death of the family pet.

Judith Kerr also wrote a semi-autobiographical trilogy for young adults called Out of the Hitler Time about the reality of life before, during and after World War II from a child's perspective. It was written to provide her children with a more realistic view of the times than they were getting from the film The Sound of Music.

Other books by Judith Kerr: The Mog series, including – Mog the Forgetful Cat (1970), Mog's Amazing Birthday Caper (1986), Mog's Kittens (1994) and Goodbye, Mog (2002). The Out of the Hitler Time trilogy – When Hitler Stole Pink Rabbit (1971), Bombs on Aunt Dainty (originally published as The Other Way Round, 1975), A Small Person Far Away (1978) and One Night in the Zoo (2009).

OPPOSITE, TOP: The original cover of Tiger featured both Sophie and her mother at the table.

OPPOSITE: That bothersome cat Mog even forgets she has her own cat flap.

OPPOSITE, FAR RGHT: The traumatic events of 1933 were described by Judith Kerr in When Hitler Stole Pink Rabbit.

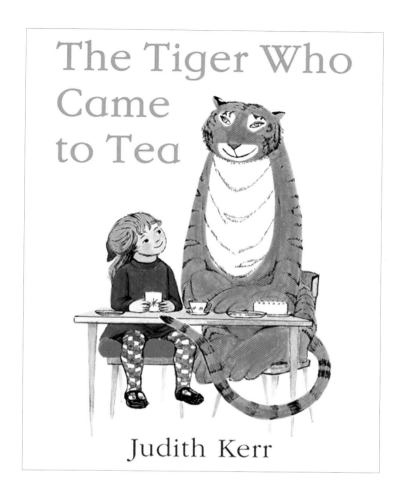

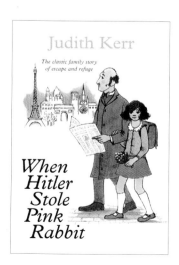

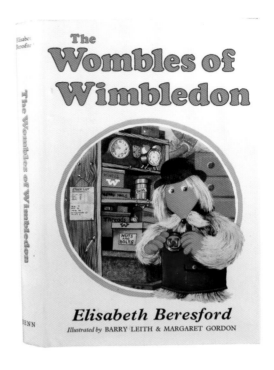

ABOVE LEFT: *The first edition* Wombles *cover illustrated by Margaret Gordon.*

ABOVE: *Later book covers used the animated characters, familiar to a 1970s television audience.*

LEFT: *Mike Batt's Wombles ripping it up on* Top of the Pops. *After masterminding* The Wombles *group, Batt went on to write a musical of Lewis Carroll's poem* The Hunting of the Snark.

The Wombles

(1968) and series

Elisabeth Beresford (1926–2010)

Up until the early 1970s, the London suburb of Wimbledon was associated with its lawn tennis tournament and little else. Elisabeth Beresford's book about the Wombles of Wimbledon Common and their recycling tidy bags, changed that forever.

For the uninitiated, Wombles are shy underground creatures who recycle the litter left by humans. They live all around the world, but Elizabeth Beresford wrote specifically about the Wombles of Wimbledon Common. In 1968, when concerns about the environment were just beginning to grow, they were ahead of their time. Their motto is "Make Good Use of Bad Rubbish."

They were created when Elizabeth Beresford's daughter kept mispronouncing the name of Wimbledon Common during a family walk on Boxing Day, 1967. Their names came from places to which the family had travelled, and their characters were based on members of the Beresford family – Orinoco for example was modelled on her son, and Great Uncle Bulgaria on her father-in-law. Beresford's daughter was the inspiration for Bungo Womble.

Elizabeth Beresford's father was a novelist, and her parents moved in literary circles. Their friends included D. H. Lawrence and Somerset Maugham; Elizabeth's godparents were the poets Cecil Day-Lewis (father of actor Daniel) and Walter de la Mare.

She began her career after World War II by ghost-writing speeches, before working as a journalist writing columns for TV and radio. She tried her hand at children's adventure stories with her first novel *The Television Mystery* (1957), and at fantasy with *Awkward Magic* (1964), the first of a series of novels. *Awkward Magic* concerned a griffin and a magic carpet, drawing comparisons with E. Nesbit's *The Phoenix and the Carpet* (1904). It wasn't until *The Wombles* (1968), however, that she found mainstream success.

The first two books were illustrated by Margaret Gordon, who defined their furry, long-nosed appearance. They were moderately successful, but Womblemania

really took off when the BBC commissioned a series of short stop-animation Wombles films in 1973. The programmes, narrated by Bernard Cribbins, were produced by Ivor Wood, the pioneering animator of series such as Serge Danot's *The Magic Roundabout*, Michael Bond's *Paddington* and for a later generation, *Postman Pat*. It was a winning formula. Scheduled to run just ahead of the early evening news it also received a large adult audience who knew Cribbins from British comedy films.

The catchy title music for the TV series, written by Mike Batt, was a surprise hit, the first of eight Top 40 entries for the Wombles which made them the U.K.'s Top Recording Artists of 1974. They even made guest appearances, in costume form, on other TV shows, for example *Top of the Pops* and *The Goodies* sketch show. For two or three years the Wombles were everywhere, on merchandise and in person. Pity the respected musicians inside those hot, heavy costumes for the Wombles musical, which played in London's West End. However, by the time a feature-length movie, *Wombling Free*, was released in 1977, the bubble had burst. Youth culture had moved on from Womblemania to punk music.

Beresford continued to write new Wombles stories right up to her death – there are some twenty books now; to this day the merchandising rights are controlled by Mike Batt and the children of Elizabeth Beresford. Womblemania still resurfaces from time to time, and in 2011 the Wombles played to screaming crowds at the Glastonbury Festival, their motto to recycle more relevant than ever.

Other books by Elizabeth Beresford: *The Television Mystery* (1957), *Cocky and the Missing Castle* (1959), *Awkward Magic* (1964), *Sea-Green Magic* (1969), and *Invisible Magic* (1978).

What Do People Do All Day?
(1968)

Richard Scarry (1919–1994)

Not many children's books act as primers for the economic systems of the Western World. Richard Scarry's *What Do People Do All Day?* does it with a deft touch and a host of cute animal characters from the microcosm of Busytown USA.

Busytown is the world in which Scarry set his most popular stories. Not for Scarry the broad strokes and simple lines of other artists: his pictures are characterised by their busy-ness.

What Do People Do All Day? introduces the world of work. "Everyone is a worker," Scarry declares in the book. And he proceeds to show how all work is connected by the chains of supply and demand. For example, Farmer Alfalfa (a goat) sells his surplus crops to Grocer Cat, who sells it on to the population of Busytown. Meanwhile Farmer Alfalfa uses some of the money he got from selling his crops to buy himself a new suit from Stitches the Tailor, and a new tractor from Blacksmith Fox with which he will be able to increase the yield of his fields. The money left over he saves in the bank.

Beyond the narrative which they illustrate, there are often little sub-plots being acted out in the background, and so Scarry's are books that children can easily lose themselves in.

Scarry covers a wide range of occupations from manual to managerial, blue collar to white. By addressing the concept of money too, it's the perfect response to any child who is beginning to ask difficult questions such as "Why can't I have this year's must-wear sneaker?" or "Why can't you come to school with me?"

Richard Scarry, of Irish heritage, was born and raised in Boston, Massachusetts. It's significant that his parents ran a shop there, well enough to be financially comfortable. Richard seemed likely to follow in the family footsteps when he enrolled in business college. Though *What Do People Do All Day?* adeptly explains the fundamentals of the economic system to children; Scarry did not enjoy the course and left it before

graduating, signing up instead to study art at Boston's Museum of Fine Arts.

After World War II he worked in the art departments of several periodicals until his career took off in 1949, first as an illustrator of other authors' books and from 1955 as an author himself. *The Bunny Book* (1955) was a collaboration between Scarry and his wife Patricia, who wrote textbooks for schools. The first of nine books in his series *Tinker and Tanker*, about the unlikely friendship between a rabbit and a hippopotamus, was published in 1960.

Scarry's first worldwide hit came in 1963 with the publication of his *Best Word Book Ever* which illustrated and spelled around 1,400 words in a series of themed double-page scenes – for example sports, and transport. It had the same engrossing density of detail that he would later draw in *What Do People Do All Day?*

Best Word Book Ever has become a much imitated classic for early readers, and a million-seller in several languages including a bilingual English-Spanish translation.

Selected other books by Richard Scarry: *Best Word Book Ever* (1963), *Best Nursery Rhymes Ever* (1964), *Busy Busy World* (1965), *Best Counting Book Ever* (1973), *Busy Town, Busy People* (1976), and *Biggest Word Book Ever* (1985).

OPPOSITE: Richard Scarry had a prodigious output of books in his lifetime, both with Golden Books and Random House. Some have been sensitively updated to reflect social changes, especially in gender roles.

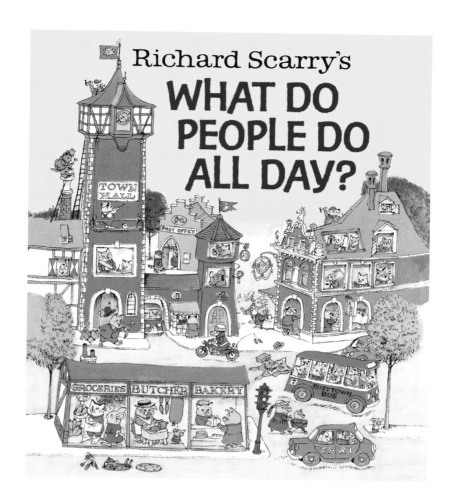

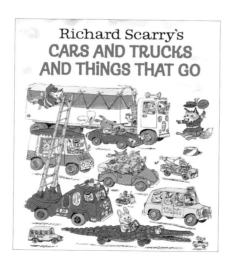

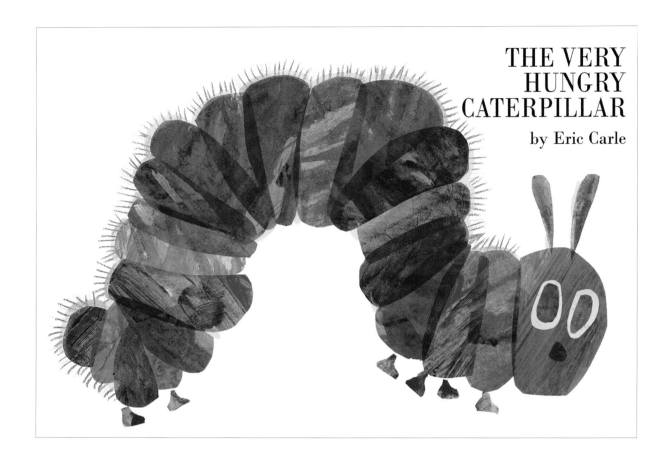

THE VERY HUNGRY CATERPILLAR

by Eric Carle

ABOVE: Eric Carle's idea started off with a hole chewed through a page by a bookworm. Thanks to his editor, the worm metamorphosed into a caterpillar.

LEFT: All the animals in the rainforest want to know why the sloth is so slow in "Slowly, Slowly, Slowly," Said the Sloth (2002).

The Very Hungry Caterpillar

(1969)

Eric Carle (born 1929)

President George W. Bush named it as his favourite children's book. It is said that a new copy of *The Very Hungry Caterpillar* is sold every minute. Demand, it would seem, like the caterpillar's appetite is insatiable.

A hungry little caterpillar emerges from its egg one Sunday. On the following six days it eats more and more. Now no longer hungry or little, it spins itself a cocoon and emerges two weeks later, no longer even a caterpillar. In the course of the book children are introduced to counting: the days of the week, the life cycle of the caterpillar, and even the folly of eating too rich a diet (especially on a Saturday).

Author and illustrator Eric Carle was inspired to write his most successful book while punching holes in sheaves of paper. The little tunnels made him think of bookworms, and he wrote *A Week with Willi the Worm*. His editor tactfully suggested that caterpillars might be more attractive to children than worms. The transformation of a caterpillar into a butterfly presented Carle with a natural ending to his story, so he happily set about making the changes. Its subsequent sales confirm the wisdom of listening to one's editor.

Eric Carle was born in Syracuse, New York, to a family of German immigrants who subsequently returned with him to Germany. There he grew up during World War II while his father, conscripted into the German Army, was held prisoner by the Russians. Carle himself was pressed into service digging trenches when he turned fifteen.

Finally able to return to the U.S. in 1952, Carle found work in the graphics department of the *New York Times*, and in advertising. His depiction of a lobster in one advertisement attracted the attention of children's author Bill Martin Jr., who gave him his first break in book illustration with Martin's *Brown Bear, Brown Bear, What Do You See?* (1967). Carle's distinctive style of collage uses sheets of paper which he has painted in brush strokes of colour before cutting them up to form his bright, lively images. *Brown Bear* introduced his artwork to a new audience, and Martin and Carle have periodically collaborated on its sequels, *Polar Bear, Panda Bear* and *Baby Bear*.

Carle credits the inventiveness of German children's picture books with his interest in unusual formats. *The Very Quiet Cricket* (1990), for example, incorporates the sound of crickets, while *The Very Lonely Firefly* (1995) contains twinkling lights. Many of his books are cut in unusual shapes, which present challenges to conventional book printers. The first editions of *The Very Hungry Caterpillar* had to be produced in Japan when no company in the U.S. was able to handle the holes in the pages supposedly made by the caterpillar eating its way through the book.

Eric Carle and his wife established the Eric Carle Museum of Picture Book Art in 2002 in Amherst, Massachusetts. It has become a mecca for all those interested in the variety and evocative history of the genre. Among the many honours bestowed on Carle, one of its greatest practitioners, the most unusual was surely the naming of a spider which disguises itself as a caterpillar. In 2019, on his ninetieth birthday, fifty years after the original publication of *The Very Hungry Caterpillar*, scientists named the newly discovered species *Uroballus carlei*.

Selected other books by Eric Carle: *Brown Bear, Brown Bear, What Do You See?* with Bill Martin Jr (1967), *The Very Busy Spider* (1984), *The Very Quiet Cricket* (1990), *Polar Bear, Polar Bear, What Do You Hear?* with Bill Martin Jr (1991), *Very Lonely Firefly* (1995), *Panda Bear, Panda Bear, What Do You See?* with Bill Martin Jr (2003), and *Baby Bear, Baby Bear, What Do You See?* with Bill Martin Jr (2007).

Are You There God? It's Me, Margaret.

(1970)

Judy Blume (born 1938)

There are four tricky subjects in children's literature – Sex, Religion, Divorce and Death. Parents find it difficult to talk about them, and so do children's authors. But not Judy Blume, who has opened up difficult conversations for older children and young adults.

While raising her young family, Judy Blume recalled that her own childhood had suffered from a lack of open discussion about the often frightening aspects of moving into the adult world. Her first book was *The One in the Middle is the Green Kangaroo* (1969), about the invisibility of the middle child. Next, she tackled the more difficult topic of racism in *Iggy's House* (1970), about the attitudes of different generations to the first black family in the neighbourhood. Her third was *Are You There God? It's Me, Margaret.*

Margaret, aged eleven, is the child of a Christian mother and a Jewish father. Her parents have not imposed any religious faith on her, although her respective grandparents wish one of them would. While she begins to think more seriously about God in his or her various forms, her pubescent friends are having altogether different thoughts. Margaret, developing later than most of her peers, fears that she is abnormal. Other girls boast of having begun their periods; other people have firm religious convictions.

But other people don't always tell the truth, and other people also have doubts. At her lowest, Margaret stops her conversations with God, but the book concludes with her entering puberty and getting back in touch: "I know you're there, God," she says. "I know you wouldn't have missed this for anything."

Are You There God? jumps right in and puts everything on the table: sex, boys, first bras, first periods, differences in religion and conflicting adults – Margaret's maternal grandparents have not spoken to her mother for years because she married a Jew. The book has been hailed for its willingness to ask difficult questions and not offer easy answers, but it has also been attacked by hard-line groups for being too frank for the age of its intended readers.

Blume next tackled puberty for boys, in *Then Again, Maybe I Won't* (1971). Twice divorced, she has twice written about divided families, in *It's Not the End of the World* (1972) and *Just as Long as We're Together* (1987). *Blubber* (1974), about bullying in school, is narrated by the bully who becomes the bullied. *Tales of a Fourth Grade Nothing* (1972) is the first of four books which focus on a character, a boy nicknamed Fudge, rather than an issue.

In 2015 she confronted death itself in *In the Unlikely Event*, an adult novel about a series of plane crashes

which really happened, in the space of fifty eight days, near her home town during her childhood. Her father, a dentist, had the grim job of identifying the victims from their teeth, something Judy Blume had blotted out until she came to write the book.

Selected other young adult books by Judy Blume: *Iggy's House* (1970), *Then Again, Maybe I Won't* (1971), *It's Not the End of the World* (1972), *Tales of a Fourth Grade Nothing* (1972) and series, and *Blubber* (1974).

ABOVE: Judy Blume wrote on subjects teenagers were anxious to learn about, which were routinely avoided in young adult fiction. Are you There God? *was a book regularly challenged in American libraries.*

OPPOSITE: It's Not the End of the World *focused on a child's reaction to her parents' impending divorce.*

Frog and Toad Are Friends

(1970) and series

Arnold Lobel (1933–1987)

Early friendships can be challenging for the very young, formed over ice cream and broken in tantrums about a shared toy. Arnold Lobel's Frog and Toad show how differing individuals can cooperate and compromise, and still remain close friends.

Frog and Toad are Friends introduced the characters in 1970, its very title spelling out the theme of this and the following three books in the series. The two friends are distinctively drawn and characterised – Frog, tall, green, easy-going, cheerful; and Toad, short, stout, brown, serious, and anxious. Lobel once claimed that they were two sides of his own personality, and the books are also about coming to terms with one's own inner tensions.

Lobel was an illustrator first and author second. Throughout the 1960s he worked on "easy readers", using a conventional approach of few words, simple rhymes and bright pictures in primary colours. He first took up art to while away the solitary hours during a long childhood illness, and perhaps it was then, alone for long periods, that he also began to think about the nature of friendship.

He met his wife Anita, another illustrator, at art school in the 1950s, and the couple sometimes worked together on books, such as *On Market Street* (1981). They lived across the street from Prospect Park Zoo in Brooklyn, and visits there with their children inspired many of Lobel's animal stories, including his early works *A Zoo for Mister Muster* (1962) and *A Holiday for Mister Muster* (1963).

By the end of the 1960s, however, Lobel was frustrated by his storylines. His desire to write stories with the weight he wished conflicted with the sorts of tales which he imagined a child might enjoy. The results, he began to feel, lacked sincerity and emotional impact. He began to write more from his heart than his head, using his own adult feelings which he believed were not so far removed from those of children. At the same time his illustrations moved from primary colours to a richer palette of shades. *Frog and Toad are Friends* was the first result of this new approach, and it clearly worked.

Lobel worked on nearly a hundred books during his life, either as illustrator or author or both. Despite the success of the Frog and Toad series it was only after his early death in 1987 that his artwork was widely appreciated. In 2008, three unpublished Frog and Toad stories were discovered in an estate sale, in a different artistic style and only in black and white. Lobel's daughter Arianne coloured them and published them over two volumes as a late addition to the series.

Arnold Lobel had worked with his future wife on a student drama production at art school, and theatre was therefore in Arianne's blood. She became a theatrical set designer and in 2000 commissioned a musical stage version of *A Year with Frog and Toad*. It premiered off-Broadway in 2002 with her husband the actor Mark Linn-Baker in the role of Toad

The simple, heartwarming stories in *Frog and Toad* showed children that even if their good deeds went unrecognised – as Frog and Toad's often were – the doer can still feel good for having done them.

Selected other books by Arnold Lobel: *Owl at Home* (1975), *Mouse Soup* (1977), *Fables* (1980), and *Ming Lo Moves the Mountain* (1982).

OPPOSITE: *The first of four* Frog and Toad *books comprised five simple stories including "A Swim", where Toad is anxious that no one sees him in his bathing suit and refuses to get out of the water. When he does, Frog laughs at him.*

Mr. Tickle

(1971)

Roger Hargreaves (1935-1988)

Mr. Tickle was the first of the Mr. Men, one of the original batch of six Mr. Men books published together in August 1971. As he approaches his fiftieth birthday, Mr. Tickle's long arms still tickle the imagination of the very young.

Roger Hargreaves, from West Yorkshire, was the creative director of an advertising business when his six-year-old son Adam asked him, "Daddy, what does a tickle look like?" Hargreaves dashed off an image of Mr. Tickle, and the remarkably successful Mr. Men series was born. There are now some ninety characters in the world of the Mr. Men and their female counterparts the Little Misses, accounting for sales of well over 100 million books across twenty-eight countries.

Each one is named for a particular characteristic – the others in that first group were Mr. Greedy, Mr. Happy, Mr. Nosey, Mr. Sneeze and Mr. Bump – and their short adventures illustrate their trait and its consequences, generally leading to a light-hearted moral life lesson. Mr. Tickle is an exception to that rule. His long arms are out of control and he gets away with his naughty behaviour, tickling authority figures such as a teacher and a policeman. The only life lesson from *Mr. Tickle* is that you never know when Mr. Tickle might tickle YOU.

Hargreaves' art is deceptively simple. He drew his characters quickly, with marker pens; but he had a cartoonist's eye for the small details that would convey character with the minimum of lines and colours. As his son Adam grew into adulthood he was rather dismissive of his father's work, which he saw as childish – until he tried to do it for himself.

When Roger Hargreaves died, having created forty Mr. Men and twenty-one Little Misses, Adam took up the reins of what was already a vast business empire of Mr. Men spin-offs – toys, TV series and other franchises. But he found it much harder than expected to write and draw in his father's style; it took, he later admitted, years of trial and error to perfect it, in the course of which he found new respect for Hargreaves senior's art and sense of humour.

Adam Hargreaves has created several new characters now, publishing them under his father's name. He has also expanded the range with occasional commercial tie-ins – for example *Little Miss Princess* to coincide with a British Royal Family wedding, and a limited-edition *Mr. Glug* for the Evian mineral water company.

Roger Hargreaves wrote other books too, including series about *Walter Worm* and *John Mouse*. The 29 books on the delightful *Timbuctoo* series are in the same style as the Mr. Men, and each named after the noise one animal makes – *Woof, Meow, Oink* and so on. Given the laughter which his legacy still produces in the young, perhaps Roger Hargreaves himself was the original Mr. Tickle.

Selected series by Roger Hargreaves: *Mr. Men* (1971), *Little Miss* (1981), *Walter Worm* (2018), *John Mouse* (1973), and *Timbuctoo* (1978).

ABOVE: Only the most revered children's books make their way onto stamps, as Roger Hargreaves' did in 2016.

TOP: Recognised the world over, Mr. Tickle rarely delivers a life lesson in his adventures.

OPPOSITE: Mr. Tall appeared in 1976, four years after Mr. Small (1972) and two years before Mr. Skinny (1978).

Meg and Mog

(1972) and series

Helen Nicoll (1937–2012), Jan Pieńkowski (born 1936)

The partnership between English writer Helen Nicoll and Polish illustrator Jan Pieńkowski lasted for over forty years and began when they worked together on children's television at the BBC in the 1960s. The incompetent witch Meg and her long-suffering cat Mog are their joyful legacy to young readers.

When Nicoll told Pieńkowski that she was thinking of writing a book about a witch, he agreed to illustrate it only on condition that none of her spells ever worked. The first result, *Meg and Mog*, was so full of fun that its publisher Heinemann immediately asked for a second one.

The *Meg and Mog* books are emphatically the work of two co-authors, not merely of an author whose work is later complemented by illustrations. Nicoll and Pieńkowski worked together throughout each book's conception, overcoming the distance between their homes by meeting halfway in a motorway service station. They also undertook research trips together, venturing to Wales to look at castles while writing *Meg's Castle*.

The humour of the books comes as much from Jan's drawings as from Helen's words. Pieńkowski, who came to England in 1946, grew up with the central European tradition of folk tales which are often much more frightening than their British counterparts. He has said that making Meg a figure of fun was his revenge on the childhood nightmares which his grandmother's storytelling gave him.

Helen Nicoll was a painstaking perfectionist, a characteristic which won her the post as one of the first female producers at the BBC. It also made her an astute entrepreneur. When an audiobook which she gave her mother proved to be disappointingly abridged, she founded Cover To Cover, which specialised in unabridged recordings of both children's and adult literature. This impressed J. K. Rowling who sold her the audio rights to the *Harry Potter* series for £5,000 before they had become such a global phenomenon. Stephen Fry recorded them, and when Nicoll sold the company to her old employers at the BBC in 2000, she excepted the Rowling titles from the deal.

Besides his work with Nicoll, Jan Pieńkowski has also collaborated with Joan Aiken, the children's author of supernatural tales. He also creates complex three-dimensional pop-up books including the widely translated million-selling *Haunted House*, and in a related field he has designed several theatrical stage sets.

Meg and Mog ventured onto the West End stage in 1981, in an adaptation by David Wood at the Arts theatre. Maureen Lipman was the inspired choice for Meg. This collaboration gave Nicoll the idea of producing audio versions of the books, with Maureen as the narrator and a colleague from the BBC Radiophonic Workshop producing the sound effects. In 2003, Meg and Mog were animated for television, with Meg voiced by Fay Ripley, Mog by Phil Cornwell and Owl by the incomparable Alan Bennett.

Meg and Mog, accompanied sometimes by their wise feathered friend Owl, appeared in seventeen books over forty years, including the final one, published in the year of Nicoll's death: *Meg Goes to Bed.*

Selected Meg and Mog titles: *Meg and Mog* (1972), *Mog's Missing* (2005), *Meg's Mummy* (2004), *Mog in the Fog* (1984), *Owl at School* (1984), *Meg's Veg* (1975), and *Meg Goes to Bed* (2010).

OPPOSITE: *Stripy cats were all the rage in the early 1970s. First there was Mog, then there was pink stripy Bagpuss on television. Mog took her last ride with Meg in 2010.*

Watership Down

(1972)

Richard Adams (1920–2016)

Richard Adams' epic tale of a colony of rabbits determined to survive, is popular with both young and old alike. Despite the subject matter, it is emphatically NOT just another children's book about cuddly bunnies and the fun things they get up to.

Although Adams always insisted that it was just a story about some rabbits, its events and characterisations evoke the sweeping classical Greek and Roman traditions of *The Odyssey* and *The Aeneid*. Like all children of his generation and class, Adams would have read these works at school.

When their warren, Sandleford, is threatened with destruction, the rabbits set out on a quest to find a new one, guided by the mystical visions of a rabbit called Fiver, and the leadership of Fiver's brother Hazel. Overcoming obstacles and dangers on the way, including a badger and a car, they arrive at Watership Down. There they must establish a new, sustainable colony and protect it from an assault by Efrafa, an aggressive neighbouring warren.

It's a heroic tale, set firmly in the landscape of Berkshire in England where Adams grew up. The village of Sandleford and the hill of Watership Down are in fact real places. The book, like so many children's classics, began life as a story which Adams improvised for his children during a car journey to Stratford-on-Avon. He was employed in the British Civil Service, but was in the habit of writing short stories to read to his daughters Juliet and Rosamund. When they pestered him to tell them another as he drove, he later recalled, he began, "Once there were two rabbits called Hazel and Fiver …" and allowed the story to unfold.

When it later came to writing the story down, Adams' boyhood knowledge of classical literature subconsciously guided him. He put considerable energy into creating a rabbit universe with its own language, culture and traditions.

For more practical details he turned to *The Private Life of the Rabbit*, a comprehensive study of the species by the naturalist Ronald Lockley, who lived for many years on an island populated only by rabbits and sea birds. (Lockley also made a pioneering nature film called *The Private Life of Gannets*.) Lockley and Adams became friends after the publication of *Watership Down*, and Lockley appears as a character in Adams' third novel, *The Plague Dogs* (1977).

Watership Down was Adams' first book. He did not confine himself to children's literature or anthropomorphised animals, although *The Plague Dogs* returns to some of the themes of *Watership Down* in a story of two dogs on the run from an animal-testing laboratory. And *The Ship's Cat* (also 1977) is a picture book for younger readers about a pirate cat, illustrated by the great Alan Aldridge – its full title is *The Adventures & Brave Deeds of the Ship's Cat on the Spanish Maine: Together with the Most Lamentable Losse of the Alcestis & Triumphant Firing of the Port of Chagres*.

Traveller (1988), his historical novel about the American Civil War, is told through the eyes of rebel general Robert E Lee's horse of that name.

In 1996 Richard Adams wrote *Tales from Watership Down*, a belated sequel, which was a collection of short stories about characters from the warren and from rabbit mythology. These fleshed out the already cohesive rabbit universe of the original book.

Other children's books by Richard Adams: *The Ship's Cat* (1977), *The Plague Dogs* (1977), *The Iron Wolf, and Other Stories* (1980, illustrations by Jennifer Campbell), and *Traveller* (1988).

Watership Down
A novel by
Richard Adams

ABOVE: *Richard Adams' debut novel was rejected by several publishers before making it into print.* Watership Down *was an immediate success and the real-life Down in Hampshire became a site of pilgrimage for the book's fans.*

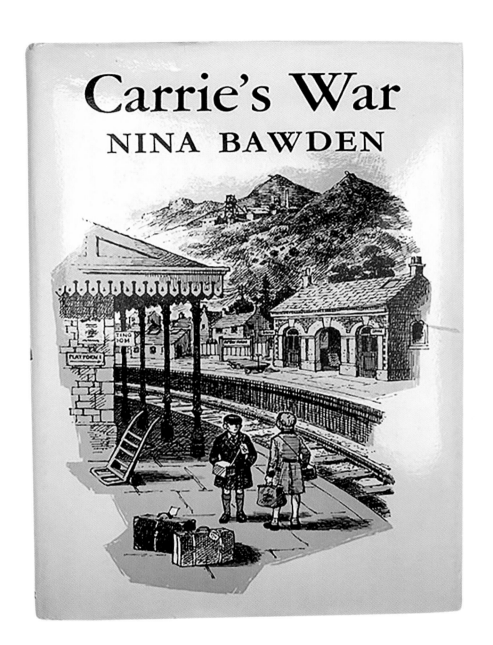

Carrie's War

NINA BAWDEN

ABOVE: *The first edition of* Carrie's War *illustrated by Faith Jaques. Nina Bawden was living in Ilford, Essex, when she was evacuated to Aberdare in Wales at the age of fourteen.*

Carrie's War

(1973)

Nina Bawden (1925–2012)

Like her character Carrie, Nina Bawden was evacuated during World War II to a mining town in South Wales. *Carrie's War* rings true because of Nina's wartime experiences and it has become a standard text for both literature and history classes in schools.

When Carrie, widowed mother of two, returns with her children to the town to which she and her brother were sent during the war, memories flood back which have haunted her since that time. It was the scene of her first kiss, with another evacuee, Albert. But as she left the town back then, she believed she had invoked an age-old curse and destroyed the lives of dear friends.

As she tells her children what happened there, she remembers how immersed in the Welsh community she became, how involved in the lives of those adults and children around her. She was caught up in the tensions between three adult siblings, nasty old Mr Evans and his two sisters – one estranged from him and dying, the other bullied by him and finding a way to escape. Was Mr Evans as bad as Carrie had believed? She hadn't been able to decide back then, and now he is gone, having died sad and alone.

It's a moving story seen through the eyes of a young girl growing up. Carrie's wartime world is as unfamiliar to her as her maturing emotions. She is becoming an adult, affected by adult conflicts both in the town and in the distant war. *Carrie's War* is understandably popular with young adults and their teachers; it is especially poignant for generations that have been spared major wars.

Nina Bawden's real life was latterly overshadowed by tragedy. In 2002 she and her second husband were involved in a train wreck which killed him and left her seriously injured. She outlived two of her three children; one son took his own life in 1981, and she survived her daughter Perdita by only a few months. Her last book, *Dear Austen* (2005), took the form of a long letter to her late husband, and tried to make sense of the accident which robbed her of him after forty-eight years.

Bawden was a well-established children's author by the time she wrote *Carrie's War*, her twenty-third novel. She was never afraid to write in widely differing genres. Her first novel, *Who Calls the Tune?* (1953) was an old-fashioned murder mystery. One of her early successes for the young was *On the Run* (1964, U.S. title *Three on the Run*), to which it might be said that *Carrie's War* served as the converse. Where Carrie is plunged into an adult world, the three children in *On the Run* are, as Bawden noted, "actually escaping, even though temporarily, from the world of grown-ups."

The Witch's Daughter (1966) is interesting for both its story and its illustrations. It tells the story of a young girl ostracised by a superstitious island community who believe her late mother cursed the sea on which it depends. The girl is named after Bawden's real-life daughter Perdita. It is also illustrated by Shirley Hughes, an author in her own right of *Dogger* and the *Alfie* series.

Bawden's *The Birds on the Trees* (1970) is different again. Nineteen-year-old Toby's middle-class parents are disappointed in him, and their constant pressure on him to do better drives him to drugs, dropping out and despair before he finally breaks the bonds and leaves home to live with his sympathetic grandmother. *The Peppermint Pig* (1976) is a nineteenth-century tale about a traumatic year in the life of two children and the pig whose escapades cheer them up. Despite the charming idea and innocent title, it's an often gruesome, violent story, highly praised but definitely one for older children.

Selected other books by Nina Bawden: *On the Run* (1964), *The Witch's Daughter* (1966), *The Birds on the Trees* (1970), and *The Peppermint Pig* (1976).

The Butterfly Ball and the Grasshopper's Feast

(1973)

Alan Aldridge (1938–2017), William Plomer (1903–1973)

From a whimsical fantasy by a prominent Victorian anti-slavery campaigner to a rock opera by a member of Deep Purple, *The Butterfly Ball* has, in its various guises, entertained the young for more than two centuries.

Liverpudlian William Roscoe (1753–1831), the original author of the poem *The Butterfly's* [apostrophe only in the Roscoe title] *Ball and the Grasshopper's Feast* (1807), was a man of many parts. Abolitionist, banker, historian, he founded the Liverpool Royal Institute and Liverpool Botanical Garden. He was a keen botanist, applying scholarship to his father's trade as a market gardener, and publishing an important work on the plant family which included turmeric, ginger and arrowroot.

Perhaps it was the importance of insects in flower propagation which inspired him to write *The Butterfly Ball*. His poem remained popular throughout the Victorian era. During the twentieth century it came to be regarded as rather archaic and quaint, although it is a landmark early example of a perennial device in children's literature, the anthropomorphised animal.

In 1973, such characters were inescapable – Paddington, the Wombles, Frog and Toad, and the rabbits of Watership Down were all relatively new arrivals on the juvenile literary scene. Into this receptive environment Alan Aldridge pitched his new illustrations for Roscoe's insect tale, inspired by a remark made to Lewis Carroll by John Tenniel, the original illustrator of *Alice's Adventures in Wonderland*, that it was "impossible to draw a wasp in a wig" for a passage in *Through the Looking Glass.*

Aldridge made his name as the art director at Penguin Books during the 1960s, when he specialised in science fiction covers which defined the era. After he set up his own studio, he designed iconic covers for the Who's LP *A Quick One* (1966), the Beatles' *Illustrated Lyrics* book (1969), and Elton John's *Captain Fantastic and the Brown Dirt Cowboy* (1975) among others.

To accompany Aldridge's images, William Plomer wrote a new and expanded version of the original poem. Plomer was Benjamin Britten's librettist and Ian Fleming's editor; the novel *Goldfinger* (1959) is dedicated to him. This new edition of *The Butterfly Ball* with its psychedelic, swirling, colourful pictures was something children could get lost in for hours. There are natural history notes at the back and puzzles to be solved in the main text; it remains a popular children's book almost fifty years later, and for historians provides a link between today and the gentle children's literature of William Roscoe's day.

At the time of its original publication in 1973, it was almost a given that a successful animal character would eventually find its way to an animation studio; once again, Paddington, the Wombles and Watership Down's rabbits are examples. So in 1974 a short cartoon based on Aldridge's pictures was released, with music by heavy metal rock band Deep Purple's bass guitarist Roger Glover. It was intended to pave the way for a full-length animated feature film, which never materialised, although Glover's full-length soundtrack was completed and released as an LP.

Aldridge subsequently worked with *Watership Down* author Richard Adams on *The Ship's Cat* (1977). Two follow-ups to Roscoe's original poem were published during his lifetime, not by Roscoe but by Catherine Ann Dorset, a popular children's poet of the time: *The Peacock "At Home"* (1807), *The Lion's Masquerade* (1807) and *The Elephant's Ball and Grand Fête Champetre* (1807). Aldridge further followed his version of *the Butterfly Ball* up with *The Peacock Party* (1979) and *The Lion's Cavalcade* (1980).

ABOVE: *Fans of Elton John's album* Captain Fantastic and the Brown Dirt Cowboy *(1975) will immediately recognise Aldridge's illustrative style.*

ABOVE: Charmed Life *introduced a parallel Britain where magic is accepted and regulated by a government department.*
LEFT: Neil Gaiman is a big fan of Diana Wynne Jones and the Chrestomanci *series. In his collection of non-fiction writing,* The View from the Cheap Seats, *a chapter is dedicated to her work and influence.*

Chrestomanci series

(1977–2006)

Diana Wynne Jones (1934–2011)

The what-ifs of history offer us a series of parallel worlds created by different outcomes of the same event – what if the Gunpowder Plot had been successful? What if the French had won the Battle of Agincourt? These are the worlds of *Chrestomanci*.

A chrestomanci, in Diana Wynne Jones seven-volume series of fantasy novels, is a supreme sorcerer. Chrestomancis exist in all her worlds. In the world at the centre of her stories, the Chrestomanci Christopher Chant is head of the British government department responsible for overseeing the use of magic, based in Chrestomanci Castle.

Chant holds the office of Chrestomanci in five of the seven books of the series. The two remaining ones look at his early life as a child and teenager. Chant's adoptive son Eric, known as Cat, proves to be his heir when it is discovered in the first book, *Charmed Life* (1977) that he has nine lives. In that opening instalment of the saga Cat must defeat his scheming sister Gwendolen, who has been stealing his lives to boost her own magic powers. Despite later novels appearing as prequels, *Charmed Life* is suggested as the best starting point for those wishing to enter the worlds of *Chrestomanci*.

Diana Wynne Jones is a vital link in the history of fantasy writing for children. She attended literary lectures by the early greats, J. R. R. Tolkien and C. S. Lewis while a student at Oxford. She has often been cited by authors such as Terry Pratchett, Neil Gaiman, J. K. Rowling and Philip Pullman as an important influence on the genre. Gaiman and Jones shared a mutual admiration, which resulted in each dedicating a book to the other. Many of her titles had fallen out of print, overshadowed by those that came after her, until the phenomenal success of J. K. Rowling's work prompted renewed interest in her work.

Beside *Chrestomanci*, she began another series in the *Dalemark Quartet*, four books of historical fantasy about an imaginary medieval land ruled by fifteen earls between whom war is common. The series starts with *Cart and Cwidder* (1975) – a cwidder is a magical lute.

Unusually for such a series, the first three books are in reverse chronological order – the second and third volumes by publication offer backstories to the first and second.

Howl's Moving Castle (1986) is the first of three books about Wizard Howl, a powerful but flawed magician who is vain, careless, and sometimes selfishly dishonest if it helps him get out of trouble. His human failings may be the result of giving his heart to a fire demon to keep the latter alive, an act which nevertheless strengthens his wizardly powers. Overlooked on its first publication, *Howl's Moving Castle* is now the most widely stocked book by Jones in public libraries, and in 2006 won the Phoenix Prize for a neglected classic. Interest in the book was partly revived by its loose adaption into an Academy Award-nominated animated feature film by Studio Ghibli and director Hayao Myazakai in 2003, which has become a cult classic among animé fans.

Jones was a prolific author with over 100 titles to her credit in a wide variety of fields, including science fiction. Her acclaimed magical fantasy output earned her the right to write several affectionate parodies of the genre. *Dark Lord of Derkholm* (1998) and its sequel *Year of the Griffin* (2000) poke gentle fun at the sometimes absurd worlds of sword-and-sorcery; *The Tough Guide to Fantasyland* (1996) is a humorous non-fiction analysis, along the lines of the *Rough Guide* series for travellers, of the rules and clichés for fantasy authors.

Selected other books by Diana Wynne Jones: *Cart and Cwidder* (1975) and Dalemark series, *Howl's Moving Castle* (1986) and Howl series, *Dark Lord of Derkholm* (1998), and *Year of the Griffin* (2000).

Dogger

(1977)

Shirley Hughes (born 1927)

Shirley Hughes has devoted her life to children's literature, with a career spanning over fifty years of illustration and storytelling. Her ability to capture simple childhood emotions in pinpoint detail have made her a children's favourite.

Among her many awards and honours, Shirley Hughes is one of a select few individuals to have won the prestigious Kate Greenaway Medal more than once. The Medal, awarded by a British association of professional librarians, is named after the great nineteenth-century children's book illustrator. Hughes' pair were awarded for her 2003 retelling of the Cinderella story, *Ella's Big Chance*; and for her most popular story, about a toy lost and (plot spoiler alert) regained: *Dogger*.

The Dogger of the title is a cuddly toy dog which its owner Dave loses at a table top sale, when someone else finds it and innocently sells it on. Every parent knows the trauma which the loss of a beloved toy can cause. It's certainly enough drama to engage the junior readers of *Dogger*. The day is saved by a selfless act on the part of Dave's sister Bella.

It's a short story with lots of pictures. By the time she wrote it Hughes had been in steady demand as an illustrator for British publishers for over twenty years. Her pedigree is unimpeachable – she was inspired to take up the profession by the work of an earlier generation of book illustrators which included W. Heath Robinson and Arthur Rackham.

After training at Liverpool School of Art and Oxford's Ruskin School of Drawing and Fine Art, she provided the artwork for some of the great British children's authors of the 1950s and 1960s – among them Noel Streatfeild, and Dorothy Edwards, whose popular series *My Naughty Little Sister* first brought Hughes' work to widespread public attention. To date she has illustrated over 200 children's books.

Her debut as both illustrator and author came in 1960 with the publication of *Lucy and Tom's Day*, a picture story of an ordinary day in the children's lives. Lucy and Tom returned belatedly in *Lucy and Tom's Christmas* (1981) and *Lucy and Tom at the Seaside* (1992). By then *Dogger* had placed Shirley Hughes firmly on the world's bookshelves. So too had another of her enduring creations, *Alfie*.

Mischievous Alfie has raced and splashed his way through seven further adventures since he first appeared in *Alfie Gets In First* (1981). Alfie is an innocent abroad, confronting life's earliest problems such as having your boots on the wrong feet. Alfie's little sister Annie Rose has also found her way into print in Alfie's wake.

In all, Shirley Hughes has written over fifty books. It comes as a surprise therefore to learn that she did not write her first full-length novel until 2015, at the age of eighty-eight. *Hero on a Bicycle* is a war story for young adults, set in Italy in 1944 and based on real events involving partisan resistance to the Axis Powers of Hitler and Mussolini.

Selected other books by Shirley Hughes as author: *Lucy and Tom's Day* (1960) and series, *Alfie Gets In First* (1981) and series, *Ella's Big Chance* (2003), and *Hero on a Bicycle* (2015).

The classic story about losing your favourite toy

ABOVE: Dogger *has parallels to another favourite item that is lost – Bonting. When Alfie finds the perfect stone in the garden he names it "Bonting" and they are going to be friends forever …*

RIGHT: Shirley Hughes' brilliance has been in capturing the emotions of children in sometimes excruciatingly familiar detail.

OPPOSITE: Snow in the Garden *is one of the more recent compilations, published in 2018.*

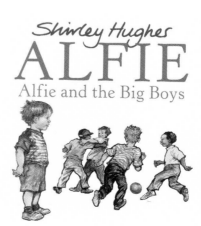

The
Snowman

Raymond Briggs

THE ORIGINAL CLASSIC STORY

ABOVE: The Snowman *has sold over five million copies worldwide. Unusually, there are no words, only pictures.*

OPPOSITE: In Fungus the Bogeyman *we follow a typical day of your average working bogeyman going about his bogeyman business.*

The Snowman

(1978)

Raymond Briggs (born 1934)

A trained artist and illustrator, Raymond Briggs brings a warm, compassionate humanity to his stories, often in spite of the coldness and inhumanity of his subject matter. From nuclear war to wintertime his comic-strip characters have captured our hearts for over forty years.

Raymond Briggs was moved to write the story of The Snowman during the winter of 1977–78, which saw exceptionally heavy snowfall in the south of England. It tells of a young boy who builds a snowman which comes to life at midnight. They explore the boy's home together before flying off over the silent, snow-blanketed landscape which inspired Briggs. Hovering over England's south coast, they watch the sun rise before returning to the house. As in so many of Briggs' stories, he mixes the magical with the melancholy. The boy's adventure – was it just a dream? – is tempered with sadness when he discovers the following morning that the snowman has melted.

An animated version of the story was produced for British television only four years after the original publication, successfully capturing Briggs' shimmering style of crayon-shaded illustration. It made several changes to the original tale. Where the book makes no mention of Christmas, the film sets it clearly at that time of year. A gift tag on a present reveals that the boy is called James (he is unnamed in the book), and far from stopping their flight at the English coastline, James and the Snowman fly to the North pole, join a party of snowmen, and meet Father Christmas. A scarf which Father Christmas gives James proves, the morning after, that it was no dream.

Briggs dealt comprehensively with Father Christmas in his first two books, *Father Christmas* (1973) and *Father Christmas Goes On Holiday* (1975). Like many of his books they explored the man behind the public persona, revealing him to be like anyone else – fed up with the "bloomin' snow" and baffled by local customs on holiday. His third book, *Fungus the Bogeyman* (1977), presented the inner thoughts of a more darkly comic character, the slimy green bogeyman weary of his task of

frightening humans. It was partly in reaction to Fungus's unremittingly unpleasant world that Raymond Briggs turned to the purity of winter for *The Snowman*.

After *The Snowman* Briggs turned to more adult subject matter – the fantasy life of public lavatory attendant *Gentleman Jim* (1980) and Jim's subsequent harrowing experience of nuclear war in *When the Wind Blows* (1982). *Ethel and Ernest* (1998) is a deeply moving portrait of his parents' marriage.

The Man (1992) and *The Bear* (1994) saw Briggs returning to some of the themes he first explored in *The Snowman* – dreams and reality, children's inner worlds and secret friends. *Ug* (2001) is a Stone-Age story about the importance of creative imagination. Throughout his career Briggs has illustrated the innermost thoughts of unlikely heroes. He helps his young readers understand what it is to be human – whether you are a bogeyman or a snowman.

Haunted House

(1979)

Jan Pieńkowski (born 1936)

Don't call it a pop-up book. It does far more – there are wheels to spin, tabs to pull, lattices to uncover and many, many doors to open. *Haunted House* is a tour de force of what librarians call the "movable book".

Haunted House, Jan Pieńkowski's most famous work, is also credited to Tor Lokvig, paper engineer. Its delicate movements had to be accurately crafted to work time and time again with each return to the book. The result treads a perfect line between humour, nervous laughter and scary surprise.

The story opens with the line "Come in, Doctor. Yes, it is a quaint old place – chilly, though …" The inhabitant of the house has called the medic for a variety of ailments. As we turn the pages we soon find out just why, for example, he has lost his appetite or has trouble sleeping. The book takes us through the rooms in the house – the hall, the kitchen, the lounge, the bathroom, the bedroom and the attic – all of which are positively infested with spooks and creepy-crawlies. "Do you think it's all imagination?" the patient asks, "Doctor?", only to find that the Doctor has fled.

There's a skeleton in the wardrobe, a ghost in the cupboard under the stairs, a crocodile in the bath and a cat in the toilet bowl. An octopus is doing the washing-up and something or someone is trying to saw their way out of a crate from Transylvania stored in the attic. Behind the door of every kitchen cabinet there is something revolting.

Without doubt, Pieńkowski's *Haunted House* took the movable book to a new level of complexity, drawing on many earlier examples. The Victorians delighted in complex paper scenes with the pages partly cut away to give depth to views of, for example, popular nursery rhymes. Pieńkowski revisited this idea for his silhouette book *The First Noel* (2000). A popular visual trick

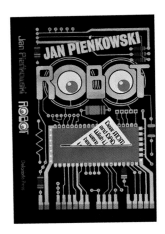

which transformed a picture of a horse into one of a zebra simply by the pulling on a tab was emulated by Pieńkowski, who used the same technique to reveal a ghost hiding behind the curtains in the bedroom.

The idea of a *volvelle*, a rotating wheel which spins to reveal different images in a window placed over it, or different alignments with items printed around it, is over a thousand years old – Persian astronomers used one to predict the phases of the moon, and the rock band Led Zeppelin incorporated one in the sleeve for their third album. Pieńkowski uses one to show the flickering flames of a fire in the lounge, and the animated contents of bottles in the kitchen.

Born in Poland, Pieńkowski's childhood was disrupted by World War II. He arrived in Britain in 1948 at the age of twelve and in time studied English and Classics at university. But art was always an interest. He drew an illustrated book for his father when he was only eight, and after university he founded a very successful greetings card business.

Before *Haunted House* he had already established his reputation as a book illustrator of other authors' books. He worked with children's authors Joan Aiken in the 1960s and with Helen Nicoll on the *Meg and Mog* series of books. *Haunted House* won him his second Kate Greenaway award.

Other movable books by Jan Pieńkowski: *Robot* (1981), *Dinner Time* (1981), *Christmas* (1989), *Good Night: a Pop-Up Lullaby* (1999), *The First Noel* (2000), *The Animals Went In Two By Two* (2003), and *The Fairy Tales* (2005).

ABOVE: *It only has six double-page spreads, but every one of them is a showstopper. A Gothic staircase folds out of the book in the first scene; a bat swings up from the rafters in the final vista.*

LEFT: *The paper engineering by Tor Lokvig on* Haunted House *is astonishingly complex, creating some stunning 3D effects.*

OPPOSITE: Robot *(1981) was another pop-up hit with excellent paper craftwork.*

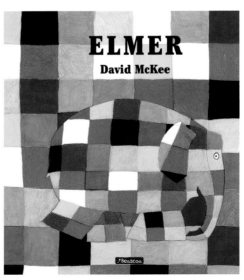

LEFT AND BELOW: Mr Benn *and* Elmer the Patchwork Elephant *both got their own television series.* Bernard, *as usual, was ignored.*

Not Now, Bernard

(1980)

David McKee (born 1935)

A great bedtime read for little monsters, Not Now, Bernard demonstrates the perils of not listening to your children when they are trying to get your attention. They might be trying to tell you something worth hearing.

Poor little Bernard is trying to get his parents to listen to him – he has something important to say. But, preoccupied with their own tasks, all they can spare him is a cursory, "Not now, Bernard." But Bernard has seen a purple monster in the garden, and when he goes outside to investigate for himself, the monster eats Bernard up. Still, his parents don't notice, and they even put the monster through Bernard's bedtime routine. "But I'm a monster!" the monster protests. "Not now, Bernard," replies his mother, and puts out the light.

Adults often find David McKee's story a little sad because it implies that even monstrous behaviour will not win the attention of some children's parents. Children on the other hand love the idea of turning into a little monster, breaking toys and biting their father's leg. To them the parents are playing along, as the final words of Bernard's mother seem to indicate. At the end of the day, all is well, all is forgiven, and children can safely go to sleep.

David McKee began his career by selling cartoons to newspapers and magazines while still at art college in southwest England. His customers included *Reader's Digest* and the late, lamented satirical magazine *Punch*. In 1964 he published his first book, *Two Can Toucan* (which he redrew and republished in 1985).

In the late 1960s he created the character of Mr Benn. Mr Benn is a mild-mannered, bowler-hatted bank clerk who visits a fancy dress shop and, through a magical door at the back of the shop, has adventures inspired by the costume he has tried on. After four books of Mr Benn's adventures McKee was approached by the BBC to develop them into a series of animated shorts. Only thirteen were made, but they have a special place in the hearts of adults of a certain age.

His series of books about the hapless King Rollo – even his cat Hamlet is wiser than he – began in the late 1970s, and he formed his own production company, King Rollo Films, to animate the stories for television. The company also animates the stories of other children's authors, including Eric Hill's *Spot the Dog* and another dog, Tony Ross's *Towser*.

McKee launched his most successful series, about *Elmer the Patchwork Elephant*, in 1989, redrawing a stand-alone book which he originally published in 1968. Elmer's skin is a checkerboard of brightly coloured squares, a happy character who loves to play practical jokes on his fellow elephants. Stories and spin-offs about Elmer account for over forty books so far.

McKee has also tackled more serious subjects with his deceptively simple text and pictures within his children's stories. *Six Men* (1972) looks at greed, power and the causes of war, and *Tusk Tusk* (1978) raises issues of prejudice and racism within its conflict between black elephants and white ones. Even when the fight is over and grey elephants start to appear, we should be on our guard against new divisions. Most of David McKee's output, however, is light-hearted and gently moral – in fact just the kind of thing that a bank clerk who lived at No. 52 Festive Road might approve of.

Some other children's books by David McKee: *Mr Benn – Red Knight* (1967) and series, *Six Men* (1972), *Tusk Tusk* (1978), *King Rollo and the Bread* (1979) and series, *Two Can Toucan* (1985), and *Elmer* (1989) and series.

Where's Spot?

(1980)

Eric Hill (1927–2014)

Not many authors can claim not only to have written and illustrated a hit series of children's stories but also to have invented a new kind of book. Step forward, Eric Hill: *Where's Spot?* is widely credited with introducing the flap to children's literature.

In the past bookmakers had sometimes resorted to extension flaps at the edge of the page; for example, to accommodate an outsize map or illustration, or to conceal the answer to a riddle. It's a feature which complicates the bookbinding process because at some point the flap has to be folded in; but in essence it is just a page which is larger than its neighbours. Eric Hill did something different.

Hill's background was as a graphic designer in advertising. When he noticed that his son Christopher, aged three, was always lifting up sheets of paper on his father's desk to see what was underneath, Hill hit on a way of harnessing the insatiable curiosity of the very young for the world around them.

He incorporated flaps into the illustrations themselves, not merely as extensions to the page. So, in the search for the errant puppy Spot, children can open the door of the grandfather clock for themselves, or lift the lid on the pink piano, or peek under the valance of the bed. Behind each of them, of course, not Spot but another animal or two lurks. The piano, for example, contains a hippopotamus with a bird on its back.

The insertion of flaps which had to be stuck onto each page was a time-consuming and costly addition to the process of book production. Most publishers shied away from the book; but Puffin Books, the children's strand of Penguin Books, took a chance. *Where's Spot?* was a bestseller within weeks. The flaps engage inquisitive young minds in the process of reading and the Spot books have been praised for their role in improving literacy.

Their simple storylines and words have been translated into over sixty languages, including the minority indigenous languages of the British Isles – Cornish, Welsh and Scots Gaelic. There are nine original Spot books, written by Eric Hill, and the series has spawned innumerable spin-offs both on paper and on television.

Spot Goes to the Farm, the sixth book in the series, was published in 1987, and such was the popularity of Spot by then that in 1993 in rural northern England a local newspaper, *The Westmorland Gazette*, replaced the traditional "Spot the Ball" competition with "Spot the Dog" – instead of pinpointing a missing football in a scene from a match, readers must guess where a sheepdog is, based on the reactions of the sheep the dog is rounding up.

Selected other Spot books by Eric Hill: *Spot's Birthday Party* (1982), *Spot Goes on Holiday* (1985), *Spot Goes to the Farm* (1987), and *Spot Visits his Grandparents* (1996).

OPPOSITE TOP: Like Dick Bruna's Miffy *and Jean de Brunhoff's* Babar, *Spot's simple illustration appealed to younger readers who learned to turn the flaps. Parental intervention is sometimes needed to stop the flap being grasped and pulled entirely out of the book. Jan Pieńkowski had also used some flaps in* Haunted House, *but as they revealed a cockroach and monster spaghetti, the desire to open them was not so great.*
OPPOSITE BOTTOM: Spot is known the world over.

Where's Spot?

Eric Hill

Spot's New Friend

Eric Hill

Spot Loves His Mommy

Eric Hill

MICHAEL MORPURGO

WAR HORSE

ABOVE: The first edition of War Horse *pictured Joey in the care of French girl Emilie and her grandfather.*

OPPOSITE: Farm Boy *(1997) continued the story of Joey and Albert on a Devon farm, but this time written from a human perspective.*

War Horse

(1982)

Michael Morpurgo (born 1943)

When your book has been adapted for the stage by Britain's National Theatre Company, and for the big screen by Stephen Spielberg, you know you've written something meaningful. But Michael Morpurgo had grave doubts about starting to write *War Horse* in the first place.

Michael Morpurgo is a master storyteller for older children. He does not condescend or sensationalise. His willingness to tell powerful tales with depth, drama and emotion draws his readers in. His books are steeped in humanity and reality.

Joey, the horse in *War Horse*, makes the same emotional journey that many soldiers did in World War I. From working on a farm he is bought by the Army and serves in the horror of the trenches. With another horse whom he has befriended, Joey is captured by German troops and made to pull artillery and an ambulance cart ferrying injured men. He witnesses his friend's death and is injured himself before being recaptured and eventually reunited with Albert, the farmboy he knew before the war. There is a sequel to *War Horse*, *Farm Boy* (1997), written in response to frequent requests about the fate of Albert and Joey after the war.

Morpurgo understands children, coming to writing after a career as a primary school teacher. In 1976 he and his wife established the charity Farms for City Children, which gives urban children real, hands-on experience of farming and the countryside. The charity played a role in convincing him to go ahead with *War Horse*.

He first started to think of writing about World War I from the horses' perspective after meeting a number of older men in his village who had all worked with horses during the conflict. He was intrigued, but had doubts about his ability to pull off such a different approach to a war story. It was a young boy called Billy, on a visit to one of the charity's farms, who persuaded him that he must try.

Billy had a very bad stammer, and his teacher urged Morpurgo not to ask the boy any direct questions because the terror of trying to speak was too much for him. The author obliged, but on the last evening of Billy's visit, Morpurgo wandered into the stable yard and saw Billy standing at the stall of one of the horses.

Billy was not just standing, but talking to the horse, words pouring out of his mouth without a hint of a stammer. And the horse was not just standing but listening, ears alert. "The horse didn't understand every word," Morpurgo recalled thirty years later, "but she knew it was important for her to stand there and be there for this child." So it was with the thousands of horses who served on both sides in the war. Morpurgo knew he had a story worth writing.

Billy does not appear in *War Horse*, but he inspired the central character of Morpurgo's next book, *Little Foxes* (1984), about a boy called Billy with a stammer whose encounters with nature fuel his growth as a human being. The Pacific theatre of World War II is the setting for another Morpurgo novel, *Kensuke's Kingdom* (1999), in which a young boy is shipwrecked on an island and befriended by a Japanese doctor left there after the war. They work together to protect nature in the form of the island's population of apes.

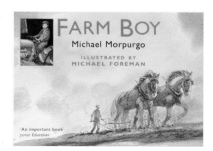

Selected other children's books by Michael Morpurgo: *Little Foxes* (1984), *Waiting for Anya* (1990), *Farm Boy* (1997), *Kensuke's Kingdom* (1999), *Private Peaceful* (2003), and *Alone on a Wide, Wide Sea* (2006).

The Sheep-Pig

(1983)

Dick King-Smith (1922–2011)

There had been pigs and paper in Dick King-Smith's family for over two hundred years. Small wonder that his most popular creation was a book about a plucky porker called Babe who defied the mocking sheepdogs.

Dick King-Smith's ancestors ran paper mills from the late eighteenth century, first in Watford, north of London, and in the twentieth century in rural Gloucestershire. They were also farmers, and their partnership with neighbours in running White End Farm in Watford led to the opening of a bacon shop in London's Covent Garden in 1825.

In Gloucestershire, where Dick grew up, the family farm provided the paper mill's canteen with milk and eggs. After serving with distinction in World War II, Dick became a farmer himself, and later a teacher, before publishing his first book, *The Fox Busters*, in 1978.

His childhood spent among the animals was the formative experience which gave King-Smith the subject matter for his prolific output of farmyard stories. By the time of his death he had written over 130 animal tales about pigs, horses, goats, ducks, mice, spiders, snails, a sloth and even dinosaurs.

His fourth, *The Sheep-Pig*, appeared in 1983. Retitled *Babe the Gallant Pig* for its 1985 U.S. publication, it tells the extraordinary story of Babe, the only pig on a sheep farm, who shows an aptitude for rounding up his woolly companions. His owner, Farmer Hoggett, enters him in the local sheepdog trials, with heartwarming results.

It's a charming tale in its own right. If it needs a moral subtext, it is that you should never judge by appearances. Nobody expects a pig to be able to control sheep, but Babe can. And everyone thinks sheep are stupid, but their response to Babe proves otherwise. Babe is the underdog, or underpig, who triumphs in the end.

Like many children's stories today, *The Sheep-Pig's* reputation is built as much on the screen version as on the original book. Combining live action from its human and animal cast with animation and animatronics by Rhythm & Hues Studios and Jim Henson's Creature Shop. The film *Babe*, released in 1995, was nominated for seven Academy Awards including Best Picture, and won the Oscar for Best Visual Effects.

Dick King-Smith died in 2011 in the city of Bath, only seven miles from the farm on which he grew up. During his lifetime *The Sheep-Pig* was also adapted as a stage play, and inspired a 1998 film sequel *Babe: Pig in the City*. The two films took $323,000,000 at the box office. As Farmer Hoggett says to Babe at the end of the original book, "That'll do, Pig. That'll do."

Other books by Dick King-Smith: *The Queen's Nose* (1983), *Sophie* (series, 1988–1995), *The Water Horse* (1990), *Martin's Mice* (1991), *Dragon Boy* (1993), *A Mouse Called Wolf* (1997), and *The Golden Goose* (2003).

The Sheep-Pig

Dick King-Smith
The master of animal adventures

ABOVE: Like so many children's novels, The Sheep-Pig *came to global attention via a film. The book had been published in the U.S. as* Babe: The Gallant Pig.
OPPOSITE: The Queen's Nose *is the story of Harmony Parker who desperately wants a pet, something which her parents won't allow.*

FRANCINE PASCAL'S

SWEET VALLEY HIGH

1

Share the continuing story of the Wakefield twins and their friends—their laughter, heartaches, and dreams.

DOUBLE LOVE

SWEET VALLEY HIGH

2

What Jessica wants, Jessica gets— even if someone gets hurt!

SECRETS

created by
FRANCINE PASCAL

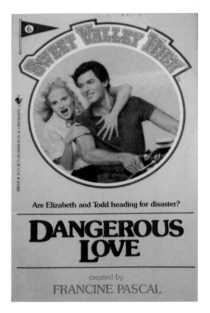

SWEET VALLEY HIGH

6

Are Elizabeth and Todd heading for disaster?

DANGEROUS LOVE

created by
FRANCINE PASCAL

FRANCINE PASCAL'S

SWEET VALLEY HIGH

37

Can Susan live with the truth?

RUMORS

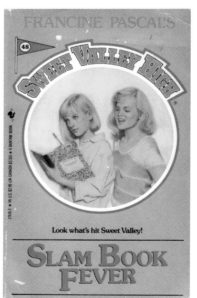

FRANCINE PASCAL'S

SWEET VALLEY HIGH

48

Look what's hit Sweet Valley!

SLAM BOOK FEVER

FRANCINE PASCAL'S

SWEET VALLEY HIGH

72

Who's the new girl at Sweet Valley High?

ROCK STAR'S GIRL

ABOVE: A teenage soap in printed form; before there was Beverly Hills 90210, *there was* Sweet Valley High.

Sweet Valley High series
(1984–1998)
Francine Pascal (born 1938)

The *Sweet Valley High* series of books, about the lives of the pupils of a fictional Californian high school, is of epic proportions. Excluding spin-offs, there are 181 titles, an average of over twelve titles a year, or more than one a month for fifteen years.

Just like the lives of the high school girls whom it reflects, *Sweet Valley High* is part long-running soap opera, part complicated romance. It revolves around identical twins: wild, outgoing Jessica and sensible, thoughtful Elizabeth. In the very first book of the series, *Double Love* (1984), they are both attracted to the same dreamboat, Todd Wilkins. The course of true love never runs smooth, and in the span of 181 episodes Todd dates both girls, sometimes concurrently.

The many spin-offs include prequels of life at Sweet Valley Elementary, Middle and Junior High. There are sequels too, following the lives of the students as they progress to Sweet Valley University, and on to adult working life. In 2001, six books chronicled the experiences of Elizabeth immediately after graduation, although no such spin-off has been written for Jessica.

Francine Pascal began writing after she met her husband, author John Pascal. They collaborated on scripts for the daytime ABC soap opera *The Young Marrieds* in the mid-1960s. Her brother was the librettist Michael Stewart, whose hits included *Hello Dolly!* and *Mack and Mabel*. John, Francine and Michael all worked on the show *George M!* which ran on Broadway for two years from 1968 to 1970, and Francine revised her brother's librettos after his untimely death in 1987.

Pascal's soap-writing background served a fitting apprenticeship for the *Sweet Valley High* series, whose episodic publication and faintly credible storylines appeared to translate the soap format from screen to book. Though Pascal is credited with the creation of the series, it was a team of ghostwriters who enabled its frequent and rapid production – her rationale was that the inclusion of multiple writers in the process provided the stories with a more universal appeal. They were not for a "sophisticated, educated audience", as Pascal suggests her earlier books had been.

Her first young adult novel was *Hangin' Out with Cici* (1977), in which a teenage girl travels back in time to meet her mother as a teenager. *Hangin'* was followed by two sequels, *My First Love and Other Disasters* (1979) and *Love & Betrayal & Hold the Mayo* (1985). Another series, the teenage romance *Caitlin* (1985–1987), takes the form of three trilogies known as Love, Promise and Forever, which followed the on-off love life of Caitlin and Jed from wooing to wedding.

After completing the core series of *Sweet Valley High*, Pascal launched a new spy and romance adventure series named after the first title of its eventual thirty-six, *Fearless* (1999). It revolves around seventeen-year-old Gaia Moore, who becomes entangled in espionage while trying to understand why she is incapable of feeling fear.

A victim of her own success, Francine Pascal has created a legion of fans hungry for the latest instalment of each series. Her prodigious output is beyond the capacity of any one mere mortal, and she has increasingly relied on an army of ghost writers to deliver new episodes of her many brands. The *Caitlin* series, for example, is now credited to teen romance author Joanna Campbell.

Other titles by Francine Pascal: *Hanging Out with Cici* (1977), *The Hand-Me-Down Kid* (1980), *The Caitlin Love Trilogy* (1988) and sequels, *Fearless* (1999) and series, and *The Ruling Class* (2004).

The Jolly Postman
(1986) and series

Janet Ahlberg (1944–1994), Allan Ahlberg (born 1938)

If Eric Hill's *Where's Spot?* (1980) tapped into children's curiosity about what lies underneath a flap, Janet and Allan Ahlberg's Jolly Postman series took it a stage further and gave their readers not only a flap to lift but something behind it to remove. What could be better than reading someone else's post?

Once upon a bicycle, so they say
The Jolly Postman came one day

The *Jolly Postman* is delivering letters to seven well-known characters from classic fairy tales – among them Mr V. Bigg, the giant who lives in Beanstalk Gardens; the witch who once held Hansel and Gretel prisoner; and BB Wolf Esq., living in the cottage that belongs to Red Riding Hood's grandmother.

Facing the cheerful rhyming verse (by Allan) and the rich illustrations (by Janet) in each case is an envelope addressed to each recipient from which the reader can remove its contents. The Big Bad Wolf, for example, is receiving a typed letter from Red Riding Hood's solicitor; the witch, living alone, is delighted to get a mail-order shopping catalogue; and Cinderella has been sent a copy of a book commemorating her marriage to Prince Charming.

The complexity of assembling such an intricate book, with its flaps and insertions, took five years to resolve before it could go into production. It was undoubtedly worth solving the problems it created; it's an endlessly fascinating book. The pictures are detailed enough for young eyes to explore over and over again, the rhymes are fun, and the thrill of opening a letter – especially one addressed to someone else – never gets old.

If you are jealous of your child having *The Jolly Postman*, there is a comparable series of books for adults by artist Nick Bantock, about a long-distance love affair between the titular characters in *Griffin and Sabine* (1991–2016), in which you can remove and read their love letters and postcards. But Janet and Allan Ahlberg thought of it first.

The Jolly Postman is as popular in the classroom as it is at home, providing a way to develop the earliest fairy-tale reading of the young with lessons about character, profession and communication. What does a postman do? Should Baby Bear accept the apology which Goldilocks has written to them after her bad behaviour in their house?

The Jolly Postman is the most successful of Janet and Allan Ahlberg's books, but it's a crowded field. They are also responsible for *Burglar Bill* (1977) and *Each Peach Pear Plum* (1978), an I-spy journey through a nursery rhyme wood. *Peepo!* (1981) is a remarkable book for babies set in wartime Britain, with holes in the pages to glimpse what's coming next. Less well known is *It Was a Dark and Stormy Night* (1993), in which a kidnapped boy keeps his captors entertained by telling stories, and through the stories works out how to escape.

Five of their books have been nominated for the Kate Greenaway Medal for children's illustration and two won the prize – *Each Peach Pear Plum* and *The Jolly Christmas Postman* (1991). The third and final title in the series, *The Jolly Pocket Postman* (1995) includes letters to Alice of Wonderland and Dorothy from *The Wizard of Oz*.

The Jolly Pocket Postman was published after Janet's untimely death. The Ahlbergs' daughter Jessica was fourteen at the time. She is now a book illustrator in her own right, and father and daughter have worked together to continue the Ahlberg legacy with books like *Half a Pig* (2004) and *The Goldilocks Variations* (2012).

Some other books by Janet and Allan Ahlberg: *Burglar Bill* (1977), *Each Peach Pear Plum* (1978), *Peepo!* (1981), and *It Was a Dark and Stormy Night* (1993).

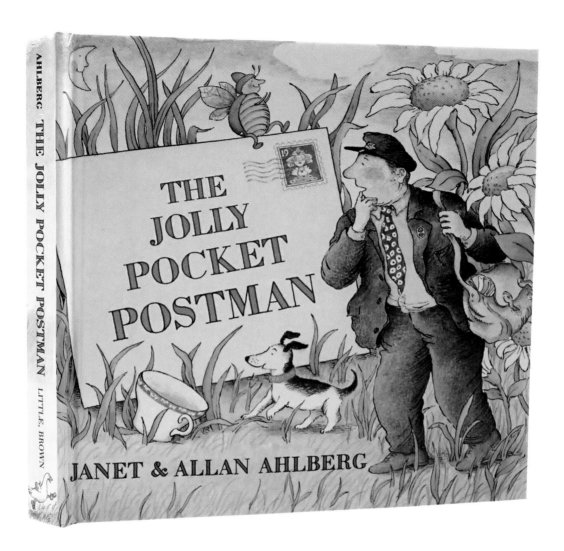

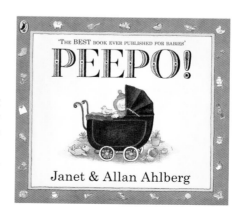

ABOVE: Janet and Allan Ahlberg's idea of linking some classic fairy-tale characters via a postman was inspired – as was the ploy of using letters inserted into the book.

RIGHT: A day in the life of a baby in the 1940s is told in Peepo, *with circles cut out to peep through to the next page.*

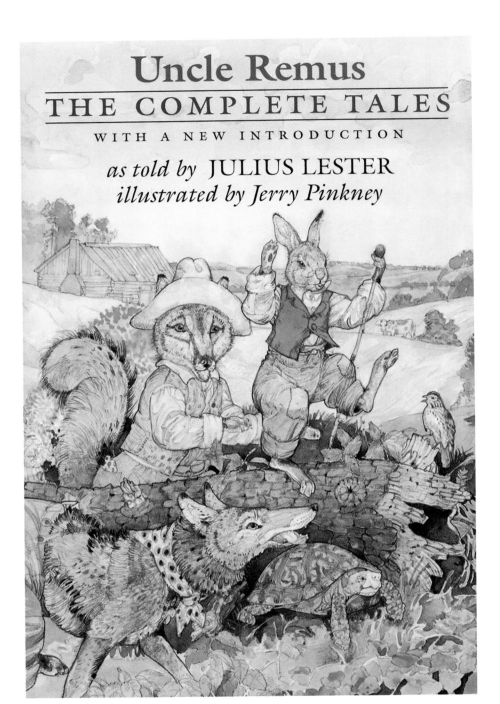

Uncle Remus
THE COMPLETE TALES
WITH A NEW INTRODUCTION

as told by JULIUS LESTER
illustrated by Jerry Pinkney

ABOVE: Author Joel Chandler Harris, a contemporary of Mark Twain, was a Southern folklorist who collected stories from the African-American oral tradition and published them under the fictional name Uncle Remus. Julius Lester took them and, together with illustrator Jerry Pinkney, gave them a new twist.

Uncle Remus: The Complete Tales
(1987)

Julius Lester (1939–2018)

The morally ambiguous Br'er Rabbit is a character many hundreds of years old. His stories and antics have been retold by the fictional Uncle Remus many times for new generations in the nineteenth and twentieth centuries.

Many of the tales of Br'er ("Brother") Rabbit have parallels in the ancient folk stories of the western and southern African continent. Senegalese folk tradition contains a similar rabbit called Leuk; and many of the same anecdotes told about Br'er Rabbit are now told in Gold Coast tales of the spider Anansi. It is therefore widely believed that the modern Br'er Rabbit arrived in North America and the Caribbean with the forced immigration of enslaved Africans into those regions.

Br'er Rabbit is a cunning trickster who gets into trouble, and gets out of it, by questionable actions. One typical story is that of the Tar-Baby. Br'er Fox, Br'er Rabbit's mortal enemy, fashions a human child out of tar and clothes it in cotton. When Br'er Rabbit sees the fox (in disguise) addressing the child without getting a reply, he punches the child for its discourtesy. Naturally he gets stuck on the tar, as the fox had hoped. When the fox reveals himself, Rabbit begs him not to throw him into the nearby briar patch. Br'er Fox promptly does so, but the thorns and spurs of the patch are the rabbit's natural habitat and Br'er Rabbit uses them to break free from the tar baby and escape.

Surprisingly, one of the first modern retellings of Br'er Rabbit appeared in the Native American newspaper the *Cherokee Advocate* in 1845 – there are many rabbit and hare legends in Native American culture, and the spirit Nanabozho is Br'er Rabbit's trickster equivalent in tales of chicanery. Teddy Roosevelt's uncle Robert was an enthusiastic collector of Br'er Rabbit stories in the second half of the nineteenth century.

Joel Chandler Harris published the first large collection of Br'er Rabbit stories, framed by the fictional narrator Uncle Remus. *Uncle Remus: His Songs and His Sayings* (1880) was immensely popular, a novel departure for children from the standard fare of European folk and fairy stories. At least nine sequels followed between then and 1948, the year in which Enid Blyton published her own retelling.

Harris was an advocate of racial integration in the Deep South. But he came in for considerable criticism as a white man appropriating black culture. This intensified with the rise of the civil rights movement in the 1950s and 1960s. By contrast Julius Lester was a Black Power activist who recorded two albums of protest music and published his first book, *Look Out, Whitey! Black Power's Gon' Get Your Mama!*, in 1968. Later, as a respected professor of African-American and Judaic literature and social history, he wrote a new, more authentic version of Harris's stories. Lester preserved Harris's Uncle Remus, but modernised some details and breathed new life into a popular but ageing canon.

The highly praised illustrations in *The Tales of Uncle Remus: the Adventures of Br'er Rabbit* and its three sequels were by Jerry Pinkney. Lester and Pinkney collaborated on several more children's books, all with an African American in a central role.

Some other children's books by Julius Lester and Jerry Pinkney: *John Henry* (1994), *Sam and the Tigers* (1996), *Black Cowboy, Wild Horses: A True Story* (1998), *Albidaro and the Mischievous Dream* (2000), and *The Old African* (2005).

The Story of the Little Mole Who Knew It Was None of His Business

(1989)

Werner Holzwarth (born 1947), Wolf Erlbruch (born 1948)

There's nothing so surely guaranteed to spring a giggle from a child (or an adult) as a bit of toilet humour. The original German title of *The Story of the Little Mole* is characteristically direct. It translates as *The Little Mole Who Wanted to Know Who Did a Doo-Doo on His Head*.

The story of the mole, who emerges from his hole one morning only to be pooped on, has sold three million copies in the thirty years since its publication. To date, children have laughed at the little mole's misfortune in thirty-three languages. The book follows the mole's search for the culprit by meeting a succession of animals and examining their droppings. In the end some flies – experts in the field – tip him off and he gets his revenge by pooping on the head of the perpetrator.

The Little Mole was Werner Holzwarth's first children's book and it remains his only collaboration with illustrator Wolf Erlbruch. Both men trained at art school – Holzwarth in Berlin, Erlbruch in Essen. Holzwarth went into advertising and copywriting, where his accounts included Lufthansa, Levi Jeans and Gillette. In the early 1980s he went to South America as a journalist for a number of German newspapers and magazines including *Stern*, for whom Erlbruch was by then working as an illustrator.

Erlbruch's first children's book commission was for James Aggrey's *The Eagle Who Didn't Want to Fly* in 1985. When Holzwarth was looking for an illustrator he chose Erlbruch, and Erlbruch introduced him to Aggrey's publisher in Erlbruch's home town of Wuppertal. *The Little Mole* was an immediate international hit and its success boosted both men's careers. Holzwarth launched his own advertising partnership in 1990 and served for a time as Professor of Visual Communication at the prestigious Bauhaus University in Weimar. But he continued to write children's books, and finally became a full-time author in 2012.

One of Holzwarth's subsequent books harks back to his time in South America. *I'm José and I'm Okay* tells humorous uplifting stories about a Bolivian boy who, not untypically in that country, is already caught up in the world of work and responsibility. Originally published to encourage literacy in LaPaz, it is based on a real child's experiences.

Erlbruch, too, entered academia, as Professor of Illustration at the University of Wuppertal. Greatly in demand as an illustrator he has also written the texts of several children's books. They often have quite serious themes: *Leonard* (1991), his first, written for his six-year-old son of the same name, is the story of a boy who turns into a dog in order to overcome his fear of dogs. *Duck, Death and the Tulip* (2008) is a tender, beautiful narrative about a duck who befriends Death. Erlbruch has said that the overarching moral of his books is that we should accept ourselves, the good and the bad in us, and do the same for those we meet.

Selected books by Werner Holzwarth available in English: *I'm José and I'm Okay* (1996) and *I Wish I Were A …* (2012).

Selected books by Wolf Erlbruch available in English: *Duck, Death and the Tulip* (2008) [as author and illustrator], *The Bear Who Wasn't There* (2014) [author Oren Lavie], and *I'll Root for You* (2019) [author Edward van de Vendel].

The Story of the Little Mole
who knew it was none of his business

30th Anniversary Edition

Werner Holzwarth and Wolf Erlbruch

One day, the little Mole poked his head out from underground to see whether the sun had already risen. Then it happened!

(It looked a little like a sausage, and the worst thing was that it landed right on his head.)

"How mean!" cried the little mole. "Who has done this on my head?"

(But he was so shortsighted that he couldn't see anyone around.)

ABOVE: Despite the enormous success of Little Mole, *there has been no follow-up from Werner and Wolf, no "afters" with the mole's protagonist. Little Mole clearly believes that justice has been done. The authors did sanction a further pop-up version, badged as* Little Mole: The Plop-Up.

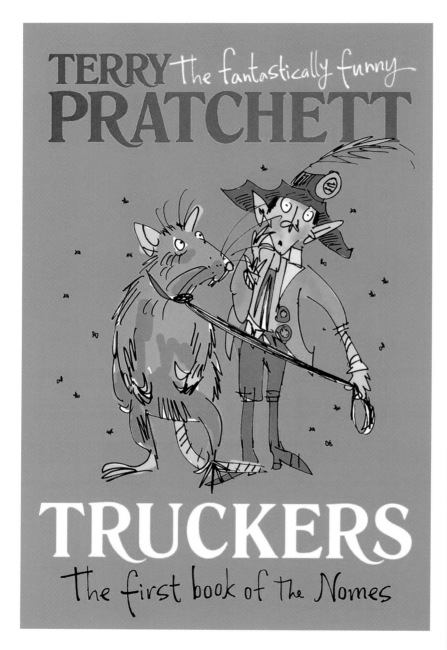

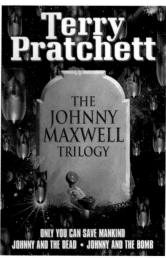

LEFT: *Mark Beech collaborated with Terry Pratchett on a number of new illustrations for his books before the author's death from Alzheimer's. Per Pratchett's request, the manager of the Pratchett estate, Rob Wilkins, fulfilled the author's wish that any unfinished work should be destroyed by a steamroller crushing his computer hard-drive.*

BELOW: Johnny and the Dead *was made into a children's TV serial for ITV in 1995.*

Truckers

(1989) and sequels

Terry Pratchett (1948–2015)

Terry Pratchett, famed for his forty-one Discworld novels, also created a world within our own world, populated by four-inch-tall "Nomes". This trilogy of books is a gleeful introduction to fantasy for young readers.

The Nome Trilogy (The Bromeliad Trilogy in the U.S.) – *Truckers* (1989), *Diggers* (1990) and *Wings* (1990) – centres on a group of Nomes who live by a motorway. Their numbers have been reduced by foxes and road deaths, and they hatch a plan to hitch a ride on a truck in search of a better future. The truck's destination is a department store, inhabited by another group, the Inside Nomes.

This second group have always believed the motto of their department store home, "Everything Under One Roof", and therefore doubt the existence of the Outside Nomes' world. They join forces when they realise that other worlds are possible, and that Nomes are actually from another planet. Together they must find a way home. *Diggers* and *Wings* are parallel sequels to *Truckers*, following various characters through different events in the same time period, to the same conclusion.

The overarching theme of the Nome Trilogy is the possibility of changing your views in the light of new evidence. The books contain regular references to a species of frog that spends its whole life inside a bromeliad plant, completely unaware of a whole world beyond it. So it is with several of the more close-minded Nomes, and therefore those who are open to new ideas struggle to convince the sceptical in their society.

The story unfolds with Pratchett's hallmark humour and puns. The Inside Nomes, for example, have names like De Haberdasheri, Stationari and Del Icatessen. It's no surprise that Pratchett, creator of the self-contained universe of Discworld, grew up reading sci-fi giants such as H. G. Wells, Arthur C. Clarke and Isaac Asimov. But his literary influences are not the usual fantasy suspects. Instead he cites a roll call of humourists including Mark Twain, G. K. Chesterton, P. G. Wodehouse and Tom Sharpe. Like all of these greats, Pratchett delights

in literary farce, a joyful exercise of wild imagination, which can lead his protagonists through absurd plot twists to a place of safety and resolution.

The Carpet People (1971), Terry Pratchett's first novel, was a children's book also about a race of tiny people whose existence is threatened and whose competing factions must accept new ideas from each other in order to survive. *The Carpet People* was Pratchett's first attempt at a flat world, which later became fully formed in Discworld. Although Discworld was not created specifically for children, it is certainly accessible reading for them, and some instalments of the canon were written especially for the young. *The Amazing Maurice and his Educated Rodents* (2001), the first of such, won the Carnegie Medal, awarded to the year's best book for children by a British author.

Pratchett returned to the fictional town of Blackbury, the setting for much of *Truckers*, for a trilogy of children's books about Johnny Maxwell, a normal boy with an unhappy home life who sees things other people don't see – ghosts, aliens and time travellers, for example. He has also written novels of alternative history for the young: *Nation* (2008), set on a nineteenth-century fictional south Pacific island, and *Dodger* (2012), a development of Charles Dickens' character the Artful Dodger in *Oliver Twist*.

Other children's books by Terry Pratchett: *The Carpet People* (1971); The Johnny Maxwell Trilogy – *Only You Can Save Mankind* (1992), *Johnny and the Dead* (1993) and *Johnny and the Bomb* (1996); *The Amazing Maurice and his Educated Rodents* (2001), *Nation* (2008), and *Dodger* (2012).

We're Going on a Bear Hunt
(1989)

Michael Rosen (born 1946)

When five children and their dog set off on a bear hunt, little do they know the challenging obstacles that will stand in their way along their journey. The danger of finding a bear is the last thing on their minds – until they find one.

A simple story with few words and much repetition has so often proved a winning formula for the picture book. Dr Seuss's *Green Eggs and Ham* is the classic example. Children's poet Michael Rosen has proved himself a master of the art. With each barrier that his intrepid bear hunters meet, they discuss the way forward in the same way:

> We can't go over it.
> We can't go under it.
> Oh no!
> We've got to go through it!

And through they go, through grass, a river, mud, a forest and a snowstorm; having conquered each obstacle, they chorus:

> We're going on a bear hunt.
> We're going to catch a big one.
> What a beautiful day!
> We're not scared.

Until they tiptoe, at the end of their hunt, through a cave. You wouldn't expect to find a bear in an English coastal cave, but they do, and across two pages they hastily retrace their steps, home and into bed. In a poignant epilogue the bear, having pursued them, is left disconsolate and alone on a beach. The story is based on an American folk song and the illustrations are by Helen Oxenbury, whose work on the book was nominated for a Kate Greenaway Medal.

Michael Rosen is a veteran author for and about children. He has written over 140 books, including aids for teachers, parents and authors. For children he has written poetry and retold traditional stories, as well as devising his own. He grew up in north-west London (where there are no bears), and began his career writing in the BBC's children's department before his left-wing views and ties to the Communist Party (his parents were members) fell foul of the corporation's employment policies.

He began instead to write poems for children, and his first collection, *Mind Your Own Business*, was published in 1974. A passionate advocate of making poetry accessible to children, Rosen has always toured schools to perform and discuss it. He has edited several anthologies of children's poetry, including *Culture Shock* (1992) and *Michael Rosen's A–Z: The Best Children's Poetry from Agard to Zephaniah* (2009).

He is not afraid to be serious with children and his *And Other Big Questions* series, co-written with Annemarie Young, discusses big moral issues for children. His most moving and personal work is *Michael Rosen's Sad Book* (2004), a book about grief which he wrote after the death of his own son, aged eighteen, from meningitis.

The majority of his output for children, however, appeals to their delight in the vulgar or silly; for example with *Burping Bertha* (2012) and *Fluff the Farting Fish* (2013). His two volumes of nonsense poetry, *Michael Rosen's Book of Nonsense* (1998) and *Even More Nonsense* (2000), are a direct link to his spiritual predecessor Edward Lear.

Some other books for children by Michael Rosen: *Mind Your Own Business* (1974), *Michael Rosen's Book of Nonsense* (1998), *Even More Nonsense* (2000), *Michael Rosen's Sad Book* (2004), *Burping Bertha* (2012), *Fluff the Farting Fish* (2013), *Uncle Gobb and the Dread Shed* (2016) and series, *Hampstead the Hamster* (2018), and *Who are Refugees and Migrants? What Makes People Leave their Homes? And Other Big Questions* (2019) and series.

We're Going on a Bear Hunt
Michael Rosen   Helen Oxenbury

Ten Little
FINGERS
and
Ten Little
TOES

MEM FOX
HELEN OXENBURY

ABOVE: Michael Rosen first performed the story on a school tour, and when asked to write the story down as a book, found it particularly difficult to transcribe the onomatopoeic sounds he'd used in his performances.

LEFT: Bear Hunt's *popularity owes a lot to the illustrations of Helen Oxenbury, whose distinctive style has graced many illustrated books over the last forty years, including* The Three Little Wolves and the Big Bad Pig *(1993) and* Ten Little Fingers and Ten Little Toes *(2008).*

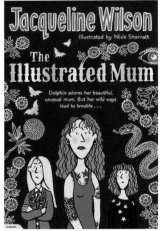

ABOVE AND LEFT: Jacqueline Wilson novels are most familiar for their Nick Sharratt illustrations. Wilson first met Sharratt after she had written The Story of Tracy Beaker, *and the two have since collaborated on countless projects – Wilson herself has lost count, and jokes that the story and illustrations are so entwined that many children often think the two live together.*

The Story of Tracy Beaker
(1991) and series

Jaqueline Wilson (born 1945)

Few popular authors have addressed the condition of being a child within the social care system. With Tracy Beaker, Jacqueline Wilson confronts the reality of life for children who have been taken into residential care.

The child without parents, whether because of wartime evacuation, death or accident, is a common character in children's literature. Harry Potter, the children in *The Lion the Witch and the Wardrobe* and *Ballet Shoes*, Lyra in *His Dark Materials*, Jim Hawkins in *Treasure Island*, Carrie in *Carrie's War*, Anne in *Anne of Green Gables* – they all start from that position. The movie *Home Alone* is an example on the big screen of absent parental figures.

It's a handy plot device for placing your protagonist in an unfamiliar situation and forcing him or her to rely on their own resources, make new friends and mature as a human being. Naturally, most authors focus on the subsequent adventures; few have taken an extended look at the everyday lives of children taken into care.

The Story of Tracy Beaker is, in a way, an inversion of the classic British boarding school story. Tracy lives in The Dumping Ground, the children's nickname for their residential care home, where she has been placed because of violence and neglect in her parental home. It's not all jolly japes and midnight feasts in the manner of Enid Blyton's *Mallory Towers* or Frank Richards' *Billy Bunter* tales. Tracy is often unhappy and displays behavioural problems as you might realistically expect from someone in her situation.

It's not all doom and gloom either, however. Tracy is ten years old, and she tells her own story the way she wants it told. "I'm Tracy Beaker," she begins. "This is a book all about me. I'd read it if I were you. It's the most incredible, dynamic, heart-rending story. Honest." She's a thoroughly and delightfully unreliable narrator who masks her vulnerability, as many such children do, through fantasy and feigned disinterest for the things that really do matter to her. She insists, for example, that her mother is a Hollywood star who is simply too busy to look after her.

Author Jacqueline Wilson's own youth was, by contrast, secure and although apt to daydream at school, she was an avid reader and compulsive writer of stories from an early age. She left education at the age of sixteen, got a job writing stories for the girls' magazine *Jackie* and was married at nineteen.

Her husband joined the police and Wilson's first books were crime novels, but she soon turned to books for children. By the time of *Tracy Beaker*, her first big hit, she had written over 40 novels – the total now stands at more than 100.

She often writes about troubled, isolated young girls. *How to Survive Summer Camp* (1985) is about ten-year-old Stella, dumped in summer camp while her mother and new stepfather go on their honeymoon. In *Take a Good Look* (1990), Mary is cut off from the world because she is partially sighted. Andy, *The Suitcase Kid* (1992), has to come to terms with her parents' divorce. In *Bad Girls* (1996), two friends bond over their isolation – Mandy is being bullied at school and Tanya, a fostered child, has dyslexia and shoplifts.

Throughout, Jacqueline Wilson writes about her subjects with an affection and a sympathy which must broaden the understanding of any young reader, whether they are going through the same things or not. It is undoubtedly for this reason that Wilson was, for a period, the most borrowed author in Britain's libraries. In an age where children are progressively turning to screens rather than books, Jacqueline Wilson has continued to inspire generations of children to read.

Some other novels by Jacqueline Wilson: *The Mum Minder* (1993), *Girls in Love* (1997) and series, *Dustbin Baby* (2001), *Hetty Feather* (2009) and series, and *The Worst Thing About my Sister* (2012).

Goosebumps series

(1992–1997)

R. L. Stine (born 1943)

In the world of book series, the sixty-two volumes of R. L. Stine's *Goosebumps* are second only to J. K. Rowling's *Harry Potter* in terms of global sales. Scary tales of the supernatural are clearly what young readers want.

By any standards R. L. Stine's work rate on the *Goosebumps* series was remarkable – an average of more than ten books a year for six years straight. Although J. K. Rowling outsold him book for book, Stine has a further twenty-five or so series to his name, ranging in length from trilogies like *Space Cadets* to the fifty-five volumes of *Fear Street*. Bookshops around the world have sold around 500 million copies of his books.

Stine, from Columbus, Ohio, began his writing career with a series of joke books for children under the name Jovial Bob Stine. Having edited the Ohio State University humour magazine *The Sundial* as a student, he launched *Bananas*, a teenage magazine, which he helmed from 1975 to 1984. So far so funny, but in 1986 he published his first horror novel, *Blind Date*.

He never looked back. After several stand-alone chillers, he published *The New Girl*, the first of the *Fear Street* series, in 1989. It was aimed at a teenage audience, and recent additions to the ongoing series have been, in Stine's words, "longer, more adult and more violent", an indication of the evolution of teenage gothic fiction since the series' initial conception.

Goosebumps is written for a younger readership and leavens enjoyably scary levels of horror with some of Jovial Bob's humour. There are no deaths in *Goosebumps* stories, no violence or drugs. Its intended audience is one growing in self-confidence but not yet worldy. The series owes its success to the simple delight of that age group in frightening itself. Stine originally wrote it with girls in mind, but found that half his fan mail was coming from boys.

Like *Fear Street*, *Goosebumps* has occasional recurring characters. But where *Fear Street* stories all take place in the same locale, the city of Shadyside, *Goosebumps* tales are set in a variety of locations, usually in order to isolate their protagonists from the support of family and friends in the ensuing adventure. Stine's characters are routinely sent to boarding school, or to a new neighbourhood, or on a camping trip, or overseas. There he subjects them to supernatural events which they overcome and from which they emerge stronger, more confident individuals. The reader, identifying with the juvenile hero, experiences their isolation and vulnerability, invests in their success and shares in their eventual triumph over adversity.

Goosebumps began with *Welcome to Dead House* in 1992, and ended in 1997 with *Monster Blood IV*, an extraordinary outpouring of creativity over six years. After the shortest of breaks, Stine returned to the series in 1998 with a first book under the umbrella *Goosebumps Series 2000*, which he completed with another twenty-four volumes between then and 2000. In addition, there have been 50 books under the brand *Give Yourself Goosebumps* (1995–2000), nineteen under *Goosebumps Horrorland* (2008–2012) and more in the ongoing *Goosebumps Most Wanted* (since 2012). To call Stine a prolific author would be an understatement.

Some other series by R. L. Stine: *Space Cadets* (three books, 1991–1992), *Fear Street Cheerleaders* (five books, 1992–1998), *Cataluna Chronicles* (three books, 1995), and *Mostly Ghostly* (eight books, 2004–2006).

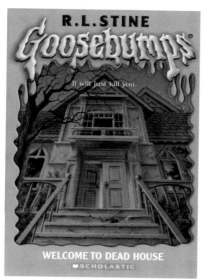

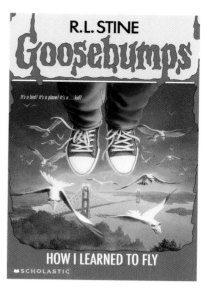

ABOVE: In an age before the Internet and despite little initial promotion, the Goosebumps *series became a viral hit simply by word of mouth between children. It was a 1990s phenomenon that soon became a franchise, with video games, plastic toys and its own land in a Disney theme park.*

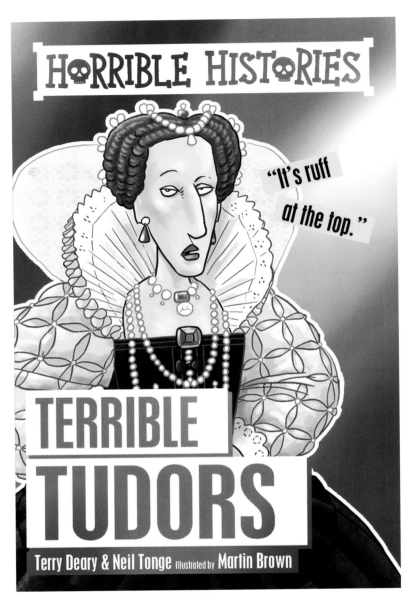

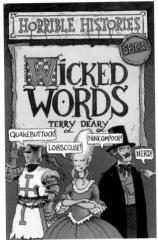

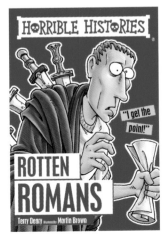

ABOVE AND RIGHT: Terry's Horrible Histories *started off with the Tudors and Egyptians and later (around March) he took a stab at infamous Romans. Deary enjoys his contrarianism; refusing an invitation to visit No. 10 and observing that "the only politician ever to have entered Parliament with honourable intentions was Guy Fawkes".*

Horrible Histories series

(1993–2013)

Terry Deary (born 1946)

Terry Deary has capitalised on the delight of children in anything gory or silly to bring the past alive. Much repackaged and reinvented for other media, the original books are an invaluable introduction to history for young minds with short attention spans.

Perhaps it was growing up in his father's butcher's shop that gave Deary a taste for the bloodier aspects of human history. His *Horrible Histories* revel in the gruesome details of times past, from *Awesome Egyptians* to *Blitzed Brits*. They're aided by his terrible jokes and the accompanying cartoons by artist Martin Brown, which emulate the cartoons often found in publications for adults. Somehow through this cocktail of juvenile mayhem, he manages to convey historical truths and a wealth of detail. Parents and teachers love the educational value, while children lap up the grizzly, giggly stories.

As a young man he joined Theatr [sic] Powys, a theatre-in-education company that gives issue-based performances and workshops in Welsh schools. Deary acted, directed and eventually wrote scripts, discovering that he had a knack for communicating with children. He trained as a teacher, taught drama in schools and began to write novels for the young.

When his publisher proposed the idea of *Horrible Histories*, Deary resisted the idea on the grounds that he was not a historian. For the first two in the series, *Terrible Tudors* and *Awesome Egyptians* (both 1993), he shared writing credits with Neil Tonge and Peter Hepplewhite (authors in their own right of many accessible history books). By the third, *Rotten Romans* (1994), he had found his feet, and wrote the book along with the remaining twenty in his own style. He finished the series in 2012, feeling that he had run out of stories to tell.

What had been proposed as a series of joke books with a historical theme became a series of history books with jokes, as Deary became more and more fascinated by the historical details he unearthed in his research that fell outside the mainstream curriculum. He became aware of the extent to which history is open to interpretation, and his *Horrible Histories* challenge the official version handed out in schools with sections like "Test Your Teacher" and "What Would You Do?"

Outside school they have regularly topped the list of books most commonly borrowed from U.K. libraries. It is not surprising that Deary is highly critical of the school system, believing that schools take all the fun out of learning, and are just a device for keeping children off the streets. It is more surprising that he is critical of public libraries, believing that books should be sold like other commodities, not merely lent. He is also scathing about his fellow historians for their lack of objectivity: "They don't write objective history … They all come with a twist."

The *Horrible Histories* have sold over twenty-five million copies around the world. Apart from being frequently repackaged in different combinations, box sets and other formats such as cartoon strips, the series has also become a very successful theatrical franchise and a merchandise brand for toys, video games, tie-ins with historical sites, and a much-loved TV series. It has also inspired similar series by other authors – *Horrible Geography*, *Horrible Science*, and *Boring Bible* among them.

Some other books by Terry Deary: *The Fire Thief* trilogy (2005–07), *Gory Stories* series (2008–09), and *Master Crook's Crime Academy* series (2009–10).

Where, Oh Where is Kipper's Bear?

(1994) and series

Mick Inkpen (born 1952)

Mick Inkpen's canine creation Kipper has been a bookshelf favourite for more than twenty-five years. Because the little dog sees the world as his young readers do, he's the perfect vehicle for early learning through reading.

When *Kipper* (1991) was first published, a perceptive reviewer for the *School Librarian* magazine commented, "an engaging little character, … a type from which series are made." Kipper's engaging innocence and curiosity about the world quickly established him as a popular puppy to rival Eric Hill's Spot. He has now appeared in nearly fifty books along with his friends Tiger, Jake, Arnold and the rest.

Mick Inkpen has put Kipper to good use. Besides the simple storybooks, there are Kipper counting books (*Kipper's Toybox*, 1992, and *Kipper's Book of Numbers*, 1999), a Kipper alphabet (*Kipper's A-Z*, 2000), with a very persistent zebra, and Kipper's books of weather, colours and opposites (all 1995).

Where, Oh Where is Kipper's Bear? (1994) is another variation – a pop-up book. Every page has some movable element as we follow Kipper in the search for his favourite toy. Birds fly out of the trees, mice shake their heads, a piglet jumps up. On the last page, in which Kipper goes to bed having been unable to find his bear, we can lift Kipper's bedclothes and find the bear for ourselves, reading a book under the covers by the light of a torch – a real light embedded in the page.

Why is this book better known than others? Like many illustrators, Mick Inkpen began his career in the world of commercial graphic design. He started out, as Anthony Browne and Jan Pieńkowski did, designing greetings cards before going into partnership with Nick Butterworth, who had been to the same school as Inkpen. The pair designed advertisements for everything from banking to bras. In 1986 they were commissioned to illustrate a series of children's books by Elizabeth Lawrence and Noreen Wetton, and tried their hands at writing and illustrating their own stories.

Both men have now become successful children's authors, separately and together. In collaboration their works include *Just Like Jasper!* (1989) and *Jasper's Beanstalk* (1990) about Jasper the cat, and *Sports Day* (1988) and *School Trip* (1990) about special days at school. On his own Nick Butterworth is best known for his series about Percy the Park Keeper, beginning with *One Snowy Night* in 1990.

Mick began his solo career with a counting book, *One Bear at Bedtime* (1987) and followed it with two What-If books – *If I Had a Pig* and *If I Had a Sheep* (both 1988) – about the things you might like to do with a new friend. *Threadbear* (1990) brought him to wider attention when it won a major U.K. award. It tells the story of a bear in search of a working squeak, and Inkpen played with the book format by including fold-out flaps.

He used flaps again in *Penguin Small* (1993), about a young penguin's journey from the North Pole to the South where the rest of the penguins have gone to escape penguin-eating polar bears. Here, foldouts give us a four-page-long whale among other delights. In the twenty-first century Inkpen has begun a new series of gentle, fantastical stories set on Blue Nose Island, all beginning with the phrase "The story starts like this", and all with Inkpen's characteristically clear-lined, comical, softly coloured watercolours.

Other children's books by Mick Inkpen: *One Bear at Bedtime* (1987), *Threadbear* (1990), *Lullabyhullaballoo!* (1993), *Penguin Small* (1993), *Wibbly Pig is Happy!* (1995) and series, *Bear* (1997), and *Blue Nose Island: Ploo and the Terrible Gnobbler* (2003) and series.

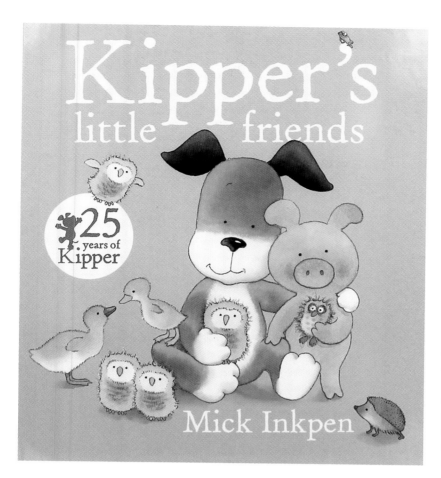

LEFT: Kipper had his first adventure in 1991.
BELOW: In Where, Oh Where is Kipper's Bear? *Kipper searches the house for his teddy. Flaps reveal that under the stairs there are the Under-the-Stairs Bears, but no sign of teddy. The final flap has an unexpected novelty (to those who can't read the cover) his teddy is at the bottom of his bed holding a torch with a real embedded light.*

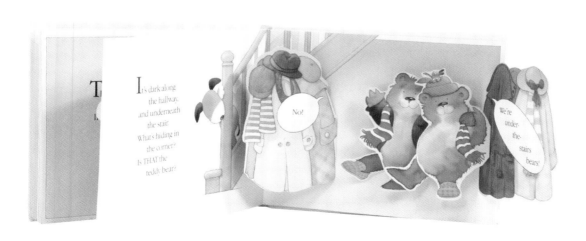

PHILIP
PULLMAN

HIS DARK MATERIALS

NORTHERN LIGHTS
THE SUBTLE KNIFE
THE AMBER SPYGLASS

INTRODUCTION BY LUCY HUGHES-HALLETT
PREFACE BY THE AUTHOR

ABOVE: The first book in the series, Northern Lights, *won the Carnegie Medal in 1995.*
OPPOSITE: Originally written as a play, Pullman was so attracted to the story and
characters of The Ruby in the Smoke *that he rewrote it as a children's book, which he*
later extended to a series of four.

His Dark Materials trilogy

(1995–2000)

Philip Pullman (born 1946)

Philip Pullman has introduced a new generation of young adults to the genre of fantasy. He is a serial author of series: the trilogy *His Dark Materials* was not his first, and a third trilogy is already underway. That's a trilogy of trilogies.

I
n fact, his first series was a tetralogy, a trilogy with an afterthought – the nineteenth-century adventures of Sally Lockhart and her friends, which began with *The Ruby in the Smoke* (1985) and finished with *The Tin Princess* (1994), published just a year before the first of *His Dark Materials*. Sally's world is not fantastical, but it is remote from our own, set in an imperial age and encompassing China, India and Europe. What begins with Sally's attempts to discover the truth about her father's death becomes a running battle with evil and a search for love.

His Dark Materials takes a Victorian world not unlike Sally's as its starting point, but it soon becomes clear that this is not a world from our own past. For a start, every human character is accompanied by his or her daemon, a shape-shifting creature reflecting the soul of the human, akin to the familiar figure of the traditional witch.

In *His Dark Materials* a dominant Religion is experimenting on abducted children by separating them from their daemons. It believes this will eradicate the sins of adulthood, which are derived from a mysterious Dust. When Lyra, the twelve-year-old protagonist of the trilogy, sees her best friend killed by this research, she determines to find the source of Dust for herself. The friend's death releases so much energy that a portal is opened to a parallel universe, the next stage on Lyra's journey and the first of several such universes in the trilogy.

The overarching theme of the trilogy is the ambiguous nature of original sin. This is a reflection, and an inversion, of John Milton's epic poem *Paradise Lost*, which Pullman has cited as a central influence on *His Dark Materials* – the very title comes from a line in the poem:

Unless th' Almighty Maker them ordain
His dark materials to create more Worlds

But where Milton saw sin as a tragic flaw in human nature, Pullman in *His Dark Materials* celebrates it as the very thing which gives human beings their humanity. This and his hostile references to the religion of the books have brought him into frequent conflict with Christian groups. It is therefore ironic that Pullman, an avowed atheist, has played God by creating several parallel worlds and ordaining the lives of their populations.

Such was the success of *His Dark Materials* that Pullman set two further stories in the same universe: *Lyra's Oxford* (2003), which takes place two years after the events of the original trilogy, and *Once Upon a Time in the North* (2008), a prequel which fills in the back story of some of the other characters from *His Dark Materials*.

He has hinted that there may be a third such book, and he has begun a new trilogy, *The Book of Dust*, in the same setting. Two volumes of it have already appeared: *La Belle Sauvage* (2017) and *The Secret Commonwealth* (2019). Lyra remains the focus, and *The Book of Dust* follows her life before, during and after the events of *His Dark Materials*. Fans will have plenty of reading from Pullman for years to come.

Selected stand-alone books by Philip Pullman: *Count Karlstein, or The Ride of the Demon Huntsman* (1982), *How to Be Cool* (1987), *The Broken Bridge* (1990), *Clockwork, or All Wound Up* (1995), *I Was a Rat! Or The Scarlet Slippers* (1999), and *The Scarecrow and his Servant* (2004).

Harry Potter series

(1997–2007)

J. K. Rowling (born 1965)

The *Harry Potter* series has broken more records than the boy-wizard has cast spells. Its author became the world's first and, to date, only billionaire author. *Deathly Hallows*, the final volume, sold eleven million copies in the first twenty-four hours of its release. It is, simply, the most successful book series in history.

The idea of an orphaned young wizard learning his craft at a school for wizards came to the author J. K. Rowling while she was trapped on a delayed British train for four hours. It was, in a way, as magical a revelation as anything that her young protagonists would experience over their seven years of study. Rowling has said that the idea came to her fully-formed, and that the epilogue to the seventh and final book in the series was one of the first things she wrote.

Each book follows a year in the school life of the friends Harry Potter, Hermione Granger and Ron Weasley. In that sense it is very much in the tradition of British boarding school stories as written by Anthony Buckeridge and, in his early days, P. G. Wodehouse. There are adventures after dark, teachers good and bad, and threats to the school. As Rowling has noted, the overarching moral of the series is that we sometimes have to make choices between what is right and what is easy. Sometimes Harry and his friends have to break rules of wizardry for the greater good.

There are also parallels with the Arthurian legends of the Middle Ages. The gothic setting of Hogwarts School, the use of Latin in spells, the creation by Rowling of fantastic beasts reminiscent of those in the illuminated manuscripts of the time, the sense of a compelling quest in many of the Harry Potter stories – all are echoes of the medieval tales of the Knights of the Round Table. Harry's mentor Dumbledore has shades of both King Arthur and the wizard Merlin about him, and Arthurian scholars see in Harry himself a reflection of Arthur's Sir Percival, whose quest was for the Holy Grail.

Death is ever-present in *Harry Potter*. J. K. Rowling's mother died while she was writing the first book, which begins with the murder of Harry's parents. The death of ever-more central characters in the course of the

series reaches its climax in the fates of Dumbledore, and ultimately Voldemort (whose name can mean "flight of death" and "theft of death" – both apt for the character). Some have seen a metaphor for Christianity in the perpetual battle with death, but some Christian groups have condemned the portrayal of witches and wizards as a promotion of satanic beliefs.

The passage through adolescence of the main characters is part of the attraction for young adult readers of *Harry Potter*, as fans of the first book aged more or less at the same rate as their heroes. More surprising was the attraction of the books to an older readership, for whom the books were eventually issued with different, more adult covers. It was the domination by *Harry Potter* of the bestseller lists that persuaded the *New York Times* in 2000 to create a separate children's list, and in 2004 a separate list for book series, in order to give other books a chance. Some mocked the move, suggesting that by the same logic the Beatles should have been given a separate pop chart in the 1960s.

It was an appropriate parallel to draw. Harry Potter has become as much an icon of Britishness as the Beatles, the Royal Family, James Bond and Sherlock Holmes. Along the way he has generated a few myths of his own. It is not true, for example, that the series has contributed to a reverse in the decline of literacy among the young; nor that there has been a marked rise in the incidence of children keeping owls as pets. It is the case, however, that quidditch, the sport of the broomstick-riding pupils of Hogwarts, is now a real sport played by *Harry Potter* fans.

Other books from the Hogwarts library by J. K. Rowling: *Fantastic Beasts and Where to Find Them* (2001), *Quidditch Through the Ages* (2001), *The Tales of Beedle the Bard* (2008), and *Hogwarts: An Incomplete and Unreliable Guide* (2016).

ABOVE: *A 20th Anniversary Edition released by Bloomsbury in 2017 featured four new covers that represented each of the Hogwarts Houses. It is Thomas Taylor's cover art for the first U.K. edition of* The Philosopher's Stone, *however, that is the most well-known.*

ABOVE: Holes *was ranked number six by the American School Library Journal among*
all-time favourite children's novels.
OPPOSITE: *Like* Holes, Sideways Stories from Wayside School *has*
been adapted for the screen.

182_____ 100 Children's Books That Inspire Our World

Holes

(1998)

Louis Sachar (born 1954)

Combining elements of fairy tale, historical novel and modern mystery, Holes tackles subjects all too rarely addressed in young adult novels in an intricate weave of storylines past and present.

The wrongful imprisonment of young Stanley for a crime he did not commit is just the latest example of a curse which has afflicted his family for five generations, beginning with his great-great-grandfather. His family's fate is intimately bound up with that of an African-American onion farmer murdered in the nineteenth century for kissing a white teacher. His killing in the waters of Green Lake prompts a drought which dries up the lake, creating the present desert.

In juvenile detention, Stanley must dig a hole in the desert every day – unknown to him, the warden is looking for buried treasure which once belonged to Stanley's great grandfather. Stanley's friendship with a fellow inmate rights many wrongs of injustice and racism in the course of the novel. The curse is lifted, and rain begins to fall once more, restoring Green Lake to its former lush glory.

The narrative of *Holes* moves backward and forward between present and past, demonstrating that all actions have unforeseen consequences. The failure of Stanley's great-great-grandfather to complete a fairy-tale quest which would have won him the girl he loved; the murder of a farmer which drove his law-abiding girlfriend to a life of crime; the theft of a pair of trainers which sent the wrong boy to jail; all these contribute to the conclusion of *Holes*. The book has won praise for addressing racial discrimination and youth imprisonment, and for delivering a rich, complex, thoughtful storyline for young adult readers.

Louis Sachar insists that there is little autobiographical content in his novels. "My personal experiences are kind of boring," he has said. "I have to make up what I put in my books." Nevertheless, his first series of novels, about the strange goings-on at Wayside Elementary School, was prompted by a period during his university studies when he volunteered as a teaching assistant at a local elementary school. He earned the nickname "Louis the Yard Teacher", and a character of that name is a regular feature in Wayside. Sachar wrote five Wayside novels between 1978 and 1995; after a twenty-five-year hiatus he has returned to Wayside with a new collection of stories for 2020.

Among Sachar's other works are the eight light-hearted books about Marvin Redpost, a red-haired third-grader always getting into trouble. He has also written seven stand-alone novels about children at various different stages of school. The idea of a curse,

the dominant plot theme of *Holes*, also appears in his earlier novel *The Boy who Lost his Face* (1989). Stanley from *Holes* returns briefly in a sequel, *Small Steps* (2006), which focuses on the difficulties of one of the other characters in *Holes* – getting on in life when you have a criminal record.

Other books by Louis Sachar:
Sideways Stories from Wayside School (1978) and series, *Johnny's in the Basement* (1981), *There's a Boy in the Girls' Bathroom* (1987), *The Boy who Lost his Face* (1989), *Marvin Redpost: Kidnapped at Birth?* (1992) and series, and *Small Steps* (2006).

Skellig

(1998)

David Almond (born 1951)

David Almond recalls that even as a child he wanted to write and would make little storybooks for his parents. His mother used to tell him that shoulder blades were what remained from a time when we were all angels. It's the sort of thing you remember as you grow up.

Almond became a teacher, publishing short stories in his spare time. When he set out to write his first novel, he had no fixed plot or idea in mind. He set it in a house like his home, with a toilet in the dining room and a garage full of clutter. When he began to write about his protagonist, Michael, he didn't know what Michael would find; to this day he claims he is still not sure quite who or what Skellig is.

Skellig is the strange creature that Michael finds, starving and grumpy, in a corner of the garage. Michael, new to the area, has no friends at school and hangs out with Mina, the home-educated daughter of a neighbour. They look after Skellig but keep him a secret. Is he human? Is he a prehistoric bird, the archaeopteryx? An owl? An angel? At the end of the book Skellig moves on, having appeared in a vision to Michael's mother in which he seemed to save the life of Michael's new, prematurely born sister.

Allusions to angels abound in *Skellig*, and even the young protagonist is named after the archangel Michael. Though the creature, which he discovers has wings but is no angel, Michael learns that shoulder blades are the vestiges of angels' wings.

Skellig, Almond's first novel, has echoes of an earlier short story for children, *A Very Old Man with Enormous Wings* (1955) by Gabriel García Márquez, whose influence Almond has acknowledged. That story is about the reactions of a small community to an angel which arrives in their midst one stormy night. Mina and Michael treat their discovery rather better than Márquez's community dealt with theirs, but Márquez reveals his angel to the outside world and Mina and Michael do not.

Skellig is a book of hope and possibility, however irrational both may seem. Besides Márquez, it also draws on the art and poetry of William Blake and, without being too heavy-handed, touches on themes of life and death, nature and evolution, family and education. It's a short book, and later Almond wrote a longer prequel to it of great merit called *My Name is Mina* (2010). The latter was shortlisted for the Carnegie Award for children's literature by a British author; *Skellig* itself won it. David Almond was honoured with the Hans Christian Andersen Award in 2010.

Some other books by David Almond: *Kit's Wilderness* (1999), *Counting Stars* (2000), *Secret Heart* (2001), *The Fire Eaters* (2003), *Clay* (2005), *Jackdaw Summer* (2008, U.S. title *Raven Summer*), *The True Tale of the Monster Billy Dean* (2011), *Mouse Bird Snake Wolf* (2013), and *The Tightrope Walkers* (2014).

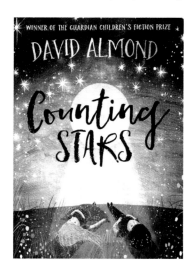

OPPOSITE: *The first edition of the book has cover art by Fletcher Sibthorp, whose abstract depiction of an angel recalls the archangel Michael. The names 'Skellig' and 'Michael' are also said to be derived from the Skellig Islands off the coast of County Kerry, Ireland, one of which is named Skellig Michael.*
LEFT: *Almond's* Counting Stars *is a collection of eighteen semi-autobiographical stories which draw on the author's childhood in North East England.*

DAVID ALMOND

Skellig

Whitbread Award Winner

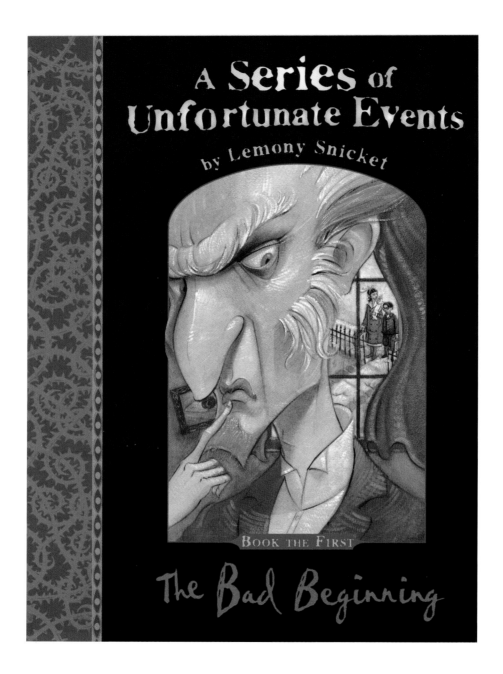

ABOVE: The metafictional style of writing sees the book's illustrations by Brett Helquist acknowledged by Snicket within the text.

OPPOSITE: The series was completed in 2006 with the publication of the thirteenth novel, aptly named The End.

A Series of Unfortunate Events
(series, 1999–2006)

Lemony Snicket (born 1970)

The thirteen books of *A Series of Unfortunate Events* have subverted the form of the gothic fairy tale for a whole generation of readers. But who or what is Lemony Snicket? Is he an author? Is he a character? A pen name? Is he for children or adults? The answer's "yes".

While researching his debut novel, *The Basic Eight* (1998), an adult comedy about high school students and satanic rituals, American author Daniel Handler sought information from a number of unsavoury organisations. Wisely preferring not to use his own name in such enquiries, he signed them Lemony Snicket.

The Basic Eight proved a hard sell. Before Thomas Dunne Books picked it up Handler received thirty-seven letters of rejection, including one from Harper Collins, who liked his style and suggested he write for children. Handler was reluctant to do so, but set about reworking an old manuscript of his, a comic gothic horror originally written for adults. Gradually Lemony Snicket began to become more than just a pen name. By the time *The Bad Beginning*, the first book in the *Unfortunate Events* series, was finished, Snicket was a fully rounded character, a children's author and the first-person narrator at the centre of his own absurd, anarchic, anachronistic, alt-gothic world.

The Unfortunate Events which Snicket describes revolve around the efforts of the orphaned Baudelaire children Violet, Klaus and baby Sunny to protect themselves from their scheming relative Count Olaf. Olaf is determined to swindle the children out of their inheritance by hook or by crook. Snicket proves to be an unenthusiastic and unreliable storyteller, relating events very much from his own perspective. As the series progresses the young heroes learn more about their parents' death and about

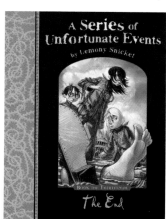

a mysterious organisation called VFD, of which their mother and father were members.

The morality of the books becomes significantly darker and more ambiguous towards the end of the Series. Good people do bad things. As the three children age, their story becomes a rite of passage towards adulthood. Little Sunny, who starts the series as a wordless infant, proclaims near the end of it that "I'm not a baby."

Lemony Snicket is perhaps a writer for older children who have already acquired a moral compass from earlier reading. Adults can find other layers in the text, which is packed full of literary and social references above the head of the average young reader. *A Series of Unfortunate Events* is designed to appeal on different levels to different age ranges, just as many family movies are today. There is something for everyone to enjoy, as adults have found with the *Harry Potter* books of J. K. Rowling.

Daniel Handler has expanded the Snicket universe with several other books. *The Beatrice Letters* (2006) are the correspondence between Snicket and Beatrice Baudelaire, the mother of Violet, Klaus and Sunny. They were published just before the final instalment of *Unfortunate Events* and included clues about its ending. *All the Wrong Questions* (2012–2015) is a quartet of books describing Snicket's own story before the events of *Unfortunate Events*.

Selected other books by Lemony Snicket: *Lemony Snicket: The Unauthorised Autobiography* (2002), *The Beatrice Letters* (2006), *All the Wrong Questions* (2012–2015), and *File Under: 13 Suspicious Incidents* (2014).

Angus, Thongs and Full-Frontal Snogging

(1999) and series

Louise Rennison (1951–2016)

Has anyone ever captured the spirit of the teenage girl better than Louise Rennison? She wrote for them as someone who remembered being one. Rudely hilarious, she delighted her target audience and horrified their teachers and parents who had forgotten what it's like.

There are many similarities between the *Angus, Thongs* series and the *Molesworth* series of the 1950s by Geoffrey Willans. Though Nigel Molesworth was younger, male, and from an earlier time, Rennison's heroine Georgia Nicolson, like Molesworth, stands for all her sex and age group with their scant respect for authority and an entirely self-centred view of the universe. Like Willans, Rennison hits the nail on the head in her depiction of a teenage mentality.

For Georgia, the universe consists largely of make-up and boys; one "Sex-God" in particular being the unattainable Robbie. "I can already feel myself getting fed up with boys," she declares at one point, "and I haven't had anything to do with them yet." The book, and the nine which follow it, take the form of Georgia's "Confessions". Rennison's genius is in being able to tap into her own memories of teenage angst with unflinching honesty and self-mocking ridicule.

Rennison developed this ability to laugh at her own disasters during her earlier career as a stand-up comedian. Autobiographical shows such as *Stevie Wonder Touched My Face* and *Bob Marley's Gardener Sold My Friend* in the 1980s and 1990s drew on her own adolescent experiences and won acclaim at the Edinburgh Fringe Festival. The *Guardian* newspaper wrote of her audiences that "she was colluding with them in a way that seemed totally genuine, as she shared an impression of herself on the edge of disaster."

Her success as a performer led to work writing for other comedians, and she contributed to a newspaper column called "Dating at 35" in a similarly introspective, self-deprecating way. In an inspired move, publishers Piccadilly Press saw in the column someone "so self-obsessed and so childish" that they invited Louise Rennison to write a teenage diary. *Angus, Thongs and Full-Frontal Snogging*, her first novel, was the result.

Rennison was determined not to be moralistic about Georgia and her friends, but to enjoy the life she was reliving through them, and to laugh about what might at the time have seemed very unfunny. Above all she wanted Georgia to come across as a decent human being, not a silly girl. Rennison's first steps in cabaret were with a feminist group called Women With Beards, which mocked men and the mess they make of the world, and Rennison lent those attitudes to her young heroine.

The book is strongly autobiographical – it is said that Rennison used the real names of childhood friends in fictionalising episodes from her youth, and forgot to change them before publication. Like Georgia at the end of *Angus, Thongs and Full-Frontal Snogging*, Louise's teenage life was interrupted when her family immigrated temporarily to New Zealand. The effect is to give Georgia a thoroughly authentic voice, one immediately recognisable to all teenage girls.

The books have been less popular with teachers. When Rennison visited schools to promote the book, she spoke in the same language about the same rude issues which obsess her character and her audience. At one public question-and-answer session in a London bookshop a teacher was so offended that he removed his class after only ten minutes – but he had to drag them out because they were enjoying it so much.

Books about Georgia Nicolson: *Angus, Thongs and Full-Frontal Snogging* (1999), *It's OK, I'm Wearing Really Big Knickers* (2001, U.S. title *On the Bright Side, I'm Now the*

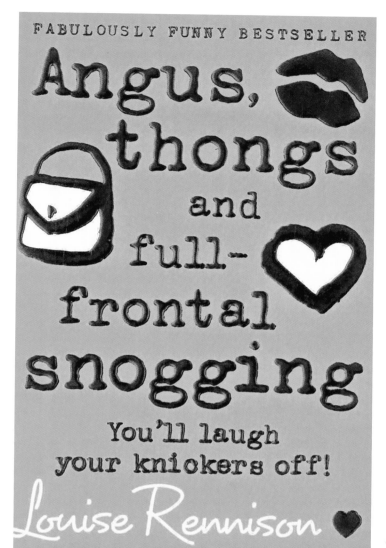

FABULOUSLY FUNNY BESTSELLER

Angus, thongs and full-frontal snogging

You'll laugh your knickers off!

Louise Rennison

LEFT: Several of Louise Rennison's titles were considered either too British or too vulgar for a U.S. audience, and were renamed. OK, I'm Wearing Really Big Knickers *became* On the Bright Side, I'm Now the Girlfriend of a Sex God *for the American market.*

Girlfriend of a Sex God), Knocked Out by my Nunga-Nungas (2002), *Dancing in my Nuddy-Pants* (2003), *… And That's When It Fell Off in My Hand* (2004, U.S. *Away Laughing on a Fast Camel*), *…Then He Ate My Boy Entrancers* (2005), *Startled by His Furry Shorts* (2006), *Luuurve is a Many Trousered Thing* (2007, U.S. *Love is a Many Trousered Thing*), *Stop in the Name of Pants!* (2008), and *Are These My Basoomas I See Before Me?* (2009).

Books about Georgia's friend Tallulah Casey: *Withering Tights* (2010), *A Midsummer Tights Dream* (2012), and *The Taming of the Tights* (2013, U.S. *Wild Girls, Wild Boys, Wild Tights*).

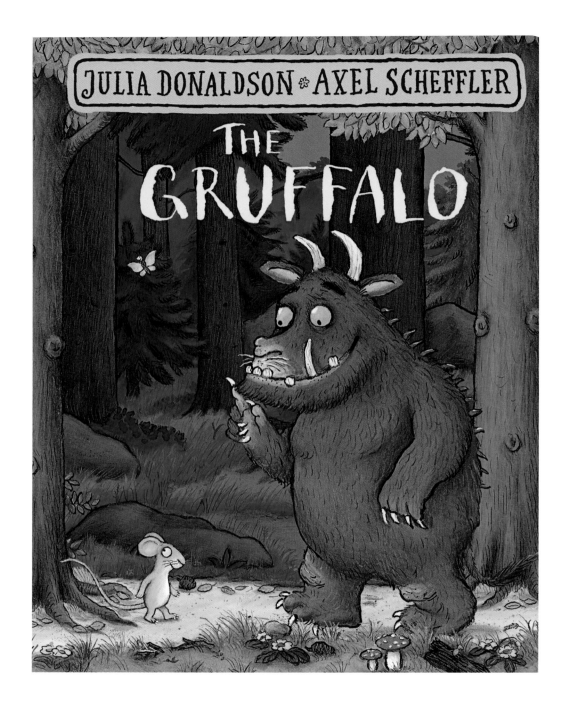

JULIA DONALDSON ✳ AXEL SCHEFFLER

THE
GRUFFALO

ABOVE: *Julia Donaldson based* The Gruffalo *on a traditional Chinese story about a girl who tricks a hungry tiger into believing she is the Queen of the Jungle.*

The Gruffalo

(1999)

Julia Donaldson (born 1948), Axel Scheffler (born 1957)

Many children's books aim to help the young overcome their fears. Few have been more popular in recent years than The Gruffalo, of which thirteen million copies have so far been sold in over forty languages. The Gruffalo is a phenomenon as much as a story.

It's a classically simple tale. A mouse, walking through the forest, encounters a series of animals that would like to eat him. To deter them, he invents a fearsome, made-up animal called a gruffalo, whose favourite food is the animal threatening to eat him. Each animal retreats in fear.

But then the mouse meets a real gruffalo, exactly as frightening as the one he thought he had invented, and intent on eating the mouse. They meet the other animals, one by one, who run away at the sight of the gruffalo. The gruffalo, however, believes it is the mouse that they are afraid of; and when the emboldened mouse threatens to eat the gruffalo, it is the gruffalo who turns and runs.

The Gruffalo owes its success to a perfect blend of traditional storytelling devices. Julia Donaldson's text is short – only 700 words – and in rhyming couplets, often repeated with only small variations for each animal the mouse meets. This repetition is a trick as old as the Norse sagas and it makes the story quickly memorable for young ears.

The use of animals instead of human beings is a tried and tested way of connecting with children, in the manner of Aesop's Fables, and Axel Scheffler's illustrations complement the simple text perfectly with bold colours and cheerfully drawn characters.

His gruffalo is a masterpiece. It has all the attributes which the mouse imagines – "terrible tusks and terrible claws, and terrible teeth in his terrible jaws," "knobbly knees and turned-out toes, and a poisonous wart at the end of his nose," "his eyes are orange, his tongue is black, he has purple prickles all over his back" – but Scheffler's monster is (if we're honest) more cuddly than scary, more an imaginary friend than an imaginary beast.

Julia Donaldson's background is in writing plays and musicals for children, and it's still the case that about two thirds of her published work is not available to the public, but intended for use in educational institutions. She performed plays and songs in schools and folk clubs, and was eventually chosen to write music for the BBC's children's programming.

It was when the lyrics of one of her BBC songs, *A Squash and a Squeeze*, was published in 1993 that she realised that the rhyming couplets of her songs could be turned to storytelling in book form. *A Squash and a Squeeze* was illustrated by Axel Scheffler, a German artist who moved to England in 1982. He began his illustrating career with a new edition of Helen Cresswell's 1967 breakthrough children's novel *The Piemakers* in 1988.

Scheffler was Donaldson's first choice for *The Gruffalo*. Although she has worked with many other illustrators before and since, the pair have to date collaborated on over twenty books, including *The Gruffalo's Child* (2004) and *Stick Man* (2008) which tells the story of the Gruffalo child's wooden toy.

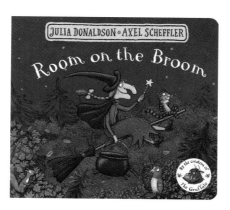

LEFT: Room on the Broom *(2001) was Donaldson and Scheffler's next collaboration after the success of* The Gruffalo.

Stormbreaker

(2000)

Anthony Horowitz (born 1955)

Young fictional heroes often find themselves involved in international espionage – think Famous Five and Uncle Quentin's "important papers" that often go missing – but Anthony Horowitz's Alex Rider novels are the most successful to have emerged in the James Bond mould.

In the nineteenth century Sherlock Holmes occasionally worked in the service of his government. But the genre of spy fiction first emerged around the beginning of the twentieth century as tensions between the European imperial powers grew. Rudyard Kipling's *Kim* and John Buchan's Richard Hannay novels exemplified the new fashion for heroes in the service of their country.

World War I enabled a new breed of spy writer to emerge, with physical experiences that provided their protagonists with a sense of credibility. Compton Mackenzie, Alexander Wilson and W. Somerset Maugham were all former intelligence officers and wrote with a new authentic voice. The approach of World War II encouraged new authors to embrace the genre, led by Eric Ambler, Dennis Wheatley and Helen MacInnes. In America E. Howard Hunt wrote his first spy novel in 1943 *before* he was recruited by the CIA in 1949, and continued writing them afterwards. After the war Ian Fleming, a former naval intelligence officer, published his first James Bond novel, *Casino Royale*, in 1953. Children's literature came relatively late to the genre, and modern novels may be said to be inspired by the Bond movie franchise rather than Fleming's original stories.

Anthony Horowitz is, as far as we know, not a spy. He was already a successful young-adult novelist before he set about creating a juvenile James Bond in the form of blond whizz-kid Alex Rider. Rider (named after the original Bond girl, played by Ursula Andress, in the first Bond movie *Dr No*) made his debut in *Stormbreaker*. It's a thoroughly Fleming-esque story, about an evil villain who intends to unleash a biological weapon on the children of Britain by giving every child a free computer programmed to release a real virus. Rider is the reluctant recruit to MI6, who must foil the plot with a combination of wit, strength and Bond-like gadgetry.

Alex Rider has appeared in a dozen novels to date, two of which have appeared since Horowitz declared that he would write no more. It's good news for fans – Horowitz's outlandish plots are exactly what the public has been taught by the Bond movies to expect of a spy story. It is no surprise that Horowitz has been commissioned by Ian Fleming's estate to write two new James Bond books so far, *Trigger Mortis* (2015) and *Forever and a Day* (2018), nor that he became the first author officially sanctioned by the Conan Doyle estate to write new novels about Sherlock Holmes, *The House of Silk* (2011) and *Moriarty* (2014).

Anthony Horowitz, who was given copies of *Frankenstein* and *Dracula* (and a human skull) by his mother at the age of thirteen, often treads a fine line between comedy and horror in his work for children. His first book, *The Sinister Secret of Frederick K. Bower* (1979), was a comedy adventure, published in 1979. In 1983 he published *The Devil's Doorbell*, the first in a young adult horror series known as the Pentagram novels, in which thirteen-year-old Martin Hopkins battles evil.

In *Groosham Grange* (1988) another thirteen-year-old, David Eliot, is the proto-Potter young wizard in a gruesome boarding school where the horrors are in part based on Horowitz's unhappy memories of his own boarding school childhood. He has more fun with Tim and Nick Diamond, a juvenile detective and his more intelligent brother with echoes of Sherlock and Mycroft Holmes. The Diamond Brothers books all have titles which parody film titles, starting with the first, *The Falcon's Malteser* (1986). Horowitz returned to the supernatural with *Raven's Gate* (2005), the first in a series of five books under the *Power of Five* banner about portals into other dimensions.

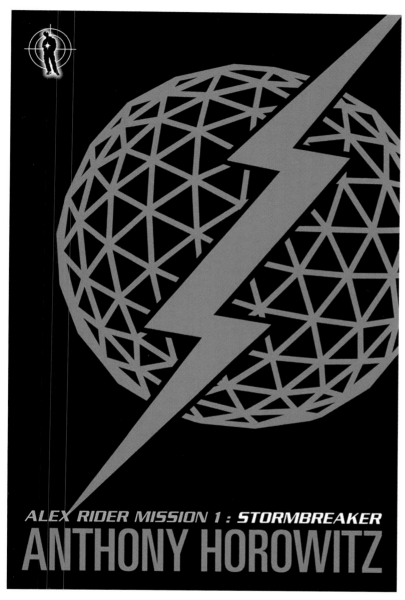

ALEX RIDER MISSION 1 : STORMBREAKER
ANTHONY HOROWITZ

LEFT: Horowitz took research for his series very seriously; for the book's sequel Point Blanc, *in which Rider deploys a crane, Horowitz climbed and operated a 150-metre crane to see it in operation.*
BELOW: One of Horowitz's earlier series, The Diamond Brothers, *has been updated with new illustrations by* Horrid Henry *illustrator Tony Ross.*

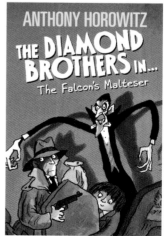

Some other books by Anthony Horowitz: *The Sinister Secret of Frederick K Bower* (1979), *The Devil's Doorbell* (1983) and series, *The Falcon's Malteser* (1986) and series, *Groosham Grange* (1988) and sequel, and *Raven's Gate* (2005).

ABOVE: Resembling Egyptian hieroglyphics, the text featured on this first-edition cover is written in "Gnommish". Each of the books in the series features similar text, and can be decoded to discover a message.

OPPOSITE: In Colfer's The Legend of Spud Murphy, *brothers Will and Marty discover a love of books through the influence of fearsome librarian Spud Murphy.*

Artemis Fowl

(2001) and series

Eoin Colfer (born 1965)

The character of Artemis Fowl, a twelve-year-old criminal mastermind, is a wonderfully subversive addition to the canon of juvenile protagonists. He's a welcome antidote to the large cast of highly moral children's characters.

Unscrupulous Artemis Fowl kidnaps a fairy and holds it for ransom, attempting to restore his family's fortune. But Eoin Colfer's fairies are not the gossamer kind and Fowl soon finds he has bitten off more than he can chew. His victim is Captain Holly Short of the Lower Elements Police Reconnaissance (LEPrecon for short) and Short's colleagues are coming for him. In a nod to the Bruce Willis movie franchise, Colfer has described the Artemis Fowl series as "Die Hard with Fairies."

Artemis Fowl is, like the *Die Hard* series, pure entertainment. There are goodies and baddies, but despite some claims by Fowl's fans, this is not an epic battle between good and evil. Both sides make morally questionable decisions – Fowl, obviously, in kidnapping someone, and some of the fairies in their willingness to unleash a troll on him without regard to the consequences.

Critics have questioned the book's literary merits – its elevation of its central character as repellent anti-hero, its re-use of well-trodden scenarios of dramatic tension, even its blatant establishment of the forthcoming sequel. As one reviewer put it, "all the familiar action-flick clichés are trotted out." But that is the nature of pure entertainment. You can't argue with the success of the *Artemis Fowl* series, which was completed after eight novels. All eight have also appeared as graphic novels, and Colfer has written a companion to the series, *The Artemis Fowl Files* (2004), fleshing out the Fowl backstory.

The success of Artemis Fowl enabled Colfer to give up his day job as a teacher. He had previously published two novels about Benny Shaw, an Irish schoolboy who learns about life after befriending a boy in Tunisia in *Benny and Omar* (1998), and about local rules in the company of a tomboy in his grandfather's village in *Benny and Babe* (1999).

Since becoming a full-time author, Colfer has launched several other series for children. His *Legends* series, three books so far, follows the escapades of two pre-teen brothers, Will and Marty. *Half Moon Investigations* (2006) is about intrepid boy detective Fletcher Moon. It's not yet a series, but Colfer has hinted at further adventures.

Colfer's stand-alone novels for the young are interesting. *The Wish List* (2003) is an afterlife fantasy with a less polarised view of heaven and hell than that of traditional Christian doctrine. It tells the story of a young girl, killed in a gas explosion, who must help the pensioner she was robbing at the time before she can be admitted to heaven. *Airman* (2007) is an alternative historical adventure set in a fictional nineteenth-century world of castles, princesses and early attempts to fly. It was shortlisted for the Carnegie Medal, British children's literature's highest honour.

Other children's books by Eoin Colfer: *Benny and Omar* (1998), *Benny and Babe* (1999), *The Wish List* (2003), *Legend of Spud Murphy* (2005) and series, *Half Moon Investigations* (2006), and *Airman* (2007).

Journey to the River Sea

(2001)

Eva Ibbotson (1925–2010)

She made her name as a children's author with humorous stories about ghosts and witches. But after the death of her ecologist husband, Eva Ibbotson could not find the strength to be funny. Instead she wrote him a beautiful, lyrical tribute in the form of a novel set in the Amazon.

Journey to the River Sea tells the story of orphaned Maia, sent from England to live with distant relatives on their rubber plantation in the Amazon basin. She has an exciting vision of what she will find there – exotic plants, giant butterflies and colourful parrots. Her English school friends are full of tales of horror about the region, including man-eating crocodiles, giant snakes and hostile local tribes. Where does the truth lie?

At first it looks as if she will not find anything. Her relatives, the Carters, keep the Amazon firmly at bay with xenophobia and insect repellents, tolerating Maia only for the money they receive for looking after her. She is not allowed to leave their clinically sterile enclave at all. Isolated, her only ally is her governess Miss Minton. But she begins to meet kindred spirits – Clovis, an actor without a troupe; and Finn, an heir to a British fortune who does not want to claim it. In their company her experience of the Amazon is transformed, into neither what she expected nor what her classmates feared, but something even richer.

Life, and location, are what you make them. Maia is open to life on the Amazon where she makes friends and sings with the local population; she makes the place her happy home. The Carters in contrast are narrow-minded, and think the Amazon is hell on earth; when a fire in their house, fuelled by insect repellent, consumes their home, it seems that hell has indeed become the place where they live.

Eva Ibbotson's life had parallels with fellow author Judith Kerr. She was born in Vienna to Jewish parents who separated when she was three. Both left Austria during the rise of Hitler, and Eva moved between them in Edinburgh, London and Paris – as she put it, "always on some train and wishing to have a home." She

returned to Austria in her writing as the setting for her children's book *The Star of Kazan* (2004).

Eva had intended to follow her father's profession in medicine, but abandoned it when she realised it would have involved vivisection. Instead, after a brief spell as a teacher, she followed in her mother's footsteps. Anna Gmeyner was a successful playwright and novelist in Austria until her books were banned by Hitler. In exile she drew on her experiences for the novel *Manja* (U.K. *The Wall*, U.S. *Five Destinies*, 1939). Ibbotson in turn based two adult novels, *The Morning Gift* (1993) and *A Song for Summer* (1997), on that time in the life of her family. Many of Ibbotson's novels, including these, have been republished for young adults.

The Morning Gift, like *Journey to the River Sea*, also celebrates Ibbotson's love of nature. If the natural environment is what defines a place, especially a wild place, then surely we must work with it to make the most of a place. This is Ibbotson's tribute to her ecologist husband and she draws her readers in as surely as the Amazon would.

Some other children's books by Eva Ibbotson: *Which Witch?* (1979), *The Haunting of Hiram C. Hopgood* (1987), *The Secret of Platform 13* (1994), *Dial-a-Ghost* (1996), *Monster Mission* (1999, U.S. title *The Island of the Aunts*), *The Star of Kazan* (2004), and *The Beasts of Clawstone Castle* (2005).

New York Times Best-selling Author of *Which Witch?*

EVA IBBOTSON

Journey to the River Sea

★ "Ibbotson dishes up her best work yet."
—*Kirkus Reviews*, starred review

ABOVE: Journey to the River Sea *garnered wide praise from critics, winning the Smarties Prize (ages 9–11), and being shortlisted for the Carnegie Medal, the Whitbread Award, and the Blue Peter Book Award.*

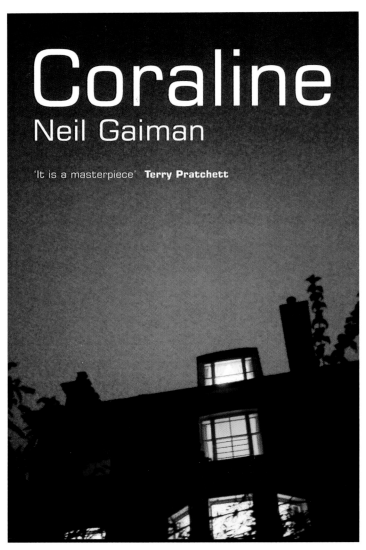

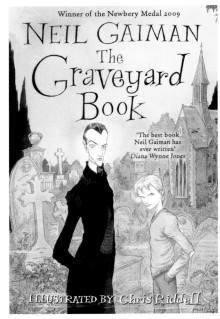

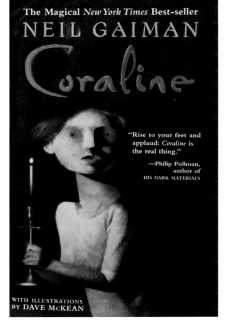

ABOVE: The original cover of Coraline, *gave little away about the terrors of "Other Home".*

TOP RIGHT: The Graveyard Book won both the American Newbery Medal and the British Carnegie Medal, the first time both had named the same book.

RIGHT: A subsequent cover of Coraline *illustrated by one of Neil Gaiman's favourite illustrators, Dave McKean.*

Coraline

(2002)

Neil Gaiman (born 1960)

What began as a typographical error has become a twenty-first-century Alice in Wonderland with a strong, fearless role model for girls as its central character. Coming from a background in graphic novels Gaiman is equally equipped to deliver demons in the printed text.

When Neil Gaiman mistyped the name "Caroline" in 1990, he liked the sound of his mistake and began to wonder what the story of someone called Coraline would be. The result, finally published twelve years later, has won numerous awards, and in reader reviews prompted its young adult audience and their parents to wish they had a friend like Coraline.

Coraline opens a door in her home which previously covered only a brick wall, and discovers a passageway to a parallel world with slightly distorted versions of her home, her parents and other inhabitants of the real apartment block in which she lives. At first everything in her Other Home seems better – better food, better toys – and her Other Mother says Coraline can have it all forever, if she will only agree to have buttons sewn over her eyes. When Coraline refuses, it becomes a battle for her soul in which she is imprisoned in a mirror and her real parents are kidnapped and held in a snow globe. Coraline must use all her wits to trick Other Mother and escape back to her real world.

Who doesn't flinch at the thought of having buttons sewn onto their eyes? Gaiman has been praised for not avoiding the powerful emotion of fear in his writing for the young, whom he believes are perfectly capable of experiencing it without distress in a fictional setting. His early reading included the horror writers Edgar Allan Poe, Mary Shelley and Dennis Wheatley, as well as the darker fantasy authors such as C. S. Lewis and J. R. R. Tolkien. He read Lewis Carroll's *Alice in Wonderland* so often that, so he claimed, he knew it by heart. All these works have exerted their influence on *Coraline.*

After a spell as a journalist – among other things he wrote a biography of pop stars Duran Duran – Gaiman began his literary career in the world of the graphic novel. His early work in this field caught the attention of industry leaders DC Comics, where he revived an old DC character, the Sandman, with spectacular results. Gaiman's *The Sandman* series (1989–96) by 1996 had begun to outsell DC's core characters Batman and Superman and is credited with attracting new audiences to the graphic novel genre, especially young women. Under Gaiman's authorship the Sandman, Master of Dreams, was joined by his older sister Death, a figure which became as popular as the Sandman himself.

Gaiman's first text-only novel was a farce about the birth of the son of Satan, *Good Omens* (1990), written in collaboration with fantasy author Terry Pratchett. Two very different fantasy novels followed before *Coraline* was completed, the very Victorian *Stardust* (1999) and the more mythological *American Gods* (2001). Gaiman has proved to be a widely read author with the ability to tackle many different genres and media. He often writes his own scripts for film and TV adaptations of his work, such as the BBC production of *Good Omens;* some of his output, for example *Neverwhere* (1996), began life as a drama before being novelised.

Because he is willing to reach dark places in his work, it is sometimes hard to draw a distinction between Gaiman's books for young adults and those for a more mature readership. *The Graveyard Book* (2008), about a boy whose parents are murdered and who grows up in a cemetery, is aimed at the young. *The Ocean at the End of the Lane* (2013), about the memories triggered by returning to the narrator's home town for a funeral is not, yet in its surreal fantasy and its depiction of deceptive appearances it has many echoes of *Coraline.*

Other books by Neil Gaiman: *The Sandman* series (1989–96), *Good Omens* (1990), *Stardust* (1999), *The Graveyard Book* (2008), and *The Ocean at the End of the Lane* (2013).

How to Train Your Dragon

(2003) and series

Cressida Cowell (born 1966)

The original *How to Train Your Dragon* (c.750 AD) is only one page long and not very helpful. Thank goodness Hiccup Horrendous Haddock III has devised a method of his own, and that Cressida Cowell has translated it for the benefit of us all.

Hiccup Horrendous Haddock III first appeared, along with his splendidly-named father Stoick the Vast, in the novel *Hiccup: The Viking Who Was Seasick* (2001). But it wasn't until he wrote *How to Train Your Dragon*, the user manual for his dragon Toothless, that he became a celebrity Viking. The book, ostensibly translated from the Old Norse by Cressida Cowell, propelled him to stardom not only on the page but in three big-screen hits.

Hiccup, Stoick, Gobber the Belch and the rest of the Vikings live on the Isle of Berk. Hiccup is unpopular and risks exile unless he can complete a rite of passage by capturing a dragon. Dragons are a constant menace but Hiccup manages to capture a small one called Toothless. He trains him sufficiently that they save the day when Berk is under threat from two sea dragons, the Green Death and the Purple Death. Hiccup and Toothless are, at last, the toast of the island.

Cressida Cowell grew up in London, but spent her childhood holidays on Little Colonsay, a tiny Hebridean island off the west coast of Scotland. Her father was a hereditary peer and lifelong environmentalist, whose ancestors founded the Pearson publishing house. The island was unpopulated except for Cressida and her family, and over three years they built their own home there from the ruined dwellings of earlier inhabitants. The only food except for what they brought with them was whatever they could catch from the sea. There was no electricity, no telephone, and no television.

In this idyllic, wild, unspoilt environment, surrounded by the sea, the family made its own entertainment and young Cressida learned to weave stories from her imagination and her surroundings. She studied English and Art at university and began to write seriously after the birth of her children. Early titles include *Little Wonder* (1998) and *Don't Do That, Kitty Killroy* (1999).

Hiccup and Toothless appeared together in twelve books and three films. Cowell has also written related titles, including Toothless the Dragon's take on *How to Train your Viking* (2006) and *The Incomplete Book of Dragons: A Guide to Dragon Species* (2014, U.S. title *The Complete Book of Dragons: A Guide to Dragon Species*).

While expanding the *Dragon* series she continued to write stand-alone titles, and also created the popular *Emily Brown* series about the things that might worry a little girl – loss of her rabbit, fear of the dark, unhappy teddy-bears and so on. She wrote *How to Fight a Dragon's Fury*, the last *Dragon* book to date, in 2015. Since then she has begun a magical fantasy series, *The Wizards of Once*, about a boy wizard and a warrior girl. Already running to three books, the wizards are proving as successful as the dragons.

Other books by Cressida Cowell: *Don't Do That, Kitty Killroy* (1999), *Hiccup: The Viking Who Was Seasick* (2001), *Claydon Was a Clingy Child* (2002), *Daddy on the Moon* (2005), *That Rabbit Belongs to Emily Brown* (2006) and series, *The Wizards of Once* (2017) and series, and *The Story of Tantrum O'Furrily* (2018).

OPPOSITE: The How to Train Your Dragon *series has been translated into thirty-eight languages. Cressida Cowell became the eleventh writer to take on the role of Waterstones' Children's Laureate in 2019, unveiling her large "To Do" list, which includes asserting every child's right to "see themselves reflected in a book".*

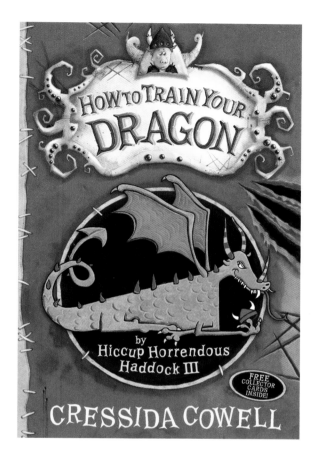

LEFT: Haddon uses Christopher's voice to shape the novel, including numbering chapters with prime numbers rather than consecutive numbers. Christopher's affinity with prime numbers stems from the fact that, much like himself, prime numbers do not fit or follow usual patterns.

BELOW: Winner of seven Olivier theatrical awards, the play based on the book opened in London in 2012, running until 2017. It also utilised prime numbers within the score; the music is based on prime number sequences and rhythms.

The Curious Incident of the Dog in the Night-Time

(2003)

Mark Haddon (born 1962)

With *The Curious Incident of the Dog in the Night-Time*, children's author Mark Haddon intended to write his first novel for adults. The result was named the U.K.'s 2003 Whitbread Book of the Year as an adult work, but it also won the *Guardian* newspaper's Children's Fiction Award.

The title comes from a Sherlock Holmes short story in which the curious incident is that there was no incident; the dog in question unexpectedly did nothing. The same could be said of the poodle in *The Curious Incident*, except that in the latter case it is because the dog has been stabbed to death with a garden fork. This grisly find sets the novel's protagonist, young Christopher Boone, on a voyage of personal discovery and growth.

Christopher is on the autism spectrum and must negotiate his way through unfamiliar social situations as he searches for the truth about the dog's death and his parents' marriage. All ends well. In fact, in a 2006 survey by the BBC, *The Curious Incident of the Dog in the Night-Time* came fourth in a public vote of the best happy endings in books – behind *Pride and Prejudice*, *To Kill a Mockingbird* and *Jane Eyre*, but ahead of Daphne du Maurier's *Rebecca*.

Haddon has been praised by the medical profession for his portrayal of autism. He insists, however, that for the book he did more research about the London Underground system than about Christopher's condition, which is a form of Asperger's syndrome. The novel is written in the first person, and for many young readers it is the first opportunity to see the world through the eyes of a person with autism. The detailed diagrams included throughout the book are used by Christopher to help him process new environments and complex emotions which, to most people, would seem relatively straightforward.

It was Haddon's publisher who suggested, perhaps with an eye to his author's existing readership, that the book be promoted to young adults as well as older ones.

His first book, for early readers, was *Gilbert's Gobstopper* (1987), which follows the eponymous jawbreaker on a voyage to the bottom of the sea and to outer space after Gilbert accidentally drops it down a sewer.

Like many of Haddon's books for the young he both wrote and illustrated *Gilbert's Gobstopper*, as he did his series of four books under the *Agent Z* banner (1993–2001). Agent Z is the *nom de guerre* of three schoolboys who delight in practical jokes; for example, putting plastic spiders in the gravy in the school canteen, or smearing the black toilet seats of the school lavatories with black boot polish.

In 2009 Haddon published *Boom!*, an updated version of his 1992 children's novel *Gridzbi Spudvetch!*. This is a wild tale of extra-terrestrial kidnap and rescue, which starts from the premise that schoolteachers may well be aliens. But as a sci-fi story it had dated quickly, in a world where cassette tapes and floppy discs were already becoming things of the past. A plea from a schoolteacher persuaded Mark Haddon to revisit his book, which had been out of print for some years. Apart from *Boom!*, he has written only for adults since the success of *The Curious Incident*.

Other children's books by Mark Haddon: *Gilbert's Gobstopper* (1987), *Agent Z Meets the Masked Crusader* (1993) and series, *Titch Johnson: Almost World Champion* (1993), *The Real Porky Phillips* (1994), *Ocean Star Express* (2001), *The Ice Bear's Cave* (2002), and *Boom!* (2009).

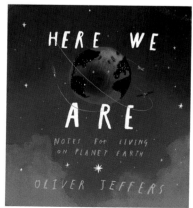

ABOVE: Jeffers says he uses empty space in his illustrations and storytelling to aid readers' imaginations, allowing people to place themselves in the story.

ABOVE: *Jeffers says he uses empty space in his illustrations and storytelling to aid readers' imaginations, allowing people to place themselves in the story.*

LEFT: *Whilst* Here We Are *was inspired by conversations with his son, before the birth of his children Jeffers primarily wrote picture books for himself, noting that while they were largely enjoyed by children, they were not the sole intended audience.*

Lost and Found

(2005)

Oliver Jeffers (born 1977)

With finely judged colour washes and a handful of lines Oliver Jeffers has drawn a touching story of how friendship begins and what it means. The book, only his second, features an animal often featured in David Attenborough's nature documentaries – the lonely penguin.

Oliver Jeffers divides his time between children's books, commercial illustration and fine art. He's the founder of an artists' collective in Belfast, where he grew up, and has exhibited in capital cities around the world from Dublin to Sydney, and from Berlin to Washington DC. His distinctive graphic style, often mixing media and incorporating chalk drawings, has boosted sales for Starbucks, Lavazza Coffee and United Airlines, among other clients.

He is best known for his children's books, in which his distinctive illustrations capture emotion as well as action. *Lost and Found*, is the story of a boy who finds a lost penguin on his doorstep and determines to take it home, in his rowing boat, to the South Pole. During the hazardous journey they keep each other's spirits up with stories, "talking of wonderful things all the way". But when the time comes to part, neither feels happy at the successful completion of their journey. As the boy rows away, he realises that the penguin wasn't lost, just lonely, and that the two have become friends.

Jeffers' illustrations give his subjects space on the page. They are uncluttered and without unnecessary detail. The boy is portrayed in an almost minimalist style – a circle for a head, a rectangle for a body, and two lines for legs. Yet Jeffers is adept at creating an expressive character, despite a face with just a hint of a nose and two dots for eyes. A tree is a green circle on a stalk. The South Pole is just ice, sea and sky – the only thing to focus on (apart from a Vegas-style sign proclaiming "Welcome to the South Pole") is the boy getting back into his boat, alone.

The simplicity of Jeffers' figurative elements lend themselves readily to animation, and the film version of *Lost and Found* (2008) won 40 international awards, including the 2009 BAFTA for best animation. Jeffers has since made further contributions to the world of animation: his long-running 2012 commercial for Kinder chocolate shows a boy playing vet with his cat and eating the chocolate which he prescribes. In 2014 he contributed a video for the Innocence + Experience world tour by his fellow Irishmen U2.

With so many strings to his bow, Oliver Jeffers is not necessarily a prolific children's author, producing at most one title a year. But what he lacks in quantity he adds in quality. The boy in *Lost and Found* initially appeared in Jeffers' first book, *How to Catch a Star* (2004), and returned in *The Way Back Home* (2007), in which he must work together with a Martian on the moon to the find, as the title suggests, their way home. The penguin joins him again in *Up and Down* (2010).

Some of Jeffers' books convey a strong sense of awareness for the environment. *The Great Paper Caper* (2008) is concerned with conserving trees for the benefit of all, and *Here We Are: Notes for Living on Planet Earth* (2017), full of humour and references to his earlier work, was written from the heart for his two-month-old son. It's about the wonderful diversity of our unique world, whose protection is everyone's responsibility.

Some other books by Oliver Jeffers: *The Incredible Book-Eating Boy* (2006), *The Great Paper Caper* (2008), *The Heart and the Bottle* (2010), *This Moose Belongs to Me* (2012), *Once Upon an Alphabet: Short Stories for All the Letters* (2014), and *Here We Are: Notes for Living on Planet Earth* (2017).

Diary of a Wimpy Kid

(2007) and series

Jeff Kinney (born 1971)

There's a wimpy kid in all of us, the one that desperately wants to be popular, famous or attractive. Jeff Kinney simply defined him for us in the character of Greg Heffley, whose online diaries received twenty million visits before they had even got into print.

*D*iary of a Wimpy Kid began life in 2004 as a daily series on the FunBrain website, a resource for teachers with educational games for children. Its author, Jeff Kinney, was already a successful cartoonist; it was the success of his "Igdoof" strip in a campus newspaper that persuaded him to become a full-time artist.

He began formulating his ideas for *Wimpy Kid* in 1998. The series revolves around Greg Heffley, who explains at the start that he is writing a journal, not a diary, and writing it only to have something to sell when he is rich and famous. Until then, he's stuck in middle school with his remarkably tolerant best friend Rowley, surrounded by fellow students and his family, all of whom he sees as morons.

Funnily enough they all get on better in life than he manages to. When the cartoon strip he and Rowley create is accepted by the school newspaper, Rowley gets all the credit. He is cast as a tree in the school play, soaked by teenagers while trick-or-treating, caught cheating in a test, and breaks Rowley's arm while using him for target practice. When he joins the School Safety Patrol in a bid to get some status, he can't resist terrifying some very young children with some worms, and is sacked.

Things never seem to work out for Greg, though the same cannot be said of Jeff Kinney. There is no suggestion that he modelled Greg on himself, but the *Diary of a Wimpy*

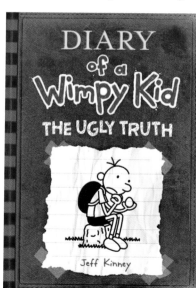

Kid has brought him nothing but success. Before it made its way into print the online version received twenty million views, while the books themselves – fourteen of them so far – have sold well over 200 million copies around the world.

There have been a number of spin-offs too. The series has generated four blockbuster movies so far, each accompanied by its own diary, a "making-of" tie-in. And in 2019 long-suffering Rowley finally made it into print in his own voice with *Diary of an Awesome Friendly Kid: Rowley Jefferson's Journal*. Greg's diaries won the Nickelodeon Kids' Choice Award for "Favorite Book" for seven of the nine years from 2008 to 2016 – and were nominated in the other two.

They've been translated into nearly sixty languages, proof that Greg Heffley really is a universal character, despite his distinctly American setting. In Germany the books are published under the prosaic title of *Greg's Tagebuch* – "Greg's Diary". But it turns out there is a word for "wimpy kid" in many languages: *dégonflé* in French, *drisyn* in Welsh, *schiappa* in Italian, *slabaka* in Russian, *wimpy wean* in Scots, *cwaniaczka* in Polish, *renacuajo* in Spanish, *ineptus puer* in Latin and *loser* in Dutch.

Other books by Jeff Kinney: *Diary of a Wimpy Kid Do-It-Yourself Book* (2008), *The Wimpy Kid Movie Diary* (2010), and *Diary of an Awesome Friendly Kid* (2019).

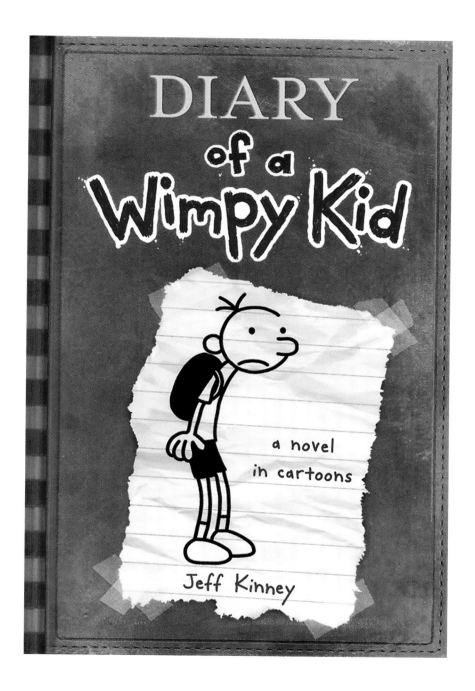

ABOVE: *Jeff Kinney's instantly recognisable stick-drawings accentuate the wimpiness of Wimpy Kid. There's none of the latest branded footwear for Greg Heffley.*
OPPOSITE: The Ugly Truth, *the fifth book in the series, sees Greg fall out with his best friend Rowley.*

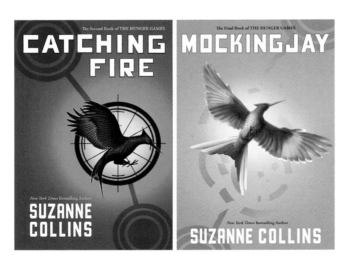

ABOVE AND LEFT: *Suzanne Collins has revealed the impact of Roman and Greek mythology on her trilogy, citing the story of* Theseus and the Minotaur, *in which seven youths and seven maidens were sent from Athens to Crete, to be thrown in the Labyrinth and devoured by the Minotaur. The Capitol's enjoyment of the Hunger Games similarly reflects the use of the ruthless Roman gladiator games as a form of popular entertainment.*

The Hunger Games
(2008)

Suzanne Collins (born 1962)

The speed with which *The Hunger Games* made the transition from page to silver screen is an indication of the remarkable success of the original book, which has become the most downloaded Kindle edition of all time.

Suzanne Collins' nightmarish vision of a dystopian, post-apocalyptic America called Panem has touched a chord with the young adult readers of the twenty-first century. Its barbarous competitive violence between children ordained by a brutal government could be suggested as an update to the reality TV age of traditional teenage fiction. Contestants, or "tributes", are killed or fight to the death until only one remains to be crowned winner of the annual Games. A conventional love triangle enhances this comparison.

Because of a failed rebellion by one of Panem's thirteen districts, the remaining twelve are forced to send a teenage boy and girl, chosen by lottery, to the annual Hunger Games, at which all twenty-four participants must fight to the death until only one remains. A consequence of the Games, now in their seventy-fourth year, is to propel the participants and subsequent victor to stardom. Each seeks to enlist the support of the audience, wealthy members of the Capitol, to whom each of the twelve districts are subjugated, and for whom the games is the highlight of their year. Tributes seek obtain valuable items by winning sponsorship from capitol members through the adoption of an image which will appeal to the spectators.

The Games themselves are as ruthless and violent as you would expect, given that contestants are forced to fight for their very lives. Contestants are also at the mercy of the Gamemakers, who control every aspect of the arena, creating literal death traps for the viewing pleasure of its audience. Alliances are made for convenience and broken for expediency. Even the romance between the two tributes from District 12, Peeta Mellark and the book's narrator Katniss Everdeen, is open to question.

The Hunger Games is a novel of the Television Age. It works as a satire of reality TV shows and indeed was in part inspired by them, as Collins has said. Which of us hasn't at some point imagined how we would conduct ourselves if suddenly put in front of a TV camera? But imaginary Panem was also shaped by real TV images of poverty, oppression, and hunger as the result of war, which fill our TV screens in every news bulletin.

Collins began her writing career with children's shows for the Nickelodeon TV channel, and she co-wrote the big screen adaptation of *The Hunger Games* herself. Her first published success was with *The Underland Chronicles*, a series of five books set in an underground world. It begins with *Gregor the Overlander* (2003), in which two overlanders, brother and sister Gregor and Boots, stumble into the Underland by accident and are caught up in its prophecies and conflicts. Collins was moved to write *The Underland Chronicles* when she found herself thinking, with regard to *Alice in Wonderland*, how much more likely it would be now to fall down a manhole than a rabbit hole, and what else one might find there other than a Mad Hatter's Tea Party.

Besides the two sequels to *The Hunger Games*, a prequel published in 2020 concerns the District 13 rebellion which prompted the Games. This later addition has been welcomed by young adults, who make up the core fanbase of the series, and whose commercial value as a consumer group has rapidly grown within recent years across all media. The wild popularity of Collins' books has put her at the forefront of this media revolution, just as Katniss's character the "Mockingjay", in *The Hunger Games*, is the inspiration for a revolution across Panem.

Other books by Suzanne Collins: *Fireproof* (1999), *The Underland Chronicles* (2003–2007), *When Charlie McButton Lost Power* (2005), and *Year of the Jungle* (2013).

Mr Stink

(2009)

David Walliams (born 1971)

David Walliams has been hailed as the new Roald Dahl for his gleefully subversive children's literature. After only eleven years in the genre it may be too early to tell, but his early promise is epitomised by the success of his second book, *Mr Stink*.

"Mr Stink stank. He also stunk. And if it was correct English to say he stinked, then he stinked as well." Thus begins, to the mock-disgusted delight of all children, the story of a smelly tramp, befriended by young Chloe despite the disapproval of her parents. The book starts as a string of jokes, mostly at the tramp's expense. When Chloe's mother's hopes of becoming a Member of Parliament are boosted by a misunderstanding about Mr Stink, the truth is exposed on national television, causing a rift between mother and daughter.

The story takes on an even more serious tone when we find that Mr Stink is actually Lord Darlington fallen on hard times after the destruction of his home and the death of his wife. With Mr Stink's help Chloe and her mother are reunited, and by the time he moves on at the end of the book he has had a positive influence on all the lives he has touched. *Mr Stink* is a plea for tolerance, and for not judging people on appearances (or smells). Those opening words say the same thing in a different way – stank, stunk, stinked, people use different words for the same thing and that's okay, as long as the meaning is clear. There is no single correct way of speaking, or dressing, or smelling.

David Walliams did not arrive on the children's literature scene out of nowhere. He was already a celebrity as a comedy sketch show performer and writer and, increasingly, as a serious actor and television presenter. Born David Williams, he studied drama in Bristol and amended his surname when he joined the actors' union Equity, which already had a member called David Williams.

His involvement in the sketch show *Little Britain*, with its provocative brand of humour, made him a household name. It ran for four seasons and a number of specials;

by coincidence the last special was broadcast in 2009, the year that *Mr Stink* was published and it became clear that a book-writing career was beckoning. Certainly *Little Britain* shares an unconventional, risqué approach to jokes with his books for the young.

Walliams revisited the idea of not prejudging someone in his fourth book, *Gangsta Granny* (2011). In it, Ben discovers that the grandmother whom he dislikes has a past as a jewel thief who dreams of one last big heist. In contrast, Alberta the *Awful Auntie* (2014) is genuinely awful and must be thwarted in her efforts to steal young Stella's inheritance. In *Grandpa's Great Escape* (2015), Jack's grandfather suffers from Alzheimer's disease but also has a secret past, which Jack helps him relive following a daring escape from Grandpa's nursing home.

Although his stories each stand alone, there is a character who recurs as a plot device in all but one of them, the kindly, helpful Mr Raj the newsagent. In all Walliams' stories a child is the hero, while adults often treat each other cruelly. Despite their humour and zany plots, there is generally a strong moral line drawn, and a heartwarming ending, although often a sense that not everyone lives happily ever after. In all these respects, Walliams very much fits the Roald Dahl mould.

Selected other books by David Walliams: *The Boy in the Dress* (2008), *Gangsta Granny* (2011), *Ratburger* (2012), *Awful Auntie* (2014), and *Grandpa's Great Escape* (2015).

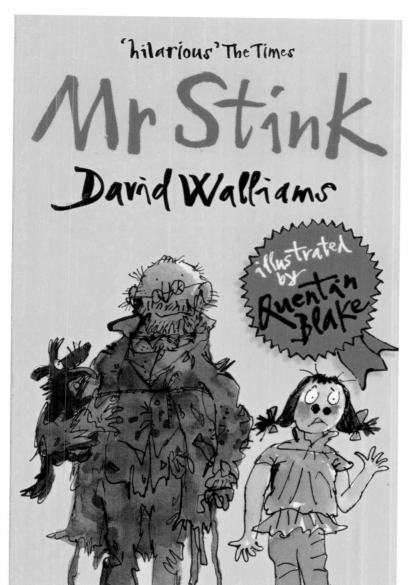

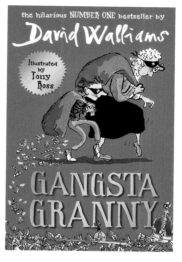

ABOVE: *David Walliams' cast of outrageous characters and situations is reminiscent of the people we met in his hit television series (with Matt Lucas)* Little Britain. *The author is never afraid of going right up to the boundaries of good taste, teetering on the edge, but ultimately staying the right side.*

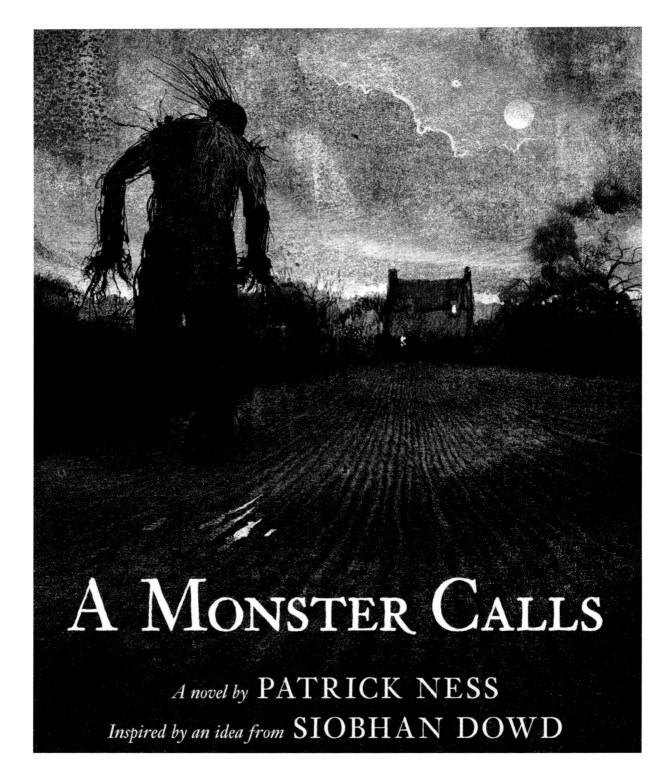

A MONSTER CALLS

A novel by PATRICK NESS

Inspired by an idea from SIOBHAN DOWD

A Monster Calls

(2011)

Patrick Ness (born 1971)

A supernatural masterpiece about the pain of letting go of the very people you want to keep closest, A Monster Calls haunts its readers long after they have finished reading. The circumstances of its conception are no less haunting.

Young Conor O'Malley's mother is dying of cancer. His father is absent, with a second family; Conor has withdrawn from school life where he is bullied; and the grandmother with whom he lives is unsympathetic. Isolated, he is woken one night from a recurring nightmare by a monster outside his window. He has unwittingly summoned the monster, a giant shape looming from the branches of a yew tree in the garden.

The monster will tell Conor three stories about previous occasions on which it was summoned, and then Conor must tell a story of his own. The monster's tales illustrate the complexities of the human condition – our willingness to deceive ourselves sometimes; our helplessness and our need to trust the help of others; and the value or otherwise of being noticed and being invisible. "Your mind," the monster tells Conor, "will believe comforting lies while also knowing the painful truths that make those lies necessary. And your mind will punish you for believing both."

Conor's story is his nightmare, in which he is clinging to his mother's hand to prevent her falling to her death in a chasm. The end, both of the nightmare and the book, is heartachingly inevitable, and Conor and the reader must accept it, no matter how much they wish it were otherwise. *A Monster Calls* has reduced people of all ages to tears.

The idea for the book was conceived not by Patrick Ness, but by Siobhan Dowd, author of four powerful novels for and about teenagers: *A Swift Pure Cry* (2006), *The London Eye Mystery* (2007), *Bog Child* (2008) and *Solace of the Road* (2009). The first two were nominated for the Carnegie Medal and the third won it.

The last two were published posthumously: *A Monster Calls* came to her as she lay dying of cancer in 2007.

Ness agreed to write it on the condition that he had free rein in how the story developed, and he described the process as "a really private conversation between me and [Dowd], and that mostly it was me saying, 'Just look what we're getting away with.'"

The book was illustrated by artist Jim Kay, who later supplied the pictures for the illustrated editions of the *Harry Potter* books. When *A Monster Calls* was published in 2011, it achieved a unique double. For the first time in their 56 year history the book won both the Kate Greenaway Medal for its illustrator and its companion award the Carnegie Medal for its author.

Other children's books by Patrick Ness: *The Knife of Never Letting Go* (2008), *The Ask and the Answer* (2009), *Monsters of Men* (2010), *More Than This* (2013), *The Rest of Us Just Live Here* (2015), *Release* (2017), and *And the Ocean Was Our Sky* (2018).

OPPOSITE: Though Patrick Ness and Siobhan Dowd shared the same literary editor, Ness never met Dowd before her death. Ness describes illustrator Jim Kay as a vital third player in the creation process, bringing to life Ness's vision of the kind-yet-frightening monster.

Another 50 Children's Books

The longer list of titles included these fine works, *But Not the Armadillo.*

1704 *The Thousand and One Nights*
Antoine Galland
(first published edition and
European translation)

1812 *Swiss Family Robinson*
Johan David Wyss

1857 *Tom Brown's School Days*
Thomas Hughes.

1863 *The Water Babies*
Rev. Charles Kingsley

1883 *The Adventures of Pinnochio*
Carlo Collodi

1900 *The Wonderful Wizard of Oz*
L. Frank Baum

1928 *Milly-Molly-Mandy* stories
Joyce Lankester Brisley

1930 *Mostly Mary*
Gwynedd Rae (Mary Plain)

1930 *The Little Engine that Could*
Watty Piper

1935 *Little House on the Prairie*
Laura Ingalls

1935 *The Box of Delights*
John Masefield

1936 *The Story of Ferdinand*
by Munro Leaf and
Robert Lawson

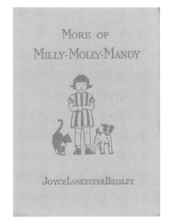

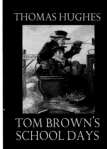

ABOVE: Two contrasting treatments of Thomas Hughes' famous novel, both with the helpful "To Rugby" signpost. Although for the top image, "To Salzburg" might be more fitting.

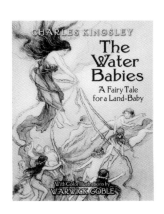

1938 *Orlando the Marmalade Cat*
Kathleen Hale

1938 *The Sword in the Stone*
T. H. White

1940 *Lassie Come-Home*
Eric Knight

1943 *Lone Pine* series
Malcolm Saville

1948 *Hurrah for St. Trinian's*
Ronald Searle

1949 *Tiptoes the Mischievous Kitten*
Noel Barr

1954 *Lord of the Flies*
William Golding

1959 *The Adventures of Asterix*
René Goscinny
and Albert Uderzo

1962 *A Wrinkle in Time*
Madeleine L'Engle

1962 *Berenstain Bears* series
Stan and Jan Berenstain

1964 *Harriet the Spy*
Louise Fitzhugh

1964 *The Giving Tree*
Shel Silverstein

1965 *Gentle Ben*
Walt Morey

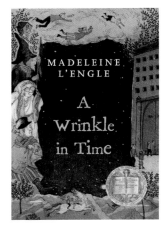

ABOVE: *Orlando the Marmalade Cat is one of the few guitar-playing cats in children's fiction. When the Owl and the Pussycat went to sea, it was left to the owl to do the strumming.*

1968 *A Wizard of Earthsea*
Ursula K. Le Guin

1970 *Mr Gumpy's Outing*
John Burningham

1972 *There Was an Old Lady
Who Swallowed a Fly*
Pam Adams

1974 *The Worst Witch*
Jill Murphy

1977 *Bridge to Terabithia*
Katherine Paterson

1981 *Goodnight Mister Tom*
Michelle Magorian

1982 *Moo, Baa, La La La!*
Sandra Boynton

1982 *The Secret Diary of Adrian Mole,
Aged 13¾*
Sue Townsend

1983 *Gorilla*
Anthony Browne

1985 *The Magic Key*
Roderick Hunt and
Alex Brychta
(Biff and Chip)

1986 *I Want My Potty!*
Tony Ross

1987 *Where's Wally?*
Martin Handford

1991 *Sophie's World*
Jostein Gaarder

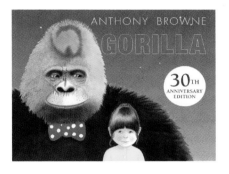

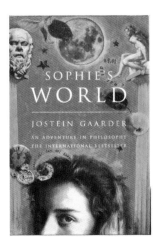

1992 *Flour Babies*
Anne Fine

1992 *Owl Babies*
Martin Waddell
and Patrick Benson

1994 *Guess How Much I Love You*
Sam McBratney and
Anita Jeram

1994 *Horrid Henry* series
Francesca Simon

2000 *I Will Not Ever Never Eat a Tomato*
Lauren Child
(Charlie and Lola)

2001 *Noughts and Crosses*
Malorie Blackman

2003 *Inkheart*
Cornelia Funke

2003 *Rainbow Magic* series
"Daisy Meadows"

2003 *You Choose*
Nick Sharratt and
Pippa Goodhart

2004 *The CHERUB* series
Robert Muchamore

2006 *The Boy in the Striped Pajamas*
John Boyne

2012 *Wonder*
R. J. Palacio

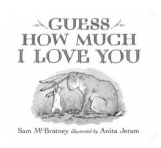

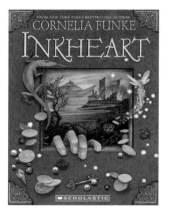
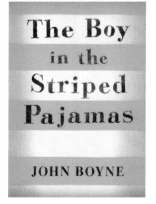

Index

ABOVE: *Terry Pratchett's* Diggers *from 1990.*

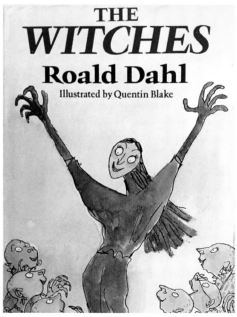

ABOVE: Roald Dahl's The Witches *(1983) turned children into mice.*

Acknowledgements

The publisher wishes to thank all the publishing houses
(particularly Puffin) of the books used in this review of beloved
children's literature. A big thank-you also to the staff of Pavilion Books
who contributed lists of favourites. Apologies to Polly Powell for not
including *Ant And Bee* by Angela Banner, but it only goes to show that
you can be the chairman of the company and still not get your favourite
on the list.

Thanks also to the following for supplying photography:

Rostrum camera images Margo Stagliano

Alamy images, pages 11, 20, 117

Anne Frank Museum, Amsterdam, page 89

Shutterstock, page 122

Also in this series:

Maps That Changed the World ISBN 978-1-84994-297-3
John O. E. Clark (2015)

100 Diagrams That Changed the World ISBN: 978-1-84994-076-4
Scott Christianson (2014)

100 Documents That Changed the World ISBN: 978-1-84994-300-0
Scott Christianson (2015)

100 Books That Changed the World ISBN: 978-1-84994-451-9
Scott Christianson and Colin Salter (2018)

100 Speeches That Roused the World ISBN: 978-1-84994-492-2
Colin Salter (2019)

100 Letters That Changed the World ISBN: 978-1-911641-09-4
Colin Salter (2019)

About the Author
Colin Salter is a history writer with degrees from Manchester
Metropolitan University, England and Queen Margaret University in
Edinburgh, Scotland. His most recent publications are *Remarkable Road
Trips, The Moon Landings: One Giant Leap, 100 Books That Changed the
World, 100 Speeches That Roused the World* and *100 Letters That Changed the
World.* He is currently working on a memoir based in part on letters
written to and by his ancestors over a period of two hundred years.